D0312783

IN THE
NIGHT
WOOD

IN THE
NIGHT
WOOD

☽

Dale Bailey

A John Joseph Adams Book
Houghton Mifflin Harcourt
Boston   New York
2018

For information about permission to reproduce selections from this book, write
to trade.permissions@hmhco.com or to Permissions, Houghton Mifflin Harcourt
Publishing Company, 3 Park Avenue, 19th Floor, New York, New York 10016.

hmhco.com

Library of Congress Cataloging-in-Publication Data
Names: Bailey, Dale, author.
Title: In the night wood / Dale Bailey.
Description: Boston ; New York : Houghton Mifflin Harcourt, 2018. | A John
Joseph Adams Book.
Identifiers: LCCN 2017058529 (print) | LCCN 2018001185 (ebook) |
ISBN 9781328490810 (ebook) | ISBN 9781328494436 (hardback)
Subjects: | BISAC: FICTION / Fantasy / Contemporary. | FICTION / Fairy
Tales, Folk Tales, Legends & Mythology. | GSAFD: Fantasy Fiction.
Classification: LCC PS3602.A54 (ebook) | LCC PS3602.A54 I5 2018
(print) | DDC 813/.6—dc23
LC record available at https://lccn.loc.gov/2017058529

Book design by Chrissy Kurpeski

Printed in the United States of America
DOC 10 9 8 7 6 5 4 3 2 1

Frontispiece illustration © Andrew Davidson

For Pam and Sally

The specific mode of existence of man implies the need of his learning what happens, and above all what *can* happen, in the world around him and in his own interior world. That it is a matter of the structure of the human condition is shown, *inter alia,* by the *existential necessity* of listening to stories and fairy tales, even in the most tragic of circumstances.

— MIRCEA ELIADE, *THE FORBIDDEN FOREST*

Gretel began to cry and said,
"How are we to get out of the forest now?"

— THE BROTHERS GRIMM, "HANSEL AND GRETEL"

ONCE UPON A TIME . . .

PRELUDE

B Y THE TIME THE MOON AROSE AND let down her golden skirts, Laura was sore afraid. In the pale light she stumbled through a ring of sinister yews into a glade where stood a single bearded oak, hoary and not unkind.

"I met you once in a dream," she said.

"And I you in my long, arboreal sleep," replied Grandfather Oak (for that was his name).

"Isn't that odd?" Laura said to the tree.

"Not at all," said Grandfather Oak, nodding sagely. "The Story is rich in coincidence."

"What kind of Story is it?" asked Laura.

And just then the North Wind swept through the trees, and Grandfather Oak shivered all his branches and dropped down a curtain of golden leaves. "It is not a happy Story," he said. "But so few Stories are."

— CAEDMON HOLLOW, *IN THE NIGHT WOOD*

1

HOLLOW HOUSE CAME to them as such events befall orphans in tales, unexpectedly, and in the hour of their greatest need: salvation in the form of a long blue envelope shoved in among the day's haul of pizza-delivery flyers, catalogs, and credit card solicitations. That's how Charles would pitch it to Erin, anyway, sitting across from her in the night kitchen, with the envelope and its faintly exotic Royal Mail stamp lying on the table between them. Yet it felt to Charles Hayden like the culminating moment in some obscure chain of events that had been building, link by link, through all the thirty-six years of his life — through centuries even, though he could not have imagined that at the time.

Where do tales begin, after all?

Once upon a time.

In the months that followed, those words — and the stories they conjured up for him — would echo in Charles's mind. Little Red Cap and Briar Rose and Hansel and Gretel, abandoned among the dark trees by their henpecked father and his wicked second wife. Charles would think of them most of all, footsore and afraid when at last they chanced upon a cottage made of gingerbread and spun sugar and stopped to feast upon it, little suspecting the witch who lurked within, ravenous with hungers of her own.

Once upon a time.

So tales begin, each alike in some desperate season. Yet how many other crises — starting points for altogether different tales — wait to unfold themselves in the rich loam of every story, like seeds germinating among the roots of a full-grown tree? How came that father to be so faithless? What made his wife so cruel? What brought that witch to those woods and imparted to her appetites so unsavory?

So many links in the chain of circumstance. So many stories inside stories, waiting to be told.

Once upon a time.

Once upon a time, at the wake for a grandfather he had never known in life, a boy named Charles Hayden, his mother's only child, scrawny and bespectacled and always a little bit afraid, sought refuge in the library of the sprawling house his mother had grown up in. "The ancestral manse," Kit (she was that kind of mother) had called it when she told him they'd be going there, and even at age eight he could detect the bitter edge in her voice. Charles had never seen anything like it — not just the house, but the library itself, a single room two or three times the size of the whole apartment he shared with Kit, furnished in dark, glossy wood and soft leather, and lined with books on every wall. His sneakers were silent on the plush rugs, and as he looked around, slack-jawed in wonder, the boisterous cries of his cousins on the lawn wafted dimly through the sun-shot Palladian windows.

Charles had never met the cousins before. He'd never met *any* of these people; he hadn't even known they existed. Puttering up the winding driveway this morning in their wheezing old Honda, he'd felt like a child in a story, waking one morning to discover that he's a prince in hiding, that his parents (his parent) were not his parents after all, but faithful retainers to an exiled king. Prince or no, the cousins — a thuggish trio of older boys clad in stylish dress clothes that put to shame his ill-fitting cords and secondhand oxford (the frayed tail already hanging out) — had taken an instant dislike to this impostor in their midst. Nor had anyone else seemed particularly enamored of Charles's presence. Even now he could hear adult voices contending in the elegant chambers beyond the open door, Kit's querulous and pleading, and those of his two aunts (Regan and Goneril, Kit called them) firm and unyielding.

Adult matters. Charles turned his attention to the books. Sauntering the length of a shelf, he trailed one finger idly along beside him, *bump bump bump* across the spines of the books, like a kid dragging a stick down a picket fence. At last, he turned and plucked down by chance from the rows of books a single volume, bound in glistening brown leather, with red bands on the spine.

Outside the door, his mother's voice rose sharply.

One of the aunts snapped something in response.

In the stillness that followed — even the cousins had fallen silent — Charles examined the book. The supple leather boards were embossed with some kind of complex design. He studied it, mapping the pattern — a labyrinth of ridges and whorls — with the ball of his thumb. Then he opened the book. The frontispiece echoed the motif inscribed on the cover; here, he could see it clearly, a stylized forest scene: gnarled trees with serpentine roots and branches twining about one another in sinuous profusion. Twisted, and bearded with lichen, the trees projected an oddly menacing aura of sentience — branches like clutching fingers, a hollow like a screaming mouth. Strange faces, seemingly chance intersections of leaf and bough, peered out at him from the foliage: a grinning serpent, a malevolent cat, an owl with the face of a frightened child.

And on the facing page:

In the Night Wood
by
Caedmon Hollow

Looking down at the words — like the frontispiece, garlanded with foliage — Charles felt his heart quicken. The age-darkened pages smelled like a cellar of exotic spices thrown open in an airless room, and their texture, faintly ridged underneath his fingers and laid through with pale equidistant lines, felt like the latitudes of a world yet unmapped. Those sly foxlike faces, peering everywhere out at him from tangles of leaf and briar, seemed to consult among themselves, a confabulation of whispers too faint to quite discern, there and gone again in the same breath. His finger crept out to turn the page.

"Charles."

He looked up, startled.

Kit stood in the doorway, her thin mouth compressed into a bloodless line. Staring at her, Charles saw for the first time — as with an adult's eyes — how old she looked, how tired, how different from her immaculate sisters, lacquered to within an inch of their lives. He thought of his grandfather, that stranger in the casket who shared Kit's jutting cheekbones and deep blue eyes. It fell upon him like a blow, that image. It nearly staggered him.

"We're leaving, Charles. Get your things."

He swallowed. "Okay."

She held his gaze a moment longer. Then she was gone.

Charles started to slide the book back into its slot on the shelf — but hesitated. He felt once again that sense of tremulous significance, as if the flow of events had been shunted into a new and unsuspected channel. As if thrones and dominions more powerful than he could imagine had stepped briefly from behind some hidden curtain in the air. The room almost hummed with their presence.

He could not surrender the book, this artifact of a life that, but for Kit, could have been his own: the manicured lawns and the vast rooms and the great library most of all. (Libraries would be the lodestone of his life.) He would have to tuck it into his knapsack and spirit it out of the house.

He would have to steal it.

As this conviction took root inside him, Charles felt a surge of panic. Terror and exhilaration vibrated through him like a plucked chord.

He wanted to flee, to cast aside the book and, for the first time all day, seek human companionship. Even the unbearable cousins would do. But he could not seem to pry loose his frozen fingers. As of its own accord, the book fell open in his hands, and he found himself flipping past the frontispiece and the title page to the text itself: Chapter One.

The initial letter of the opening sentence was inset and oversized and bound in ornate runners of leaf and vine. For a moment, his inexperienced eye could not decode it. And then abruptly, the entire phrase snapped into focus.

Once upon a time, it said.

2

BUT FOR THE BOOK, Charles might have forgotten the entire episode. For all Kit ever spoke of it, the whole day might have been an elaborate fantasy inspired by their itinerant existence in a succession of cheap walk-up apartments, sustained by a series of minimum-wage jobs ("Fired again," she always told him ruefully when one of them headed south) and well-meaning but feckless boyfriends, most of whom exuded a sweet-smelling haze that Charles would many years later come to recognize as the scent of pot.

But the stolen leather volume had a way of turning up anew with each fresh move — in a box of mateless socks or shoved in among the well-thumbed paperbacks on Kit's bedroom shelf. Finally, home sick one afternoon in Baltimore — they'd only just moved; he must have been nine or ten at the time — Charles actually *read* it.

The story showed up in his dreams for days thereafter, a hallucinatory montage of great trees pressing close upon a woodland path, a terrified child, a horned king, his pale horse steaming at the nostrils in the midnight air. Afterward, Charles could never be quite certain whether to attribute the eidetic quality of these images to the book itself or to the feverish condition he'd been in when he read it. He meant to go back and have another look, but the pressures attendant upon being the new kid at school (he was always the new kid at school, and a bookish, nerdy kid at that) intervened.

By the time he did try to go back, two or three moves later, the book had evaporated, vanished in one of the more recent relocations. And this time it really was forgotten.

It might have stayed that way had Charles not enrolled in a seminar in Victorian nonsense literature fifteen years later. He'd been on his own for years by then (sometimes it felt like he'd always been on his own, like he'd spent more time parenting Kit than vice versa), a scholarship kid who did well enough as an undergraduate English major to snag a teaching assistantship at one of the big state Ph.D. mills. There, he divided his time between a derelict apartment in the student ghetto, cramped classrooms, where he held forth on the merits of the thesis statement to bored freshmen only four or five years his junior, and the classes he was taking, where the air was thick with intellectual posturing and professional anxiety. He'd enrolled in the nonsense seminar out of necessity, when the class he'd really wanted — a course in literary theory taught by a fading Ivy League *enfant terrible* who planed in once a

week to teach his classes and then promptly vanished—filled up before
he could get in.

So it happened that Charles—at twenty-five, still scrawny and bespectacled, still a little bit afraid—found himself in the university library one cold February evening, reading up on Edward Lear. He'd just
started nodding when his eye chanced upon a footnote referencing an
obscure Victorian fantasist by the name of Caedmon Hollow. Now almost entirely forgotten (Charles read), Hollow had written only a single book: *In the Night Wood.*

The title jerked Charles fully awake. The library was silent, cool,
and all but abandoned at this late hour. A hard snow ticked against the
windows, but despite the chill, a thick column of heat climbed through
him. Rereading the footnote, he felt time slip. He was a child again,
alone in his grandfather's enormous library with the cries of the dreadful triumvirate of cousins sounding far away beyond the great arched
windows. Long-forgotten details from that single feverish reading
flooded through him: a full moon looking down through the mists
of the Night Wood; the Mere of Souls, black in its midnight glade; a
child flying through the whispering trees; the Horned King upon his
pale horse.

"Shit," he whispered, setting aside the book. He stood and made his
way across the reading room to a bank of terminals and tapped the title
into the catalog. A few minutes later, clutching a call slip in one hand,
Charles caught an elevator to an upper floor. Walking the labyrinth of
stacks and dragging a single finger in his wake, *bump bump bump* across
the spines of the books, Charles nearly missed it.

He supposed he'd been expecting the same beautiful, leather-bound
volume he'd plucked from his grandfather's shelf. The library's copy was
infinitely more practical, a thin, sturdy book bound in blue boards—or
rebound, he surmised when he flipped it open to find the same baroque
frontispiece. It was a woodcut, he saw, the lines strong and sure.

Wily faces peered out at him from behind the boles of the ancient, lichen-shrouded trees, their great splayed roots knuckling down
into beds of rich, damp soil. As he gazed at them, the faces seemed
to shift and draw back into the foliage, only to appear again, peeping

out at him from some neighboring bower of wood and leaf. He imagined that he overheard their whispered conversations in the air around him.

He started back toward the elevator, flipping to the first chapter, that opening invocation —

Once upon a time

— ringing in his head. When he turned the corner and collided with someone strolling the other way, Charles had a brief and not unpleasant impression that he'd been enveloped in a feminine cloud, faintly redolent of lavender. Caught off balance, he threw out his arms to catch himself —

"Watch where you're going!" the girl cried.

— and went over backward. He thumped to the floor, his glasses flying one way, his book the other. He was still scrambling for the former when the cloud of perfume enveloped him once again.

"Steady there," the girl said. "You okay?"

He blinked at her owlishly. "Yeah, I —" His fingers closed over his glasses. He fumbled with them, and she swam briefly into focus, a small, lean brunette in her mid-twenties, with a prominently boned face and wide-set hazel eyes, bright with amusement — not beautiful, exactly, but . . . *striking,* Kit would have called her. Out of his league, anyway, that much was sure. "I guess I wasn't looking where I was going."

"I guess not."

She took his hand and heaved him to his feet, startling him all over again. "Steady," she said as he snatched at the nearest shelf. He was still trying to get his glasses adjusted — he thought he might have bent the frames — when she reappeared with his book.

"What was it you were so intent on, anyway?"

"Nothing," he sputtered. "It was — I —"

Waving him into silence, she flipped the book over to see for herself. She laughed out loud. "Small world."

"What," Charles said, still fussing with his glasses. "You've read it?"

"Once upon a time, long ago."

"Not many people have read it."

"Not like I have," she said.

"What do you mean?"

"You wouldn't believe me if I told you," she said, shoving the book at him. "Here. Hold still." Shaking her head, she reached out and straightened his glasses. Maybe they weren't bent after all. "Better?"

"Yeah, I guess so. Thanks."

"You bet." Reaching out once again — Charles forced himself not to step back — the girl brushed a speck of imaginary dust from his shoulder. "All set?"

"Yeah, I mean — Yeah."

"Good."

Smiling, the girl slipped past him into the stacks.

"Wait," Charles said. "I wanted —"

But she was already gone, leaving a perfect girl-shaped vacuum in the air before him. "Shit," Charles said, turning to look after her, but the library was cold and empty, a forest of nine-foot shelves branching off as far as the eye could see.

Then, in one of the few courageous acts in his life up to then, he gave chase. He turned the corner of one row of stacks and accelerated. "Hey," he called. "Wait up." And when he reached the next intersection — almost at a run — he nearly collided with her again. She was waiting there, leaning against a shelf, arms crossed, a sly smile upon her face.

"You're aching for a concussion today, aren't you?" she said. "You sounded like a herd of wildebeests. I thought you were going to brain yourself."

"I wanted to ask you something," he said. "I wanted to know what you meant by 'small world.'"

"That's a complicated answer."

"Let me buy you a cup of coffee." Once the phrase passed his lips, the room seemed suddenly airless. He was not the kind of man to ask strange women out for coffee. He was, in fact, not the kind of man to ask out women at all — not for lack of interest, but for lack of confidence. Assuming rejection, he found it easier to save everyone the trouble. So when she said —

"Sure. Coffee sounds good."

— he exhaled an audible sigh of relief.

3

HER NAME WAS ERIN, her secret unexpected (to say the least).

Coincidence, Charles called it. Coincidence that he had plucked down that book in his grandfather's library (she dismissed it all as chance). Coincidence that he had gone on to seek a Ph.D. in English. Coincidence that on a late night in the library with snow slanting out of the black February sky, he should run (literally) into the great-great-exponentially-great-something-or-other of Caedmon Hollow himself, who might have influenced, in subtle ways, Charles's pathway to this place.

Fate, he thought. The Worm Ouroboros. The snake biting its own tail. He had come full circle. And for a moment Charles glimpsed a vast, secret world, intersecting lines of power running just beyond the limits of human perception — a great story in which they were all of them embedded, moving toward some unimaginable conclusion.

As secrets go, it wasn't much of one, Erin confided. The branch of the family that had immigrated to America had generations ago fallen out of touch with the family that remained behind in England — there might have been some kind of conflict, a formal break. She didn't know, or much care. But Caedmon Hollow had remained with them, as a legend if nothing more: an eccentric figure out of the distant past, who'd squandered much of his abbreviated life in drinking and debauchery, squandering as well the talent that had enabled him to eke out but a single volume of fiction.

"Everyone in the family reads it at some time or other. It's like a ritual," she said. "It's not really a story for children, is it? It's hardly a story at all, more like the ravings of a man half mad from drinking."

"I suppose it is," he said, recalling the strangely vivid nightmares his own reading had produced. "But it has a kind of power, doesn't it?"

"I guess so. I haven't forgotten it, anyway."

"Is there more, do you think? Unpublished?"

"Methinks I hear your grad-student heart beat harder," she said. "On the hunt for a dissertation topic, are we?" And when he blushed — he could feel the heat creeping up his face — she touched his hand, and he flushed still harder. "Teasing," she said. "You can have my crazy old great-great-whatever. It hardly matters to me."

So it began, their introduction to the fuel that love feeds upon: stories.

That night they shared their stories — the beginning of them, anyway, as they understood them then. They started at the surface as the best stories do. So they talked about their graduate studies (their *gradual* studies, he said, venturing a rare joke). They talked about their crummy apartments and their crummier cars. He talked about the pressure to publish. She talked about the Law Review.

And then, as the best stories do, they deepened.

They *talked*. She was an orphan, alone in the world. Her parents had died in a car accident three years ago. In a way, Charles was an orphan, too. Kit had hardly been a mother to him, and in his freshman year of college she'd moved to a commune in Nova Scotia. He hadn't seen her since.

Dreams and aspirations, two cups of coffee, then three. They were both too wired to sleep, so they repaired to her apartment to talk some more. She checked his head to make sure he hadn't injured himself when they'd collided, his lips brushed hers, and one thing led to another, as these things will.

Everything important that had ever happened to him had happened in libraries, Charles thought, drawing her down to him on the bed. Then he stopped thinking at all. They married six months later.

They lived happily ever after.

I

HOLLOW HOUSE

───────────

A T MIDNIGHT, BY MYRIAD WAYS and strange, through trees parted before her to direct her path, Laura crept down to look into the Mere of Souls, whence the Sylph had dispatched her. Of a time you could see things in the water, or so Laura had learned in the Sylph's Tale, and she went to her knees, enamored of these mysteries. But no matter how she tilted her head or squinted her eyes, she could see nothing but clots of leaves rotting in the depths below.

Then the waters began to boil and the *Genii* of the Pool thrust his head above the surface. Weedy hair coiled around his face. His eyes were narrow and blue and cold. "What brings you to this place?" he said in tones thick with the thunder of distant waters.

Laura gathered up her courage and spoke, her voice quavering. "I was told in a Story once upon a time," she said, "that you could see your Fate in the Pool if only you believed hard enough. And I believe very hard."

"Some things are better left unseen," the *Genii* rumbled, "and the Mere of Souls may lie."

— CAEDMON HOLLOW, *IN THE NIGHT WOOD*

1

THEY HADN'T SPOKEN for almost an hour—not since Harrogate, where he'd had some trouble with a roundabout and the solicitor's car had vanished, eclipsed by traffic—when Charles Hayden caught his first glimpse of the Eorl Wood.

In the days prior to their departure from their home in Ransom, North Carolina, with its attendant griefs and sorrows, Charles had fooled himself into thinking that maybe, just maybe, things would be okay after all—that the quiet stranger who shared his home was the outward face of a new Erin, a sadder, wiser Erin, tempered, but no longer paralyzed, by knowledge of the myriad ways the world could betray you. He had fooled himself into believing that with enough time and effort, with enough patience, he might yet reach the core of warmth inside her. He had supposed that the core of warmth was still there.

Last night over dinner at the hotel, this pleasant illusion had crumbled around Charles. And over breakfast this morning with the solicitor—her name was Merrow, Ann Merrow—Erin had been pensive and morose. During the chaos at the roundabout, as Charles had whizzed around the circle in futility for the second time, Erin had roused herself long enough to point at one of the branching exits.

"I think it's that one," she'd said, and Charles had whipped the car across three lanes of traffic. He caught a flash of the sign mounted high above. *Ripon and Points North,* it read. Then a lorry blew by with an aggrieved blast of the horn, and he'd yanked his attention back to the road. There had been a time when a stunt like that would have elicited an impassioned orgy of outrage from Erin. Now, however, she barely blinked. Charles supposed she'd just as soon the truck had crushed the car like an aluminum can. If you got right down to it, he supposed he wouldn't have much minded it himself.

Ahead, traffic cleared and the solicitor's dusty blue Saab came into view. "Sorry," Charles said, but Erin hadn't replied. The last vestiges of Harrogate fell away in the rearview mirror and the alien Yorkshire terrain drew up around them, a rugged patchwork of hand-stacked stone walls, rolling pasturage, and narrow-windowed eighteenth-century farmhouses, the forbidding line of the moors looming always up behind them like the shoulders of sleeping giants, blanketed with earth.

It was a bleak prospect even on this clear April morning, and Charles found himself thinking of the Brontë children, tubercular and strange, more than halfway mired in fantasies wrested by sheer force of desperation from this unrelenting landscape, the remote Haworth parsonage and the churchyard before it, overcrowded with the dead. The present seemed to lie lightly on the land here, as though the narrow span of gray pavement, where the solicitor's car hove momentarily into view at the crest of each new ridge, might simply melt away like a dusting of fresh snow, unveiling the bones of an older, sterner world.

That thought put him in mind of Caedmon Hollow and his own strange fantasy wrested from this same hostile terrain all those years ago — more than a century and a half now; Caedmon Hollow might almost have known the Brontës — and Charles felt a surge of excitement at the prospect of Hollow House awaiting them. In that moment of anticipation, he could almost forget Erin's brooding silence, the trouble with Syrah Nagle, and — and the rest of it. He could almost forget it all.

Ahead, Merrow turned into a still more narrow road. It ran downhill between retaining walls of stacked stone for maybe half a mile. Then the road broadened, the walls drew away, and they were in civilization again, or what passed for it out here, anyway.

Suddenly they were in Yarrow. The village was old and steep, crowded into a rift between the hills. Merchants hugged the high street — a newsagent with a white cat drowsing in the front window; a pub, its lot crowded with the noon rush; a hardware store; and a florist (Petal Pushers, Charles noted with a humorless snort). At the far end of town before a crumbling stone house, Charles saw a sign reading *Yarrow His-*

torical Society. He made a mental note to come back and have a look at the place. They weren't likely to have anything useful, but you could never say for sure.

He glanced at Erin, but if the change in scenery had made any impression on her, it didn't show. Merrow made two quick turns, each road more narrow than the last. If they met an oncoming car, they would have to pull over to let it pass. Charles had the fleeting thought that in leaving Yarrow they had passed through the last outpost of the modern world.

The terrain here was sharper, more unwelcoming, the hills rising steeply on either side. The pavement wound through rugged outcroppings of stone and patches of wiry brush. Charles cracked the window and let the slipstream flow in, freighted with the scent of heather and flowers just coming into bloom, and cooler than it would have been back home.

Except this was home now, wasn't it? Home and a fresh start. He glanced at Erin. She seemed to have dozed off. She'd tilted her head against the back of the seat and closed her eyes, and for a single heartbreaking moment, as the midmorning sunlight etched silver the line of her profile, she looked like the girl he had married nearly a decade ago. Then the car dipped into shadow, and the sorrow around her eyes and in the set of her lips sprang into relief.

Charles frowned and looked away, the thought echoing inside his head: a fresh start. God knows they needed it. Drumming his fingers on the wheel, he studied the road, ascending a sharp hill. The solicitor's car hung at the crest a moment, then plunged out of sight. Yew trees clustered against the sky, their tips just visible above the ridgeline.

Anticipation flickered in him once again.

Beside him, Erin opened her eyes. "We there?" she murmured.

And then they topped the ridge. The valley bottomed out endlessly before them, and suddenly the Eorl Wood was there, bigger than Charles had expected, and more forbidding. The trees began halfway down the slope, like the wall of an ancient fortress, a palisade of enormous alder and elm and gnarled oak. The wood spread as far as the eye could see — lime, olive, jade, a thousand shades of green, fading here and there into glossy emerald patches of darkness.

When Charles saw it, his first thought was that he understood, really understood, the environment that had shaped the nightscape of Caedmon Hollow's mystifying book. His second thought, coming fast on the heels of the first, was that the wood was collectively alive, a single vast organism spilling out across the valley in wild profusion, bigger than the eye could comprehend, improbably, impossibly bigger, that it was sentient, watchful, and that somehow —

— *how?* —

— it had been awaiting them.

"Jesus," Erin whispered, and it was all Charles could do — the impulse took an active effort of will to resist — not to step hard on the brake and wrench the car back toward Yarrow.

Too late to turn back now.

Momentum seized them, the gray pavement blurring as the car gathered speed. At the base of the decline, Merrow signaled left and disappeared into the trees. If Charles hadn't seen it happen, he would have missed the turnoff entirely.

He almost missed it anyway. He braked hard — the road ended in a turnaround maybe two dozen yards past the entrance — the force of the deceleration pressing him into the upholstery. He swung the car around and squared up to the entrance.

It gaped under the trees, a tunnel hewn into the flesh of the wood itself, flanked by stone columns shrouded in vines. Engraved words, eroded almost flush with the stone, were visible on the pillar to the right: *Hollow House,* and below that, *1848.* There had been a gate there once, but no more.

A taillight flashed deep in all that emerald gloaming. Charles reached out for Erin's hand. "We're here."

"So we are." She gave him a forced smile in return, but her fingers remained dead in his grasp.

Charles sighed. He turned on the headlights, touched the gas, and nosed the car between the columns. The wood took them. When the sound of their engine died away under the trees, no evidence of their passage remained.

They might never have come that way at all.

2

An oppression of trees drew up around the car, and a doomed sense of claustrophobia seized Erin Hayden. For a moment it was all too much — the dark closing down upon them and the tires whispering their incessant tidings of arrival on macadam crumbling with time and carpeted with dead leaves.

Most of all it was the ancient oaks pressing close to the road, like old men, lichen-bearded and a little deaf, stooping close to listen. She imagined them straightening up as the car slipped by, leaning their hoary heads together to pass the news, a stir of leaf and branch rippling ever outward before them.

There was something disturbing about the idea, something watchful and abiding about the gloom under the trees. It was too much, too close.

She glanced at Charles, his face masked in streamers of light and shadow. He looked tired, haggard with something more than jet lag. She almost reached out to him, maybe would have, but an overhanging branch slapped at the windshield, startling her, and she turned away instead.

That was when she saw the child: a little girl clad in a simple white dress, maybe kindergarten age —

— *Lissa's age* —

— or maybe a year older. She stood on the leaf-scattered shoulder of the road, staring toward them, so close she might have reached out and touched the car as it sped past.

"Charles?"

"Hmm?"

"Did you —" She broke off. She did not want to say it. It had been nothing, a trick of the eye, a flash of sunlight through the forest canopy or a patch of fog breathing up from the damp soil. *We see what we want to see,* her therapist had told her. As if that helped.

"Did I what?" Charles said.

"Nothing," she said.

She was tired of seeing things.

For months after the funeral, back home in Ransom, she'd caught glimpses of Lissa everywhere, through a scrim of raindrops on the windshield as she wheeled by the kids at the bus stop or in the baleful fluorescent glare of the grocery store, just turning the far corner of an aisle. Something familiar in the set of the mouth or the flash of shoulder-length hair.

Then she'd blink and see that Lissa wasn't there after all. The girl at the bus stop would shift the angle of her gaze and her face would fall into unfamiliar lineaments. Meeting the grocery store specter afresh among the frozen foods, Erin would see that she was younger than she had thought, that she had dark hair and a squared-off jaw, that she looked nothing like Lissa at all.

She'd mentioned it to Charles once and he'd flinched as if she'd struck him. After that she'd never brought it up to him again.

Until last night.

Last night, over dinner at the hotel, she'd seen Lissa once again.

One moment Erin had been sitting at the table, jet-lagged and silent, spooning an indifferent soup into her mouth. The next, she'd glanced up, reaching for her water glass, and the girl had been there: Lissa, a slim blonde apparition, standing silent in the dining room door. Erin gasped, and the water went over with a crash.

"Shit," she'd said, half rising as she reached to right the glass. When she looked up again, the girl —

— *Lissa* —

— was gone.

"Here, let me get that," a voice said at her shoulder. The landlady — a kindly heavyset woman, her gray hair pulled back from her round, smiling face — leaned over her, dabbing at the table with a cloth.

"What happened?" Charles was saying, but Erin ignored him.

"That girl," she said, sinking back into her seat.

The landlady paused, the damp rag in one hand. "Girl?"

"There. She was in the doorway."

"Did *she* cause this?" The landlady straightened, abruptly stern. "Sarah," she called. "Sarah, you come in here right now. Always underfoot, that one," she added, swiping at the spill, an expanding island of dampness in the linen cloth. "Sarah!"

"Listen —" Charles began, but Erin overrode him.

"It's not the girl's fault. Really. She startled me, that's all. She looked so much like —"

Then the girl was there, eyes downcast, her hands clasped behind her back, and the words —

— *my daughter* —

— died on Erin's lips.

The girl, pudgy and thick, with a fringe of dark hair veiling her eyes, looked nothing like Lissa. Nothing at all. Lissa had been airy, ethereal, like some elemental spirit that had settled inexplicably among them. This girl — Sarah — looked sullen and coarse, grossly earthbound.

"Sarah," the landlady said, "have you been sneaking around again?"

"N'ome. I just walked by the door. I didn't mean anything."

The landlady gave the spill a final swipe. "That should do." She snapped the rag at the serving station. "Bring me that pitcher, child. Quickly now."

Charles stared at his plate, his mouth set in a thin line, while the girl complied. She moved slowly, cradling the pitcher in her small hands. She studied Erin from under her bangs as she refilled the glass.

The landlady smiled. "I'm very sorry."

"No need to apologize," Charles said. "Accidents happen."

"Ever since her mother passed . . ." The landlady shook her head. "Can I get you anything else?"

"No," Charles said. "Thank you."

"You'll let me know if you need anything, then." The landlady turned back to the kitchen, herding the girl before her. Just before the child disappeared, she glared back at the table, and for an instant — the space of a heartbeat — she reminded Erin of Lissa once again. It was like the blink of a camera shutter: Sarah, pudgy and resentful; then Lissa. Lissa glaring back at her, her eyes reproachful and unafraid.

You let me die, those eyes said.

Then the shutter blinked again and Lissa was gone.

"Charles —"

His hands busied themselves with his silverware.

There was something wounded in his silence, something fraught and sorrowful. He looked like a little boy, scowling at his shoes lest a flash of further intimacy send pent-up tears spilling down his cheeks. Erin had wanted to touch him then, too, and in that moment of weakness, a confessional impulse seized her. A fresh start, he'd said. And why not? You didn't start fresh with lies.

"Charles—"

His knife chattered against the rim of his plate. A dull reflection alighted trembling on the flat of the blade. He stared at the table.

"I saw her, Charles. It was her. I mean . . . I know . . ."

Then he *did* look up, his face pale and cold, his expression set.

"She's gone, Erin. She's—" He drew a breath, shook his head, sighed. "She's . . . gone." He stared at her a moment longer. "I'm sorry," he said. He hesitated as if he wanted to say more, and then, biting his lower lip, he pushed back his chair and left the dining room.

"Ma'am?" The landlady stood in the kitchen door, wiping her hands on a towel. "Is there something wrong with the meal?"

"No," Erin said. "The food was fine. Everything's fine."

But everything wasn't fine. Nothing was fine. Nothing would ever be fine again. Erin leaned her head against the cool window and focused on the thrum of the tires, the hum of the engine. It would be all right, she told herself. Everything would be all right.

Yet the wood, vast and green and vigilant, still oppressed her.

Gone, Charles had said.

He was right, of course. That was the hell of it. Last night at dinner, she had seen not Lissa but another child, a dark, heavyset child with griefs and burdens of her own. If Erin's heart had chosen to see something else, it was an illusion, nothing more.

Perhaps she'd gone mad. Sane women did not see dead children cruising the canned fruit aisle when they did their weekly shopping. Sane women did not see ghostly shapes in the shadows underneath the trees.

Charles downshifted, and the engine's tone deepened. Tidal pressure swelled through her as the car leaned into a curve. A bulwark of ancient, moss-damp stone—ten feet at least, and maybe taller—shot up from the forest floor before them like the fossilized spine of a buried dragon. As the car hurtled toward it, Erin's heart quickened.

Then the road dipped and a narrow aperture, hardly wider than the car, appeared in the stone. The car shot under an archway. The suffocating omnipresence of the wood, that sense of contained energies churning just beyond the range of perception, retreated. An instant of speeding darkness followed — how thick the wall must be! — and then they surfaced on the other side, into a treeless meadow, sunlight breaking across the windshield.

Charles slowed as the road dropped down into a deep, round bowl carved into the heartwood. He nosed the car up to a second wall — hand-stacked stone, perhaps waist high or a little higher. He killed the engine.

Erin reached for her satchel. "I guess we're here," she said.

3

THEY GOT OUT of the car and stood there in silence, transfixed.

About a hundred yards away, Hollow House — three stories of gray, castellated stone — stood at a slight elevation, moated by sculpted grounds, meadow, and walls. Like a stone cast into a pool, Charles thought. Axis mundi, still center of the wheeling world.

"Something else, isn't it?" Merrow said.

Something else indeed. The photographs had not done justice to the house's implacable aspect — its grim solidity, its tower and turrets, its dormers and crow-stepped gables.

Merrow said, "The original structure burned in —"

"Eighteen forty-three," Charles said. "Everything but the library."

Merrow gave him a perfunctory smile. "You've done your research."

"Charles is all about research," Erin said, adjusting her bag. "It must be hell to heat."

Merrow laughed. "It's been decades since the entire house was in active use. Mr. Hollow — Edward, that is, your immediate predecessor — lived in a thoroughly updated suite of rooms, though 'suite' hardly does it justice. It has good proximity to the library — handy for your research, Mr. Hayden. In any case, you'll find Hollow House quite livable, I should think." Merrow led them along the perimeter of the wall. "Shall we?"

"Where's the gate?" Charles asked.

Merrow uttered something that might have been a laugh. "There's a gate for deliveries in back. Otherwise the wall is unbroken, one of the house's eccentricities. I thought you'd prefer the front view — a formal introduction, if you will. Here we go." She waved at a set of stone risers built into the wall — a stile, Charles thought, summoning the word out of dusty memories of some obscure Victorian novelist — Surtees maybe.

"Let me give you a hand," Charles said, but Merrow ignored him, flitting up the stairs on her own, so that he found himself gazing at the curve of her rear end, sleek beneath her clinging skirt.

She looked down at him from the crest of the wall. Charles averted his gaze, heat rising in his cheeks. "You'll want to be careful," she said. "It's a bit steep." Before he could reply, she started down the other side.

Charles followed, the steps slick beneath his feet. He paused atop the wall to reach for Erin's hand.

"I've got it, Charles," Erin said.

The steps on the other side were broader and overgrown with moss. He'd just reached the bottom and turned back to look at her when Erin's foot slipped. Charles lunged for her too late. She slid helter-skelter down the stairs, spilling her satchel, and smashed to the earth on one shoulder, breath bursting from her lungs with a plosive grunt.

"Are you all right?" he asked, but she waved him away.

"I'm fine." She pushed herself to her feet, wincing, and reached for her ankle. "Just get my stuff."

But Merrow was already collecting it: makeup and lipstick, her passport, an assortment of pens and pill bottles. A sketchbook. A framed photo. Merrow stood, looking at it. "Your daughter?" she asked, scraping mud off the edge of the frame. "She is very beautiful. The glass has cracked, but that can be mended easily enough, can't it? Are you sure you're okay?"

"I just twisted my ankle. I'll be fine."

She didn't look fine. Mud streaked her jeans. She was flushed. When she took a step, she favored the bad ankle.

"Here, let me help you," Charles said.

"Really, Charles, I'm fine." And then, relenting, with a small smile, "Walk it off, right?"

"I guess so," he said.

"Well, let me get your bag, at least," Merrow said. "Come on."

Together — with Charles and Merrow hovering to either side of Erin — they made their halting way toward the house. By the time they'd reached the stairs, six of them, climbing to a square portico, the door had been opened from within. A stout, fifty-something woman in full Mrs. Danvers livery — black skirts, white apron, even a black cap with her gray hair pinned up underneath — descended to meet them. It was like seeing a nurse in whites, complete with cap, in your local emergency room.

"Ah, Mrs. Ramsden," Merrow said.

Mrs. Ramsden smiled. "Here, let me help you, now," she said, reaching for Erin's arm, and together they hobbled up the stairs into Hollow House.

4

THEY STOOD IN a vaulted entrance hall, like children in a tale, long lost and returned at last to break the spell that had been cast over their ancestral home. A great chandelier illuminated the tapestries and framed portraits that adorned the walls. Doors to the left and right stood closed. The high archway before them framed a long, luxuriously furnished salon.

"I saw you fall," Mrs. Ramsden said. "That stile is a menace. I don't know how many times I've told Mr. Harris we need to do something about it." She sighed in exasperation with Mr. Harris as she led them through the salon, past twin oaken staircases that curved like the necks of swans to the gallery above. The balusters had been carved with an intricate motif of leaf and vine. Cunning foxlike faces peered out at them as they passed. "Anyway," she added, "welcome home. The house isn't always lit up this way, but we wanted to put her best face forward for you. I'd hoped to give you the grand tour, but I don't think you're in any shape to enjoy it, Mrs. Hayden. Let's get you upstairs and see if we can't find some ice for that ankle."

They went up a back staircase to what had been Mr. Hollow's living quarters: a house inside the house, Charles thought, and a luxuriously appointed one: polished floors and plush oriental rugs, Victorian-era furniture, built-in bookcases stocked with neat rows of leather-bound books. Capacious, high-ceilinged rooms — study, sitting room, dining room — radiated off the large central foyer, where a grand staircase curved up to an open gallery. "There are four suites and a maid's room upstairs," Mrs. Ramsden said, leading them down a wide hall into a breakfast room lined with windows, providing a panoramic view of the lawn. There was a second stone house down there. A cottage, really: a single floor, with narrow windows.

"That's Mr. Harris's house," Merrow said, putting Erin's satchel on the table. "He's the estate's steward."

"We do hope you'll be comfortable here," Mrs. Ramsden said as she got Erin settled. "I'll get you some ice."

Merrow took out her phone. "Let me see if I can find you a doctor."

"Please don't bother. I just twisted it."

"It's no bother," Merrow said and turned away, holding the phone to her ear. By the time Mrs. Ramsden returned with a dish towel and a large plastic bag of ice, Merrow was saying, "Yes, I expect you to come out here, John. We're speaking of the new mistress of Hollow House. Yes, three should be fine. Yes, I'm sure she'll survive until then. Good. Thank you, then."

She ended the call and smiled — a little tightly, Charles thought. "Dr. Colbeck will be here at three," she said. "Can you endure it for a couple of hours?" When Erin nodded, Merrow turned to Mrs. Ramsden. "Does Mr. Harris intend to join us?"

Mrs. Ramsden hesitated. "See, we thought you'd be arriving a little bit later. Mr. Harris ran into Yarrow. I expect him back directly."

"Not the day I should have chosen for a trip into the village," Merrow said. "Well." She looked at Erin. "You seem to be in good hands. If there's nothing else I can do for you . . ."

"You've done more than enough."

"Then I'll be off." At the doorway, she turned. "Keys. Mustn't forget the keys." She reached into her purse and withdrew a heavy key ring. "I've marked the important ones. Mr. Harris will have to help with the others."

A doorbell rang in the foyer.

"I suppose that's him," Mrs. Ramsden said.

"No doubt," Merrow said. "I'll let him in on my way out. In the meantime, if you need anything, please do ring me up. You have my card." And then, smiling at Erin, "I'm sure you'll be up and about in no time."

5

"THE HOUSE OPERATES on a skeletal staff, sir," said Cillian Harris as he led Charles through the salon. "Mr. Hollow kept just enough people on to maintain the property—groundskeepers and housemaids. It'll be a bit of a lifestyle change, sir."

Charles glanced at Harris. He looked more like a linebacker than a steward: mid-thirties, with a thatch of unruly dark hair and a crooked nose—not unhandsome in a rough-hewn kind of way. His eyes were bloodshot, and though the man seemed sober enough, Charles was almost certain that he'd caught the scent of whisky on his breath.

It was just past two o'clock.

"Mrs. Ramsden sees to the living quarters and supervises the housemaids," Harris was saying. "She'll arrive most mornings around seven. I'm always available. I live in the cottage. You may have noticed it from the breakfast room. I manage the estate." And then, almost as an afterthought, he said, "Under your direction, of course."

"Well, let's work on a more informal basis, then. Why don't you call me Charles?"

"I couldn't do that, Mr. Hayden. All my life I served Mr. Hollow, and my father before me, and never once did I call him by his given name. Mr. and Mrs. Hayden you must be to me, by force of habit if nothing else."

Charles reminded himself that he was an interloper in a foreign land. The custom of the country and all that. "If you insist."

Harris nodded. "I understand that you intend to do research."

"Yes, Caedmon Hollow, his book —"

"I know his book all right." Then, hesitant, as though he felt he was overstepping his bounds, "Never should have written it, if you want my opinion."

Not really, Charles thought, but he said nothing.

"Well, you'll want to be back before the doctor arrives," Harris said. "Let's just have a glance into the library."

6

"Tea?" mrs. ramsden said.

"Why not?" Erin said.

Mrs. Ramsden busied herself setting out the service: cookies on a platter, sugar cubes and cream, floral teacups and saucers. Everything had the pearly, translucent glow of bone china. "It's been a long trip from America, I warrant. You must be tired."

"Exhausted."

"As soon as I set out your tea, I'll leave you to rest."

"Why don't you join me instead? I'd enjoy the company."

"I'm sorry, ma'am. I fear our different stations in life preclude such intimacies."

"Oh, dear, Mrs. Ramsden, I am thoroughly middle class, I assure you."

"Mr. Harris wouldn't approve."

"Well, Mr. Harris works for me now."

Mrs. Ramsden offered her an uncertain smile.

"I insist," Erin said. "We'll finish up before he comes back. Charles will spend half an hour in the library alone."

"I'll have to get another cup."

"Use that one."

"Oh, that's for Mr. Hayden, ma'am."

"We can get him one when he gets back," Erin said. "Please, sit down. What's your first name, anyway?"

"Helen, ma'am."

"Helen it is, then." Wincing, Erin leaned forward to extend her hand. Mrs. Ramsden's — Helen's — was dry and cool. "I'm Erin. It's a pleasure to meet you."

"Likewise, ma'am. Let me just pour the tea."

"Sure. If you'd reach me that satchel, too, I'd truly appreciate it. I'd get it myself, but —" She laughed without mirth at her predicament.

"Why don't I see about fresh ice?"

"It's fine. Really. Just hand me the satchel. And please, have a seat. I mean it."

"Yes, ma'am."

The "ma'am" was going to have to go, too, Erin thought. Baby steps. At least they were moving in the right direction. The satchel, on the other hand, was a mess: her sketchbook smeared with mud, her pens and pencils jumbled at the bottom. And the photograph, of course, the glass broken, as Merrow had said. It was unbearable to look upon it, impossible not to. She had to force herself to set it aside and dig out her meds, nearly two dozen jumbo-sized plastic bottles. She counted them, to be sure. She'd been doctor shopping, hoarding, afraid of not being able to get what she needed — *wanted,* her therapist would have said — in this benighted country. Effexor for the depression. Trazodone and Ambien to help her sleep. Her medicine chest, Charles called it. Her personal pharmacy.

Sometimes she hated Charles.

She shook out a Klonopin — she had half a dozen prescriptions for anxiety, Ativan, Xanax, you name it — and dry-swallowed the pill; then, impulsively, she shook out another one.

Mrs. Ramsden was right about one thing, though: the journey had been too much. The girl at the hotel. That small figure watching from the roadside. *We see what we want to see,* as her therapist had said, adding, *Be careful or you'll learn to love your chains.*

She did not want this. She wanted to be free.

She would never be free.

Mrs. Ramsden — Helen — sat down at last. Sugar and cream, a shy smile across the table. She ignored the vials of medication. She cleared her throat. "You'll want to know about the household, of course," she said. "Mr. Harris handles most matters, but he generally gives me free rein in domestic affairs. In addition to myself, there are seven maids. They keep up the larger portion of the house. I'll introduce you to them soon. I had hoped to do so today, but you'll want to rest your ankle. I maintain the residential section myself, so you can expect to see me daily."

"I hope we see a lot of each other. I imagine I'll be lonely all by myself out here."

Mrs. Ramsden hesitated. "I'm sure you'll have plenty of company as soon as you recover from your fall."

Which was hard to imagine. She and Charles hadn't entertained in nearly a year now. Even the usual visits after . . . after Lissa . . . had been difficult affairs for all involved. While everyone had been generous and kind — their sympathies had certainly been genuine — the unacknowledged specter of Charles and Syrah Nagle had haunted every interaction, dividing her even from her closest friends in the end. You could not easily speak of it, yet you could hardly ignore it. So after the initial flurry of visits — the inundation of more food than she and Charles could ever eat, the follow-up phone calls, the two or three lunch invitations that she had declined — their social life had dwindled to nothing.

"Now, as to the matter of cooking —"

"We'll cook for ourselves, Mrs. Ramsden."

"I always cooked for Mr. Hollow."

"Charles and I have always cooked for ourselves," Erin said. But this too was a fraught subject, wasn't it? Her parents had both been functioning alcoholics. The car wreck that had killed them — Erin had been a sophomore in college by then, and the drinking had escalated as soon as she moved out — had been no chance accident. By the time she was twelve, Erin was taking care of her own meals. Even in the early days of their marriage, she and Charles, both of them busy with careers, had more often eaten meals alone than together. Only after Lissa made her debut had Erin made a concerted effort to be home for dinner. Nor did she drink, at least in those days. She would not repeat the mistakes of her parents — or so she had vowed.

Now it didn't matter, of course.

Now nothing mattered.

She glanced at Lissa's photograph, helpless to stop herself, but if Mrs. Ramsden noticed, she didn't say a word. She merely said, "You're in no shape to cook, are you? And I would wager that your husband is indifferent in the kitchen at best. Husbands usually are. You could use some meat on your bones, if you don't mind me saying so."

"Mrs. Ramsden —"

"I serve promptly at five. I will brook no protests, Mrs. Hayden."

"Can we at least revisit it after I'm on my feet again?" Erin asked, amused that Mrs. Ramsden, for all her deference, had already maneuvered her into asking permission. She had a feeling that she wouldn't be doing much cooking. Which was just as well, she supposed. It wasn't like either one of them had spent much time in the kitchen in the last year.

Mrs. Ramsden let the question pass. She smiled. "You're an artist."

"I sketch," Erin said. It was a new endeavor, but it came easily to her. She'd loved drawing as a child. "I'm teaching myself."

"May I see?"

Erin hesitated.

"I don't mean to pry."

"No, it's fine." Erin pushed the sketchbook across the table to her.

As Mrs. Ramsden flipped the pages, Erin turned her cup in its saucer, staring at the crest she'd seen at the top of so many letters from the Hollow estate over the last few months: a capital H entwined in green and gold foliage. It put her in mind of the first edition of *In the Night Wood,* passed from hand to hand down the generations of her family, the baroque initial letter of each fresh chapter. Someday, she supposed, she would have passed it on to Lissa.

"They're very well done," Mrs. Ramsden said, turning a page. "You have an eye." She looked up. "It's all the same girl, isn't it?"

Erin bit her lip. Nodded.

"The girl in the photograph there?"

She couldn't bring herself to answer.

7

"Erin?"

Alone in the breakfast room — Mrs. Ramsden had gone about her duties, whatever they were — Erin closed the sketchbook and looked up. The Klonopin had kicked in. She stood outside her emotions, aware of them but detached, an observer of her own inner life. The meds insulated her from her grief and anger, nothing more.

"Dr. Colbeck is here," Charles said from the door.

Indeed he was. He towered over Charles, a gaunt, ginger giant: ginger hair, ginger beard, all knobby elbows and knees. Six-three or -four, at least, and vastly underfed. Ichabod Crane, she thought. Ichabod Crane was to be her doctor.

"Dr. Colbeck."

The ginger stranger actually bowed slightly. He put a black medical bag on the table and took in the rows of pill bottles arrayed in front of Erin without expression.

"You'll excuse me if I don't get up."

To his credit, Colbeck ignored this witticism. He smiled. "Please, call me John," he said. Then: "So you're the Americans who've inherited Hollow House. You've been much anticipated hereabouts."

"Warmly, I hope," Charles ventured.

"Of course. You'll find the natives friendly enough, I think."

"Did you grow up here?" Charles asked.

"Born and bred. My training eroded my accent somewhat; for good or ill I am uncertain."

"Then you knew our benefactor?" Erin asked.

"Only in a professional sense. I took on Dr. Marshall's practice ten years ago, when he retired. Mr. Hollow needed little care. He came of hardy stock. He lived to ninety-seven, and I doubt he was sick a day of it until the final crisis overtook him. He was a reclusive man. Cillian Harris attended to most of his affairs."

"You'll find us more approachable, I hope," Charles said.

"I'm sure I will." Colbeck cleared his throat. "Let's have a look at that ankle."

He knelt and took the ankle in question into his big hands. Erin winced, the pain brief but not insignificant. Then Colbeck was saying, "You appear to have a sprain, Mrs. Hayden, and a minor one at that. You should be up and around in a day or two. In the meantime"—he opened his bag, which, despite the rank of shiny instruments on view, disgorged nothing more sinister than an ankle brace—"in the meantime," he said, "you seem to be doing the right things. Rest and elevation and ice, though no more than twenty minutes at a stretch. Compression"—he held up the brace—"helps as well, and you'll need some support when you get back on your feet. Easy enough, yes? I can fetch some crutches from the car, if you like."

"Why don't you—" Charles started to say, but Erin overrode him.

"I think I'll be fine."

"I think so, too. The brace should be sufficient. Weight is the key. What your ankle wants is weight. Twenty-four hours, and then you'll start trying to get up and around, won't you. You can alternate acetaminophen and ibuprofen for pain every two hours or so. Three or four days and you'll be good as new."

He leaned over to close his bag, and that was when his gaze fell on the photograph. "Oh my, she's a lovely young girl. Your daughter, I presume."

"Yes," Charles said. "Our daughter. Lissa. Back home."

The words hung in the air like undetonated bombs. Erin could not speak, but if Colbeck noticed anything, he didn't acknowledge it. He just snapped the bag closed and stood, saying, "Nobody mentioned anything about a daughter."

8

CHARLES SAW COLBECK OUT.

In the dooryard, the doctor said, "What happened to your daughter, Mr. Hayden?"

"I'm sorry?"

"Your daughter. She must be, what, five, six at the most? One doesn't usually leave a child that age behind when one plans an indefinite stay abroad." He turned to look at Charles, his eyes knowing.

Charles stared back, something tightening in his chest. "I'm not sure it's anything for you to concern yourself with, Doctor." Just at the edge of rudeness, maybe a hair across.

If Colbeck noticed, he didn't seem to care. He said, "You may have noticed that your wife had twenty-two vials of medication on that table, Mr. Hayden. I counted. You may also have noticed how remote Yarrow is. Unless you intend to drive to a surgery in Ripon every time you have a head cold, I'm likely to be your physician. It is in fact my business to know."

Colbeck held Charles's gaze. Charles looked away, surveying the green mass of the Eorl Wood. "She died," he said.

"And your wife?"

"She hasn't adjusted well. She blames me. There was an accident."

"An accident?"

"And that really *isn't* your business, Dr. Colbeck."

Colbeck didn't push it, though Charles, still staring at the wood, could sense his scrutiny. After a time, he said, "How long ago did this happen?"

"Almost a year ago. I could name the time to the day and hour if you must know. In your capacity as my physician."

Colbeck didn't take the bait. He sighed. After a time, he said, "I can offer you little in the way of comfort. I'm very sorry for your loss. I'm very, very sorry. Words are inadequate. But your stay here won't heal matters between you and your wife. It may not heal at all, and if it does, it will leave a scar, quite a bad one. Sometimes marriages survive the loss of a child, more often not. In cases where one spouse blames the other . . ." Colbeck shrugged. "In the meantime, it might help to talk about it."

"Erin was seeing a counselor at home."

"And you?"

"No."

"Perhaps you should consider it."

"Perhaps."

"I can give you the names of some good people. You'll have to drive into Ripon for that, but I think the trip might be worth it."

"That would be fine."

"But you won't go."

"No."

"Your wife —"

"I doubt it."

"Well, I'll ring you with the names all the same," Colbeck said.

Charles turned to face him. "I should check on Erin now."

Colbeck nodded. "Ice, twenty minutes on, twenty minutes off, Mr. Hayden. Try to get her up and moving tomorrow. It will be tender for a while."

"Yes."

"Good afternoon, then."

"Thank you for coming out."

"You're quite welcome." Colbeck paused. "At the risk of overstepping my bounds, Mr. Hayden, may I offer you two further pieces of advice before I go?"

"Why not?"

"In the matter of your wife, I counsel patience. These things take time. Fits and starts. Two steps forward, one step back is the rule. But even such halting progress gets you there in the end."

"And the second bit of wisdom, doctor?"

"I should steer clear of the wood if I were you."

"Why is that?"

"People get lost, Mr. Hayden."

"I'll be careful."

"Do. And ring me if you need anything."

With that, Colbeck put his back to Charles. He strode with long steps across the yard to the stile. On the other side, he wheeled around a battered pickup — it might have been red once, but had long since faded to a dull, no-color brown — and disappeared into the trees. Charles stood there, knowing that he should do as Colbeck had said and go in to check on Erin. But the doctor's closing words lingered in his mind: *I should steer clear of the wood if I were you.*

Charles turned his gaze back to the forest. He had an obscure sense that something was watching him from the line of trees, but when he scanned the wall, there was nothing there.

9

NOTHING ELSE HAPPENED that day.

Except that Charles and Erin slept in separate bedrooms, as they had every night since Lissa died.

Except that, somewhere in the deepest trough of morning, Charles opened his eyes.

He stood by the bed, dreaming of a black combe where a shallow stream hurried over a bed of broken stones and a green moss grew. The window had been flung open and a breeze caressed his bare skin, beckoning him toward the deep purple sky where a horned moon hung like a child's toy, and the night wood, girdling the great house, whispered green thoughts in its green and leafy shade.

II

YARROW

WHEN LAURA TOLD HIM OF THE little creatures in the trees with their daemonic physiognomies, the Helpful Badger said, "All manner of Folk live in the Wood. And they are all abroad under the Moon, for this night they must shrive."

"They frighten me."

"They are more often capricious than they are cruel," the Badger said. He yawned and scratched a flea, adding, "There is only one whom you must fear. When you encounter Him, you must summon all your strength and courage and bring all your wit to bear."

"Must I encounter Him?"

"The Story requires it of you," the Badger said.

"But who is He?"

"I dare not say his name. But He long ago seduced the Wood Folk into betrayal and grievously wounded their rightful Lord, whom He banished into the Outer Dark. And now the Wood Folk must bow before him and shrive their sin in secret."

"How will I know Him when He comes?"

"He wears a crown of horns."

— CAEDMON HOLLOW, *In the Night Wood*

1

IT WAS HAUNTED, of course, Hollow House.

But they were all haunted — Erin and Charles, Cillian Harris, Mrs. Ramsden, too. And though Mrs. Ramsden's sins and failures and regrets, like those of Ann Merrow or Dr. Colbeck, have but glancing significance in this story, they were each of them protagonists in other tales, with their own dramas, their flights of joy, and their plunges into sorrow. Once upon a time: no life too humble, no event too insignificant.

Every story is a ghost story.

It was the photograph that haunted Erin and Charles, or, more precisely, the loss that it signified. A kindergarten photograph of a blonde girl, three-quarter profile, her hands crossed neatly upon the table in front of her, but otherwise unposed — her giggling smile (no doubt the photographer had ventured some joke), the soft curve of her jaw, her milky complexion — all this trapped behind a spider web of shattered glass.

For Erin, the photo was like a shallow well in a dry season. She dared not drink of it too often — yet she could not help herself. She drew it in her sketchbook time and again, laying out the lines of Lissa's visage, lending it dimension and form with each careful stroke of her pencil. And then she would turn the picture to the wall and keep working, as if by this obsessive reproduction she could score the image into the tissue of her brain and heart. She would not forget her daughter's face.

Already she could feel it slipping away.

For Charles the photo was like a jail, prisoning away the grief that could any moment escape to overwhelm him. As long as Lissa was locked behind the glass he could manage his days by rote — not unaffected, but functional at least. Erin feared forgetting. Charles longed for it. The burden of his sin (for so he thought of it) was too much to bear. Yet memory could not be contained. The shattered glass made the metaphor manifest. Looking at the photo now, he felt an inconsolable longing to go back, to start over and do everything right.

And Cillian Harris? Who could say? But he'd stiffened, like a man taking a small electric shock, when his gaze fell upon the photo that first day in the breakfast room. Briefly, to be sure — a breath, no more — but Charles had observed it nonetheless, and wondered.

The glass would have to be replaced, of course.

"I can't look at her like this," Erin said, too much reminded of the horrors of the day that Lissa had died. And now that Lissa had escaped, Charles had to lock her away once more.

He took the car and drove into Yarrow, to the hardware store he'd seen on the way to Hollow House. But Lissa had arrived before him. He saw her in a small child — was it her? — holding her mother's hand as she leaned forward to smell the early spring flowers that bloomed in pots outside Petal Pushers. And worse yet, he saw her on the front page of the newspaper racked before the newsagent: the *Ripon Gazette,* the photograph unnerving, the headline worse: A FAMILY'S AGONY. He stepped inside, pressing his coins with tremulous fingers into the hand of a gruff man who barely acknowledged him, his eyes fixed on the television behind the counter.

Outside, in the bloodless English sunlight, Charles turned his attention to the paper:

> The search continued for a missing six-year-old Tuesday near Yarrow. Mary Babbing was last seen riding her bicycle in front of her family home toward dusk last Sunday. Investigators —

Too much. Charles moved to discard the paper. He could not do so. Lissa stared up at him from the front page in lurid color. He folded it instead, tucked it under his arm, composed himself, blinking back tears.

Okay, then.

Mould's hardware was next door.

2

CHARLES TOOK A DEEP BREATH, pushed his way inside. The narrow space beyond felt claustrophobic, though the store wasn't crowded. A single customer, lean, with a hank of dark hair hanging over his forehead, studied the packets of seeds on a wire rack. Charles nodded as he slipped past to the counter at the back of the store.

A tall, fleshy man stood there, wiping his hands on his apron.

"Ah, the stranger among us," he said in a thickly accented voice. But Charles was the one with the accent here, wasn't he — the stranger, as Mould (was he Mould?) had pointed out, in a strange land. Mould or not, the man was old, seventyish and hale, bald but for the unruly wisps of gray that clung to the sides of his head, thin of lip, bulbous of nose, tufted of eyebrow and ear. Eyes of pale, penetrating blue peered at Charles over half-rim glasses. Charles wasn't sure he liked the eyes. They seemed to see more than they had any right to see. The old man extended his hand. It was callused, the thick, ridged nails clogged with crescents of grease. He was Mould after all, Trevor Mould. He said the name as they shook hands, and Charles winced, not at the name but at the fact that he seemed to have inserted his hand into a vise.

"Charles Hayden," he said.

"No doubt. We're glad to have you here."

"True enough," the seed-packet man said, joining them at the counter. He introduced himself as Edward Hargreaves, adding, "Hollow House hasn't had anyone to warm its bones for near two years now. Longer if you think of how Mr. Hollow grew toward the end."

"Wouldn't leave the house," Mould said. "I hadn't seen him for years by the time he finally passed." He reached out a hand. "Let's have a look at that, shall we?"

Charles passed the photo across the counter.

"So beautiful at that age, aren't they? Six, I'm guessing."

"Five. Five and a half, she would have said," Charles said, his neck burning.

Mould tilted his head. "Left her at home, did you?"

"Back in the States." Not a lie, he told himself, but — something else. He couldn't say exactly what. An omission, nothing more. Yet a lie by any other name —

He hesitated.

The truth would come out sooner or later. Given the amount of research it had taken to track Erin down to inform her of the inheritance, Merrow almost certainly knew. And now Colbeck knew. How long before all of Yarrow did as well?

He spoke without conscious volition. "She —"

"What's that?"

Mould had turned to the rear counter to study the photograph.

"Nothing," Charles said. "She couldn't make the trip," he said, for to speak it aloud was to acknowledge it as a true thing — to acknowledge his role in it. He swallowed.

"What happened to the glass?"

"My wife. She dropped it. She took a spill on the stile."

"She's all right, I hope?"

"Twisted her ankle. She'll be on her feet again before the week's out."

Hargreaves shook his head. "Funny thing that, isn't it? That wall."

"Both walls," Mould said. "Must have been a hell of a lot of work. Hard to say whether the intent was to keep something in or something out."

"They say," Hargreaves added, "that old Mr. Hollow kept the place closed up in the last years of his life. Wouldn't so much as permit an open curtain."

A chill passed through Charles. There was something haunting about the idea of the old man thrice imprisoned, inside the house, inside the great encircling walls.

"We can fix this up for you," Mould said. "Later this afternoon, say? Joey, the one that does the glass cutting, he's down to the King for lunch. He'll be back in half an hour or so, and I can put him right on it. Say an hour. I hate to make you drive all the way back here."

"That's fine. I wanted to look in at the historical society."

"Quiet village, Yarrow," Hargreaves said. "I warrant you won't find much there."

"I'm interested in Caedmon Hollow."

Hargreaves grimaced. "Not fit for children, that book."

"Leave the man be, Ed." Mould looked up. "If you tire of the historical society, you can always stop in at the King for a pint, can't you? Anyway, we'll have it ready for you." He held out his hand as though he were finalizing some complex financial agreement, and once again, reluctantly, Charles inserted his hand into the vise.

"An hour, then," he said.

3

CHARLES DIDN'T KNOW what he'd expected from the historical society: brochures advertising local attractions, maybe? Recessed lighting illuminating framed photos and polished glass display cases?

But no. The society was very much a work in progress. The foyer was gloomy and close. It smelled musty. The rooms beyond—the two Charles could see, branching off a broad hallway with a stairway to the right—were largely barren of any such displays. Framed photographs listed on their hangers. A handful of dusty exhibit cases stood half obscured by stacks of cardboard boxes.

"Hello?" someone called from the interior.

"Hello."

A door opened and closed. In the shadows at the end of the hall, a figure appeared—angular and tall, female, beyond that he couldn't say. The woman wiped her forehead with a cloth.

"Just here for a look about, are you?"

"I thought it might be interesting."

"Ah. So you're the American who's moved into Hollow House."

"That's right."

"You're the talk of the town."

He peered closer. "We are, are we?"

"Down to the King, you are," she said. Then: "Feel free to have a look. We don't have much, I'm afraid."

"It looks to me like you have quite a lot," he couldn't help saying.

"A lot of rubbish. That's what I'm here for, to excavate it all and figure out what's worth keeping."

"I thought you were the docent."

"That, too. Listen, give me a minute to finish up. I'm sorting papers in the back here. Papers, papers everywhere and nary a drop to drink."

Suddenly he liked her, this shadowy stranger at the far end of the hall.

"Then I'll show you around a bit," she said. "I'll want to wash my face first, if you don't mind."

"And if I do?"

Was he flirting? An image of Ann Merrow's taut rear end, muscles flexing as she climbed the stile, flitted through his mind. And then, worse yet, an image of Syrah Nagle —

He shunted the thought away.

"I'll wash it anyway," the woman said dryly, and with that she was gone.

Charles wandered into the adjoining room. He glanced at a set of photos — the high street from some distant era — picked up a stiff, yellowing copy of the *Ripon Gazette,* put it down again without bothering to read the headline, and ran a finger across the dusty surface of a glass display cabinet, leaving a long, clean snail's track in its wake. He paused before a case of medals and fading ribbons. A yellowing index card pinned to the wall above it read, in faded typescript, *Yarrow has contributed its share of young men to the conflicts of*—

Charles turned away.

What on earth was he doing here, in a museum dedicated to a place where almost nothing had ever happened? Even Caedmon Hollow was an obscure figure in the annals of Victorian lit — a footnote, nothing more.

He'd hung his future on a footnote.

A wave of doubt swept over him. The scholar-adventurer indeed, he thought, turning to the next display, another constellation of fading black-and-white photographs: lean, grim-looking men posed beside farm animals and antiquated tractors, a young boy holding a prize ribbon against his chest. Black and white. Nobody smiling. *The*

Yarrow Agricultural Fair began in the early 1800s and remains an institution —

Sighing, Charles drifted to the far end of the room. More photographs, he thought — but no, that wasn't quite right. The images predated modern photography: daguerreotypes, and more than that, daguerreotypes of Hollow House. The first showed the place in ruins, roofless, the great rectangular stones of the exterior blackened by fire. The ones that followed — there were six of them, marching in a straight line across the wall — showed the house in various stages of reconstruction, culminating in an image of it in pristine condition.

Charles leaned forward to study the central image more closely: the roof framed with great beams, stacks of lumber and stones in the dooryard below.

"Probably our best thing, that," the woman said at his shoulder. "So far, anyway."

Charles turned to face her, high-cheekboned and pale-complexioned, with a cap of close-shorn blonde hair, hazel eyes, a scattering of freckles across the bridge of her narrow nose. There was a smudge of dust over her right eyebrow. Apparently she hadn't washed up after all. Or not very well, anyway.

"I'm Silva North," she said.

"Charles Hayden." He took her outstretched hand.

"Well, Mr. Hayden —"

"Charles."

"Charles, then." She nodded at the framed images. "The construction occurred between 1844 and 1848, following a fire that consumed most of the original manor house. The library and part of the salon survived, though badly damaged. Hollow's wife, Emma, was not so fortunate. Tradition holds that Hollow set the fire himself, though why he might have done so is unclear. The book came out —"

"In 1850, to little fanfare," Charles said. "Hollow committed suicide the next year."

Silva North smiled. "I see that you've developed an interest in Hollow House since you've taken up residence."

"Before that, actually. I'm working on — that is, I'm contemplating — a biography."

"Rather limited audience for that, I should think."

"I hope my book will change that."

"Well, you're in the perfect spot. There must be tons of stuff buried in that old pile."

"I'm hoping so." He hesitated, surveying the rat's nest of boxes and papers. "I don't know what your collection —"

And now Silva North laughed out loud, a rich, throaty laugh, not unkind. "Our collection," she said. "Is that what brought you to our humble historical society?"

"I take it *you* are the society."

"In a manner of speaking. The village pays me a modest stipend — all too modest, I'm afraid. And I get to live in the upstairs flat rent-free."

"In return for?"

"In return for going through boxes. I decide what to keep and what's rubbish. Mr. Sadler, who used to live here, died. Quite a pack rat, he was, with an eye to local history. That must have been twenty years ago. I was a girl. He left the house to the village, and they've been shoving boxes in here ever since. I volunteered to clean it out and put it in some order, open it to the public. A deal was struck, and here I am."

"But why?"

"I have about half of a master's in history from the University of York. And I'm interested in the village's past. Unfortunately, it has produced no one of any great significance aside from our eccentric author. Strange book. Not quite right for children, is it?" She raised her eyebrows. "No white rabbits checking their watches."

"No indeed." Charles hesitated. "I was hoping that if you ran across anything about Hollow, you'd be willing to share. Have you?"

"The daguerreotypes, obviously. They were stashed away in a box of Mr. Sadler's gas bills. God alone knows how they got there. Nothing else so far, I'm afraid." She studied them. "They'd make splendid plates for your book, wouldn't they?"

They would, Charles was about to say, but just then he heard the door open at the end of the hall, the patter of small feet in the corridor. The high, sweet voice of a little girl interrupted them, saying, "Mummy, I'm thirsty." Charles turned, reeling when he saw the child, maybe five years old, six at the most, with blonde curls and blue jeans and an elfin and expressive face. The earth slid away beneath his feet. Subsidence, old ghosts rising up inside his mind: *Lissa,* he thought.

Charles stepped backward, Silva's hand steadying him as the world came once again into focus: the musty smell of the place and the child in the foyer, the labyrinth of boxes.

Jesus, was this what Erin —

"Are you okay?"

"No, I" — deep breath, tears stinging at the corners of his eyes — "yes, of course, I —"

No words came.

Then Silva's hand was gone. He could still feel its warmth on his back. "Who's Lissa?"

Had he said it aloud?

He shook his head. "My daughter. She's my daughter."

Was, a malicious inner voice put in. *Was your daughter.*

"Still back in America?"

Always and forever, he thought. But all he said was "Yes."

"You must miss her very much."

"I'm thirsty, Mum."

"Just a minute, Lorna."

"They look very much alike," Charles said. "It gave me a shock."

"It must have. You look as though you've seen a ghost," said Silva. "You need to come upstairs for tea."

What he needed was air. "That's very kind of you," he said. "I don't mean to be rude —"

"You dropped your paper." She held it out to him as he turned away. The *Ripon Gazette,* Lissa staring out at him from the front page.

"Mary Babbing," Silva said. "Tragic."

Steadying himself, he said, "What happened?"

"No one knows, do they? She just evaporated. You expect things like that to happen in York or London. But not here."

"Did you know her?"

"She was a classmate of Lorna's." And then, looking at her daughter, "We shouldn't —"

"Of course not."

Silva shook her head. "It's a horrible thing," she said.

4

CHARLES KNEW ABOUT horrible things. Charles knew about ghosts.

On the way back to Hollow House, he parked in the turnout by the vine-shrouded pillars, the Eorl Wood looming up around him. He sat there, the car idling, his hands clenched on the wheel. Then he picked up the photograph and tore back the butcher paper Mould had wrapped it in.

Lissa gazed up at him, once again imprisoned behind her wall of glass. Only she wasn't, was she? She'd escaped, after all. He'd seen her at the Yarrow Historical Society. He'd seen her in the *Ripon Gazette.* As if to confirm it, Charles reached for the newspaper in the passenger seat and unfolded it on his lap. He placed the photo beside it: Lissa and this other lost child, Mary Babbing. Who could say what horrors she might have endured?

A FAMILY'S AGONY, the headline said.

He leaned his head against the headrest, closed his eyes.

When he opened them again, he saw a figure in the Eorl Wood.

It gazed back at him, a green shadow in a green shade. Like a man, but not a man, antlered like a stag in rut. Cernunnos, he thought. The Horned God or King. The avatar of the Night Wood. He stared, breath frozen in his lungs. He blinked. The figure was gone, not there. It had never been there at all.

Charles shook his head. He put the photograph on the seat beside him, crumpled the newspaper into the space underneath, and eased the car into gear. He accelerated between the pillars and sped into the darkness underneath the trees.

5

HOLLOW HOUSE ENVELOPED them.

As Erin's ankle healed, she and Charles explored their new home, children in a haunted mansion in a tale: the downstairs rooms, the dining room to the right of the entrance hall, the drawing room to the left. The vast salon with its twin staircases and the adjoining library, accessible by lustrous wooden doors at either side of an enormous fireplace. And beyond that a handful of smaller rooms: the music room, the game room, an office where Cillian Harris managed the estate's affairs. Bedrooms and sitting rooms opened off the gallery encircling the salon, everything luxurious, everything ornate but for the servants' quarters on the top floor: narrow, dormered chambers with rusting iron bedsteads, vestiges of another era.

And everywhere the motif on the balusters repeating itself: leaves and vines, those cunning vulpine faces. They peered from mantels and window casings, from finely wrought moldings and armchairs. Stealthy and gamesome, they retreated into the foliage in one place only to peep out anew in another, entire rooms subtly aswarm—a trick of the eye, unsettling and strangely beautiful.

Lissa would have loved it, Charles thought, but they did not speak of her. They rarely spoke at all.

Work would save them, Erin's therapist had once said.

So they went to work, each in their separate orbit. Charles took refuge in the library, all burgundy and leather, with heavy velvet curtains and plush carpets, a long table, and an antique silver globe mapping a world that had long since passed out of existence. Everything polished, everything gleaming. Comfortable chairs surrounded the cold fireplace. And books, ranks and ranks of them, stood shelved on every wall, behind glass doors with shrewd faces looking down from the corners of their frames.

"You'll want to keep the curtains closed," Mrs. Ramsden told him. "The spines of the books would dry and crack in the sunlight. Many of them are first editions, Mr. Hayden, quite valuable. A nice dim room and saddle soap once a year, that's what they want."

"I'm sure they do," Charles said. And then: "Personal documents, Mrs. Ramsden. Anything relating to Caedmon Hollow? Any ideas where to start?"

"Cabinets on the west wall, perhaps, though anything that old is more likely to be in the archives downstairs."

"Archives?"

"It was Mr. Hollow's little joke," she said. "What it really is is boxes, Mr. Hayden. Boxes and boxes and boxes. You have your work cut out for you, I'm afraid." Then: "Will there be anything else, sir?"

"No, thank you," he said.

And then he was alone, overwhelmed by the task before him.

6

ERIN, ON THE OTHER HAND, riding a smooth Xanax wave, set up in the dining room of the residence: sketchbook, pencils, and art gum erasers arrayed across the table. And Lissa's photo, of course. She flipped through the pages of the sketchbook. Lissa and Lissa again. Page after page of Lissa. Erin had been an attorney once, trafficking in matters of ultimate finality: wills and estates, the complexities of the human heart, fear and love, envy, hunger, loathing, and desire. Families in grief and horror, families shattered, divided against themselves: the territory of ambiguity, the kingdom of the gray.

She'd closed her practice after the accident. She could no longer stomach the work. She lived in binary now.

Ones and zeros.

Before and after.

With every passing day, the before was increasingly lost, bleached out by time and grief and the medication that did not salve the pain but only dulled it.

The after didn't matter.

She turned to a clean page, tapped a pencil against her teeth.

Mrs. Ramsden — Helen — put down a tray at Erin's elbow: strong coffee, cream. Already, she'd mastered their tastes.

"Thank you, Helen."

"You're quite welcome, ma'am." And then, turning back at the doorway: "I wonder if I might have a word with you."

Erin looked up. "Of course."

"It's just . . ." Mrs. Ramsden approached the table. She picked up the photograph, stared at it for a moment, put it down. "I wanted to say how sorry I am for your loss."

"My loss?"

"It's a small place, ma'am. There are few secrets here."

Erin put down the pencil. She bit her lower lip. "I suppose so."

"If there's anything I can do. If you want to talk . . ."

"That's very kind of you."

Mrs. Ramsden smiled.

"I don't want to talk," Erin said. She reached out and turned the photo facedown on the table. She tried to say it kindly: "I just want to be alone."

"If I've overstepped —"

"No, Helen, please. I just — I can't talk about it."

"I understand, ma'am," Mrs. Ramsden said. She nodded, slipped back into the kitchen.

Erin reached into her pocket for another Xanax, swallowed it with a sip of coffee, waited for it to unspool in her bloodstream. She stared at the blank page. After a time — she couldn't say how long, the minutes had slipped away on the Xanax tide — she picked up her pencil and began to draw. She didn't think, simply let her hand follow its own imperative. She might have been drawing in her sleep.

She supposed she'd gotten just what she wanted. She'd never felt so alone.

7

PLAINCLOTHES DETECTIVES CAME out from Ripon two stormy days later. Charles met them in the entrance hall, where they stood closing their umbrellas: McGavick, a burly man in his late fifties, his unruly hair sprinkled with gray, and Collier, close-shorn, younger by a decade and a half, compact and fit, his face prominently boned.

They talked in the library.

"I can remember coming out here as a boy," McGavick said. "Mr.

Hollow used to hold lawn parties in the summer. Music, and lights in the trees at nightfall. And games: toad in the hole and football on the lawn. Before that wall went up and you had to come scrambling over the stile just to get near the place." He shook his head. "The old man turned queer in the end, he did." He looked up. "I trust you and your wife are finding the place to your liking."

"We're settling in."

"Ah, good. I wonder if she might join us."

"She's indisposed, I'm afraid." Charles hesitated. "Our daughter . . ."
He couldn't bring himself to say it.

McGavick shook his head. "Of course. Village life. Everyone knows everyone else's business. It's a terrible thing, the loss of a child."

A cramped silence followed.

Collier prowled the room. He paused by a window to pull back the drapes. Rain lashed the glass. Beyond the great wall, the Eorl Wood tossed its leaves beneath a lowering sky. Collier looked at Charles's MacBook on the table, fingered the stack of papers he'd so far unearthed, useless every one of them. "You've been working."

"Research. I'm thinking of doing a book."

"You're a writer, then?"

"A professor," Charles said, thinking of Ransom College. "Used to be, anyway."

McGavick nodded. "Always thought I might like to write," he said. "Some of the things you see in this line of work —"

"What's your book about?" Collier asked Charles.

"A biography, actually. Of Caedmon Hollow."

"Now *that's* a book," McGavick said, "that *Night Wood* thing. The way that little girl — what was her name? Livia?"

"Laura."

"That's right," McGavick said. "I remember now. You think she's going to find her way out. That's the way these things are supposed to go."

"She has to figure out what she's lost before she can escape," Charles said.

"But she never does, does she? Who among us is lucky enough to do that? The book is true to life that way. That's what I like about it."

"I don't imagine it's literary criticism that brought you all the way out here in the rain," Charles said.

"No, I'm afraid not," McGavick said. "I wish it was. It's a far more sober matter than that."

"It's the girl," Collier said. "The one who disappeared in the village."

"Mary Babbing," McGavick said, shaking his head ruefully.

The name caught in Charles's throat like a fishhook. He thought of the newspaper crumpled under the seat of the car, the photos he'd placed side by side: twinned girls, an ocean apart. A FAMILY'S AGONY. How easy it was to imagine: the child snatched off the street, the wheels of her bicycle still spinning, sunlight flashing off the whirling spokes. There were holes in the world. People fell through them all the time, while elsewhere dogs were scratching their fleas in the sun and someone was eating a sandwich at a clean table with a white linen cloth and lilies in a vase. Who knew the breadth of human suffering, its weight and depth?

"Are you all right, Mr. Hayden?"

"I saw it in the paper. She— The girl looked very much like my daughter." He swallowed. Took a deep breath. "You think she's dead."

McGavick sighed. "I wouldn't like to say one way or the other. But it's a possibility we have to consider, naturally. The reason we're here is, well, the wood . . ." He shrugged. "If you wanted to . . . dispose of . . ." He lifted his hands, left the rest unsaid.

"We know you haven't been here long, Mr. Hayden," Collier said. "But if you've noticed anything, anyone in or around the wood . . ."

Charles thought of that green shadow in the trees.

"Are there squatters in the forest?" he asked.

Collier's interest quickened. "You've seen someone, have you?"

"No. I just— I wondered, that's all," Charles said. "You should talk to Cillian Harris, the estate steward. He's been here his entire life. If anyone could help you, he could."

"We'd intended to," McGavick said. "Perhaps you can point us in the right direction."

"He lives in the cottage," Charles said.

He led them out through the salon, past the music room to a back entrance that had been intended for the servants when the house had been built. Charles supposed they used it still, the housemaids and Mrs. Ramsden, Cillian Harris, too. The three men stood at the threshold, staring out at the rain. The cottage lay downslope a hundred yards or so.

"Thank you," McGavick said, unfurling his umbrella. "We'll find our way from here."

He followed Collier down the steps into the rain. He turned back to look at Charles. "Again, Mr. Hayden, my sympathies. It must be unbearable."

Charles nodded, thinking of Lissa and Mary Babbing, too. Another dead child. McGavick might be loath to say the words aloud, but Charles had seen them in the man's eyes. The world was full of dead children. There were more of them every day. "Did you search the wood?" he asked.

"We did what we could. There's more wood than can be searched properly, really. If she's in the wood, she's likely lost for good. Like the girl in that book. Laura." McGavick laughed without mirth. "There are stories, you know. Old wives' tales." He shrugged, lifting a hand in farewell as he turned away. "Thank you for your time, Mr. Hayden."

Charles stood at the door, watching them walk down the lawn. The cottage glowed through the billowing gray wings of the storm, but Harris didn't seem to be home. He wasn't answering, anyway. Charles would have given up the enterprise as a loss, but McGavick wasn't so easily discouraged. He hammered on the door again — and this time Harris opened up, emitting a wedge of golden light into the gloom. McGavick held up a badge. Harris stepped outside, closing the door behind him.

Whatever business the three men had to conduct, they conducted it in the rain.

8

THE FOUL WEATHER PASSED. Charles woke early, weary of being trapped in the library, and let himself outside. He clambered over the stile in the gray, predawn light and trudged toward the outer wall, wet earth sucking at his boots. The forest crowded the sky, dwarfing the great rampart. Close up, Charles put its height at twelve feet, maybe more, and half again as thick, grown over with vines the size of fire hoses, dispatching everywhere runners of imperial green. He pressed his hand flat against it, half expecting to feel something, the thrum of the secret powers of the earth, ley lines or echoes of Neolithic magic.

New Age nonsense. He felt nothing.

He turned, slopping his way through the weeds, keeping the wall to his left. He paused at the first of the stone archways. A moss-grown tunnel lay beyond, awash in shadow. At his feet, almost hidden among the tussocks, lay a shattered gate, rusting slowly back to earth.

Charles probed at it with the toe of one boot and took a breath of damp English air. He kicked a clod of damp English earth. England, oh England. This green and pleasant land. The whole country was a sopping mess, he thought as he strode on. He felt a sudden sympathy for Erin, tagging along on his futile quest for redemption, as though a book on an obscure Victorian fantasist could somehow salvage everything — his life, his marriage, his paltry excuse of a career.

The dean at Ransom — Hank, a bearded giant of a man — had given him a year's sabbatical.

"I made Syrah the same offer I'm making you," he'd said that afternoon in his sun-bright August office. Outside, the semester was gearing up. Students were trickling back to campus, bellowing greetings across crowded parking lots. In dusty offices, faculty bent to their syllabi. A ragged game of ultimate Frisbee had erupted on the quad.

"What did she say?"

"She resigned a week ago. I don't know where she is or what she plans to do."

"Hank —"

"Jesus, Charles, what were you thinking?"

Sighing, the dean tapped a bobblehead Freud that sat on the corner of his desk. The old Vienna fraud nodded his assent. *Yes, Charles, what were you thinking?*

Charles said nothing. He hadn't been thinking. Thinking hadn't been part of it.

"I went to bat for both of you with the board, Charles. This is the best I could do. They wanted to dismiss you outright. Look, you've got to take this. It'll give you a year to get back on your feet, look around on the job market."

"And if I refuse? If I decide to teach out the year?"

"You'd risk having your contract voided."

You'd risk. Charles had been in academia long enough to read that code. He'd be fired for certain.

The blue envelope had arrived just as the year turned, five long months later. Charles hardly believed it then, and there were a dozen times in the month and a half that followed when he hardly believed it all over again. Yet belief didn't factor into it. A small army of judges and solicitors had spent more than a year running one branch of the family to ground here, another to earth there, until finally there was only one branch left. Erin's branch.

The pressure to find the next job eased — not because he didn't want a job, but because he wanted the *right* job. The kind of job you get coming fresh off a biography that triggers the kind of wholesale reappraisal that Melville had gotten in the 1920s. And now he had the time — not to mention the access to a potentially sizeable body of unique sources — that enabled him to do it. But what of Erin? What was she to do, stranded in this desolate place?

And another question, one so self-serving that Charles could barely bring himself to speak it, even in the privacy of his own mind: what if she divorced him, dividing him from all that he hoped to achieve here? And why wouldn't she? The ties that bound them had long since dissolved. Syrah, Lissa . . . most of all his own actions — they'd all played a role in that. What did he and Erin share but grief and recrimination, each to the other a constant grinding reminder of all they had lost?

The sun had edged over the trees by the time he reached the second archway. Charles looked down at Hollow House, toylike from this perspective. The wall seemed huge by comparison, primordial, ancient beyond reckoning. Framed in wisps of ground mist, the aperture looked like a passage to the underworld. Not even the ruins of a gate remained here, but at the far end of the passageway, one survived unbroken, black and depthless against a field of green murk. Charles stepped inside. The tunnel curved gently upward. A clammy draft rose to greet him. He thought of that shadow in the trees, those great antlers branching, and almost turned back. But that had been his imagination, nothing more. He moved forward instead, trailing the fingers of one hand along the mossy stones of the wall, waving the other before him to clear any cobwebs. His boots squelched in the muck. The air stank of it, a dank, organic fetor: Ouroboros, he thought. Time was cyclical, life perpetually blooming out of the lees of the past.

Outside the wall, the wood pressed close.

A bird lifted its voice.

Charles heard its cry, muffled and far away. Neither in nor out of the wall he stood, but buried underneath, in between, at a kind of threshold dividing the house and its grounds from the Eorl Wood. A liminal space, he would have told his students: possibility yet unmade.

He pushed on. Closer, the gate took on texture and depth. The rust-pocked iron had been wrought into the semblance of a face: cheeks of stylized leaves, narrow eyes, branches curling up like horns to entangle themselves in intricate scrollwork. Cernunnos again, older than Christianity or the Romans who had foisted it upon the Celts, who had held this land for five hundred years before the Romans came.

Pagan sorcery.

He lifted his fingers to touch the face.

He'd expected the gate to have rusted fast. But it gave when he put his shoulder to it, swinging open with a shriek of corroded hinges. The Eorl Wood stood on the other side, a maze of enormous oaks, their thick roots knotted over stone outcroppings. The leafy canopy hundreds of feet overhead diffused the light, choking off undergrowth: a vast mossy labyrinth, a moted green haze.

He stepped into the forest.

9

A WEEK SLIPPED BY.

They settled into routines.

Most mornings, Charles stretched his legs in the wood, taking care never to stray too far from the wall. He spent the rest of the day foraging in the library for the ghost of Caedmon Hollow.

Erin, too, was looking for ghosts — in Lissa's photo and in her sketch-book and most of all, perhaps (to Mrs. Ramsden's unspoken distress), in the Eorl Wood. She stood at the windows for hours at a time, staring out at the forest, thinking of the child she'd seen among the trees, hoping somehow, impossibly, to catch another glimpse of her.

But there was never anything there.

She went to bed early, she drank wine with dinner, and when Cillian Harris came to speak to her about the estate's affairs — "in your capacity as the heir," he said — she empowered Charles to act on her behalf.

Charles and Cillian agreed to meet at ten a.m. in the office.

Charles arrived early. It had been a dry, cool morning, and he'd spent more than an hour tramping in the wood — longer than he'd intended, leaving him too little time to get anything done before the appointed hour. He went back through the salon to the office, hoping that Harris might already be there. But the room, paneled in dark wood, with an or-nate claw-footed desk and a matching table, stood empty.

Charles glanced at his watch. He had half an hour to kill.

He wandered back into the corridor and peeked into the music room (frilly, feminine) and the smoking room (more dark paneling, and brass cuspidors, for Christ's sake). He imagined a Victorian dinner party, the male guests retreating here for cigars and conversation before joining the ladies in — where? The drawing room? Something else he supposed he'd need to know for the book.

He entered the game room, which apparently functioned in both senses of the word. Mounted trophies — a lion; a boar of some kind or other; a bird on the mantel, its wings outstretched — gazed down upon the pool table in the center of the room. Charles took a cue down from the wall rack and leaned over the slate, sighting down a ball that wasn't there. Wonder what Caedmon Hollow had played, if he'd played at all? Billiards? Pool? Snooker? And what was the difference, anyway? And the trophies — who was responsible for that savagery? He felt at a loss, adrift in his own ignorance. How in hell did anyone ever learn enough to write a biography?

"Ah, Mr. Hayden, there you are."

Charles looked up. Harris stood in the doorway, looking more than ever like a linebacker stuffed into a business suit, his hands clasped behind his back. "Mr. Harris. I hope I didn't keep you."

"Not at all, sir. I'm just now ready."

Charles straightened. He nodded at the table. "Do you play?"

"Not well, I fear."

"What do you play?"

"Snooker. Quite popular."

"You'll have to teach me sometime. I've never played anything but eight ball myself."

"As you wish, sir." Then: "Shall we have a look at the estate's records?"

"Absolutely." Charles racked the cue and smiled. "Lead on," he said.

10

THE RECORDS WERE mind-numbingly complex: real-estate holdings well beyond Hollow House and the Eorl Wood, a complex web of bank accounts of various types, a tangle of investments too complicated for someone of Charles's bent to ever unsnarl. But the gist of the presentation seemed to be that the Hollows had been quietly wealthy — *very* wealthy — for an extremely long time. Charles didn't glean much beyond that, though he listened dutifully, once in a while even venturing a question — no doubt of the ignorant variety — just to let Harris know he was paying attention.

And occasionally — when they leaned over to examine a document or look at something Harris had pulled up on his laptop — Charles thought he caught the scent of whisky. He recalled the faintest hint of that same earthy odor on the steward's breath the day of their arrival — nothing he could be sure of, either then or now. Hell, it could be —

Harris was wrapping up his presentation, closing his laptop, packing his papers away. "Do you have any further questions, Mr. Hayden?"

Have you been drinking? Charles wanted to ask — it was not yet noon, after all, and this man administered the entire estate — but he couldn't bring himself to broach the topic. Instead, he found himself saying, "What do you know about the wall?"

Harris looked up from his bag. "Which wall, sir?"

"Well, the outer one, I guess. Who built it?"

"I don't think anyone knows. Some say generations of Hollows built it; the land's been in the family for hundreds of years. I shouldn't like to think how long. Others say the Romans. And still others say the Celts."

Charles thought of that dank, narrow tunnel and the blur of emerald light beyond the gate, the ranks of ancient trees, flinging out thick roots, gnarled and misshapen, to claw at the rocky English soil. And moss, everywhere moss, thriving in the deep-scored runnels of bark, flourishing in a moist carpet on the forest floor.

"But why build it in the first place?"

Harris hesitated. "Well, as to that . . ."

"Yes?"

"Old wives' tales, mostly. The people of the wood."

"The people of the wood?"

"Dangerous folk, wood folk. So my gran used to say when I was a lad. Not to be tampered with." He laughed. "Thinking of your book, sir?"

"I suppose."

"Well, I wish you luck, Mr. Hayden." Harris shouldered his bag. "If that's all . . ."

"Yes. Sure. Thank you for your time, Mr. Harris."

"Likewise, sir," Harris said as he ducked out, leaving Charles standing distracted in the office, thinking of the thing he'd seen — or thought he'd seen — in the wood. Thinking of Cernunnos and Caedmon Hollow and the Horned King. Thinking of Lissa and Erin and all that he'd lost, or thrown away.

11

"DID YOU FIND anything useful today?" Erin asked over the meal Mrs. Ramsden had left warming in the oven: roast beef and potatoes and vastly overcooked vegetables, vintage English fare. She left promptly at six every day, departing to attend to her own husband's dinner. "He'd starve without me," she'd once confided to Erin, adding, "Don't trouble yourself with the dishes. I'll take care of them in the morning."

They ignored this prohibition — washing up seemed the least they could do — and they ignored the dining room as well, taking their meals in the breakfast room where Erin and Mrs. Ramsden sometimes had tea. Erin's art supplies — she was drawing more than ever (obsessively, Charles thought) — had colonized one end of the dining room table, which was long and ornate, with two great chandeliers hanging overhead. Charles had once joked that they should eat there anyway, sitting at opposite ends of the table and bantering at the top of their lungs, the echoes of their voices gathering in the shadows high above them, like a synod of ghosts consulting among themselves in matters of the grave.

But there was no banter, only the subterranean idiom of their relationship since the accident, neither casual conversation nor open argument, the oblique discourse of a marriage in distress, of things unsaid — of things that maybe could not be said — running just under the surface of the most prosaic interactions.

Had he found anything useful?

"Nothing," he said.

Nothing of Caedmon Hollow, anyway, though there had been all too much of the man's descendants generations removed, mundane treasures precious to someone in their time: flowers pressed between the pages of an album (by whom, and why?), troves of impassioned love letters (still smelling faintly of some imagined perfume) and their matter-of-fact progeny, too often void of affection: courtships gone sour over decades of marriage. And photographs by the boxful, decades of them. Snapshots gave way to posed family portraits in washed-out colors, and these to sepia-toned images of imposing, sober men, unsmiling and bearded, with watch chains dangling at their bellies. Some of the pictures had names penciled on the back, but others remained enigmatic, glimpses of an irretrievable past.

Stories, always more stories — but those were not his to tell.

This was the curse of archival research: you couldn't know for sure that there wasn't something important to your story there (letters,

notes, perhaps a manuscript itself) until you'd sifted through the entire mess. Things got lost, misplaced along the way, and they turned up
in the most unlikely places: Boswell's *London Journal* in the haylofts of
Malahide Castle. A partial manuscript of *Huckleberry Finn* in a Los An-
geles attic.

He sighed.

"You sound frustrated," Erin said.

"I am, I guess."

"Well, you're only getting started."

"Why don't you come down to the library tomorrow, pitch in? I'd
love the company, and it might do you some good."

She pushed food around on her plate. "I'm fine, Charles."

"I'm not sug—"

"Aren't you, though?"

He supposed he was. She'd turned inward, warming herself at the
coals of her grief. He'd flipped through half a dozen of her sketchbooks.
He'd found Lissa on every page: faithful reproductions of Lissa's school
portrait progressing, as Erin had gained skill and confidence, to entirely
original images, drawn from memory as much as model: Lissa sitting on
her bed with her legs folded in front of her (crisscross applesauce, kids
called it), or standing in the doorway to the kitchen, her backpack on
her shoulders: first day of kindergarten, tears and smiles, on the threshold of her inaugural step into the unsheltered world, an odyssey cut
abruptly short. He would not think of that, though in forbearing it he
thought of little else. In his way, he was as obsessive as Erin. Not for the
first time Charles thought his project might be a hollow one, pun very
much intended: a shell to contain the radioactive core of his guilt. Busy-
work. Were they really so different, he and Erin?

Yet at least he'd turned outward to face the world.

"Maybe you should branch out, do some original work."

"I'm branching, Charles. I'm doing some original stuff."

"I'm not talking about—"

"I know what you're not talking about. You never talk about it. Neither one of us does."

He didn't take the bait. "I'd love to see the new pictures."

"They're not ready to show."

Because they don't exist, he thought. Aloud, he said only, "Ah."

He took a sip of wine. The wine cellars were impressive, another asset in Cillian Harris's protracted accounting — one that he and Erin had, by unspoken agreement, committed themselves to depleting, it seemed. It was wasted on Charles, though. He had no palate. Wine was wine. He could have been drinking swill straight out of a box.

"Well, when they're ready," he said.

"Sure."

They were silent then, listening to the sound of their marriage calve around them, like a glacier, like sea ice, as fragile and as cold.

"Pass the salt, please," he said.

12

CHARLES WAS WRONG.

There were new pictures, though Erin couldn't say where they came from. The blackest tenements of her soul, maybe, summoned into light by some chance cocktail of medication and emotion — fury, sorrow, regret. Once invoked, however, the images could not easily be exorcised. She doubled up on the Xanax, topped it off with a Klonopin, drank wine until she felt numb — and still they haunted her. At night, she could not sleep for thinking of them. By day she poured them out upon the page.

Came Mrs. Ramsden, bearing coffee.

"Something new?" she asked. "May I have a look?"

"No," Erin said, closing the sketchbook.

She could not bear to look upon them herself.

13

ANOTHER DAY IN the library.

At five p.m., Mrs. Ramsden fetched Charles to the residence to take a call on the landline, a wall-mounted phone with an actual rotary dial and a thick black handset, heavy as a bludgeon. Charles hadn't even known it worked. The voice on the other end sounded tinny and far away. At first he couldn't make it out.

"I'm sorry?"

"It's Silva North," the voice said. "From the historical society."

She needn't have said the latter. The name alone had conjured her into being before him: the cap of blonde hair, the sprinkle of freckles across her nose, the wide mouth. He moistened an imaginary finger and erased the smudge of dust over her eyebrow.

"Are you there?" she said.

Charles collected himself. "Right here," he said. "How are you, Ms. North?"

"Silva. And I'm sorry to bother you, but I seem to have run across something that might interest you. Actually, I know it will interest you. Why don't you and your wife — what's her name?"

"Erin."

"Why don't you and Erin join me for a pint at the King, say eight-ish?"

"Eight it is," Charles said, his heart lifting within him because, well, she'd found something related to Caedmon Hollow, obviously, a glimpse into the past, a window, a doorway, if he was lucky. Yes — and why not admit it? — because he'd thought of her in the days since his visit to the historical society: the way she'd steadied him when her daughter —

— *when Lissa* —

— had come into the room, her voice and her hand warm upon his back. *You look as though you'd seen a ghost* and *You need to come upstairs for tea.* Perhaps he should have gone. He'd wanted to see her again anyway, though he had not, maybe *could* not, acknowledge it. She reminded him of Syrah Nagle, another tall woman, and also beautiful in an unconventional way — something else he did not want to think about, and in trying not to do so, did.

Which was why he was distressed when Erin did not want to go.

"It will be good for you," he said.

"I'm tired of you telling me what's good for me." She stood at the windows in the breakfast room, gazing out into the gathering twilight. She did not turn to look at him.

"That's not what I mean. It would be good for us. It's no good just sitting out here and brooding."

"I'll decide what's good for me, Charles."

Me, he thought. As though *us* no longer existed. And maybe it didn't. Maybe it couldn't be salvaged. Maybe she didn't *want* to salvage it.

"Go on, Charles. This could be the break you've been waiting for."

He hesitated. "You sure you'll be okay?"

"If I need you, I'll call." Then, turning to face him at last: "I really don't mind."

So he went alone, leaving her there to gaze out into the twilight, though what she hoped to see there he could not say.

14

THE KING — *The Horned King,* the sign over the door announced, triggering within him a frisson of unease — was a high, beamed room with the bar at the back and a brindled cat upon the hearth, its legs folded underneath it, eyes half-lidded in bliss or feline disdain. Patterned tile, brown and green upon the floor, upholstered benches and tables along one wall, booths along the other, brass and dark wood and buttoned leather, everything gleaming in the dim. The yeasty ghost of beer, not unpleasant, permeated the air. The room was lightly populated. A couple of old men played checkers by the fireplace, a handful of people drank at the tables. Except for Trevor Mould at the bar, they were all strangers to Charles. He didn't see —

"Charles."

Silva waved at him from the shadows of a booth. He walked over and slid in across from her.

"Hello there," she said over a pint of dark beer. "Your wife isn't joining us?"

"She isn't well, I'm afraid. She sends her regrets." He looked around for a server, but there didn't seem to be one.

"You have to go to the bar," Silva said.

"I see. What would you suggest?"

"Pint of the Smith's Dark Mild, perhaps."

"Can I get something for you?"

She lifted her beer. "No, thank you."

At the bar, he nodded at Mould, said hello.

When the barman — the landlord, Charles reminded himself —
joined them a moment later, Charles put in his order. "So you're the
American out at Hollow House," the landlord said. Charles introduced
himself. He reached over the bar to shake hands. "Armitage," the man
said. "Graham Armitage. I trust you're settling in all right."

Charles considered the many and complex answers to this question
as Armitage drew his beer. "Fine," he said at last.

"A great lot of house, that."

"It is."

"She's been empty too long," Armitage said. "It's good to have someone there to warm her old bones."

As though the house were dead somehow, or dying.

The thought lingered, disquieting, as Charles returned to the booth.

"Cheers," Silva said when he sat down, lifting her beer. "To Caedmon Hollow."

The beer tasted of caramel and chocolate. She'd chosen well. "You've
found something, then."

"I have. Buried in a box of the *Yorkshire Gazette*."

"The *Yorkshire Gazette*?"

"A newspaper," she said. "This particular run from the 1840s and
'50s, so they're a nice find all on their own, and given the dates, they
could be relevant to our project."

"Our project?"

"That's right." She leaned forward. "I'm proposing a partnership,
Charles. Share and share alike. *In the Night Wood,* however obscure it
may be, is perhaps the only thing of note that's ever happened here. If
we can dig up sufficient primary sources for your biography, Caedmon
Hollow's story could be the centerpiece of Yarrow's little museum —
perhaps quite valuable if your book is a success."

Charles hesitated, thinking of Syrah Nagle and their disastrous collaboration. A harmless enough enterprise, he'd thought, yet it had led to his present nightmare in the end, hadn't it? Or maybe he'd been fore-doomed from the moment he plucked down that book from his grand-father's shelf, or from his chance encounter with Erin in the library, surely something that could only happen in a tale. Perhaps stories had no beginnings or endings at all. Perhaps they simply branched out for-ever, like rivers, one from another, enveloping you for your brief span, each life a story within a story, intersecting with thousands of other sto-ries to make — what? The story of the world, he supposed. But did he want to risk being swept up into this particular eddy again? A shared project, an attractive woman . . .

"Well, what do you think?"

It need not be the same story, he thought, another partnership. Peo-ple change and grow, else a story would not be a story in the first place. "Why not," he said, and after they'd sealed the pact with another toast: "So what have you found?"

She slid a large zipper-lock bag across the table to him. Inside —

"Don't open it. It's quite fragile."

— she'd placed a single small sheet of laid paper with a square of card-board to stiffen it. The page was age-yellowed, crumbling around the edges. A small sketch of the Horned King — Charles's heart quickened — had been roughed in at the right corner. Lines of cramped handwrit-ing, illegible in the poor light, ran margin to margin everywhere else on the page. Charles peered closer, willing himself to puzzle it out. There were three distinct chunks of text — the middle section broke into brief, telegraphic bursts studded with ellipses — but the words made no sense. They weren't even words, just random sets of letters, numbers, and sym-bols. Only they weren't entirely random, were they? That had to be a date — 1843 — at the bottom, in which case —

"A cipher," he said.

"But whose?" she asked. She tapped the drawing with the end of one fingernail, and he thought of Hollow's book, of Laura's terrible adver-sary. He thought of the figure he'd seen in the wood. He thought of the rusty gate and the name of the pub in which he sat: the Horned King at every turn.

Perhaps he was going mad.

He took a sip of his beer, chocolate and caramel upon his tongue. "You think Caedmon Hollow wrote this?"

"The date's right," she said. "Look, the left margin is ragged. It's been torn out of some kind of book. If it survived and we can find it —"

"If we can solve the cipher —"

"And if Caedmon Hollow did write it —"

"Lot of ifs," he said.

"It's a place to start at least."

"There's nothing on the back?"

"No."

"And you checked the box thoroughly?"

"Of course I did," she said. And then, "Rule number one. Don't patronize me, Charles. I am not stupid. You can be sure that I inspected the box thoroughly. Not to mention the neighboring one. And the one after that. Every box I open, actually."

"I apologize."

She nodded.

"We'll need to make a copy of it," he continued. "Transcribe it. Can I —"

Take it, he was going to say, but a commotion — raised voices, a curse — distracted him. Distracted them both. "I won't serve you, Cillian," Armitage was saying. "You're drunk. You need to go home and sleep it off."

Cillian Harris was leaning over the bar, his head drooping. He cursed again, viciously.

The pub had gone quiet by then.

"Now, Cillian," Trevor Mould put in, touching the other man's elbow, but Harris shook him off.

"Bloody hell," Silva said. "Please excuse me, Charles."

Harris looked up as she approached. When she reached out to him, he sagged into her arms. She whispered something close at his ear. Harris nodded.

"I'll see him home, Graham," she said.

"He can't keep coming in here like this, Silva. I'll ban him."

"I said I'd take care of it."

"See that you do, then."

Silva said nothing. She nodded at Charles as she steered Harris to the door. When it swung closed behind them, conversation began to pick up. Charles pondered this development over his beer. Given that he'd twice caught the scent of whisky on Harris's breath, he wasn't entirely surprised that the man had turned up drunk. But he hadn't expected a link between Silva North and Cillian Harris, whatever that connection might turn out to be — though there must be a web of connections in a village like Yarrow, intertwining stories invisible to an outsider. He looked at his fellow patrons, trying to plumb their depths, realized that he, too, was the subject of occasional scrutiny — the outsider among them — and turned his attention back to the page on the table. He took out his phone and snapped a picture of it. Then he simply stared at it, as if deciphering it required nothing more than his concentrated attention. When he'd exhausted both his beer and his patience — when it had become clear that Silva wasn't returning and he'd have to take the cipher into his own keeping, at least for now — Charles stood.

As he passed the bar on his way out, pinching the baggie gingerly between the fingers of one hand, Trevor Mould waved him over. "Can I stand you a beer, Mr. Hayden?"

"Why not?" Charles said.

He slid onto the neighboring stool and rubbed his hand across the bar to ensure that it was dry before laying down the baggie. Armitage came over to take his order: another pint of the Dark Mild.

"Sorry you should have to see that, Mr. Hayden," he said, "being it's your first night in the King and all."

"No need to apologize. I'm not surprised, actually."

"No?" Mould said.

Charles hesitated. Perhaps this was breaking some kind of confidence. Still: "I've noticed that he smells of whisky. At the house, I mean. All hours of the day."

"Have you now?" Mould drained his beer. "That's not like him at all."

Armitage busied himself wiping down the bar. "Recent development, this drinking. He's a decent man, Mr. Harris. Not averse to lifting a pint, but no drunk, I can assure you. I never thought the day would come when I might have to ban him. This old lush on the other hand." He jerked a thumb at Mould.

Mould laughed and pushed his glass across the bar. "I'll have another one."

Armitage spirited the empty away, conjured up a fresh glass, and drew a pint of something called Old Brewery Bitter. Armitage shaved the head, let it settle, topped it off. He nodded and moved down the bar to take someone else's order.

"Silva seemed to calm him down all right," Charles said.

"Ah, well, that's a knot to unravel," Mould said. "Quite the romance those two had. Gone off on each other now — at least Silva has — but there's Lorna, isn't there?" Harris was Lorna's father? This was surprising news — another story, but not one Charles had expected. "She'd not trade the child for all the tea in China, I'm sure, but if it hadn't been for Lorna, she'd have a whole different life. Finished at York and gone off into the great world, one way or another. Funny the way things turn out." He shrugged. "What is that you have there, if you don't mind my asking?"

Charles pointed to the drawing. "You recognize him?"

"Aye. See his picture on the sign outside every night. For your book?"

"How did —"

"Word gets around," Mould said. "People talk." He shook his head. "Strange book, that *Night Wood*."

Armitage had drifted back into earshot. "Wouldn't let my children read it, that's sure," he said, and Charles sighed, wondering how often he was going to have to listen to some variation of this particular theme. "It's a nasty book," Armitage continued. "And the wood isn't much better."

"Oh?" Charles said.

"There's some what say it's haunted," Armitage said. "Call it the Elf Wood and say the fairies live there. That they kidnap little ones and carry them off to their own country. Like the child in the book, what's her name?"

"Laura," Charles said. Then, to Mould: "Did you tell your children these stories?"

"That I did. It wouldn't do to have them wander off in there and get lost, would it? There are dangers in the world, Mr. Hayden. Remember young Mary Babbing."

"Aye," Armitage said. "Now there's a real tragedy for you."

"They haven't found her yet?" Charles asked, thinking of his visit from McGavick and Collier.

"Not so much as a hair," Mould said. "The parents are mad with grief."

Of course they were. Charles knew about madness, he and Erin both. They knew about grief. He thought of the twin photos, Mary Babbing and his own lost daughter, each alone gone off to that undiscovered country from whose bourn no traveler returns. *You think she's dead,* he'd said to McGavick, and McGavick, sighing, *I wouldn't like to say one way or the other.* But, he wanted to know, had Charles seen anything in the wood? And Charles had, or thought he had, or had anyway imagined he had: that strange horned figure reproduced on the page in the baggie, there and gone again, the blink of an eye: Cernunnos, Caedmon Hollow's Horned King, the forest lord who had abducted Laura into the fairy realm. Death. That was the real truth of *In the Night Wood,* wasn't it, the deep, unspoken catastrophe at the heart of the tale? Had Hollow, too, lost a child? Charles could not bear to think of it. Not now. Not here.

An oppressive heat gripped him. He thought he might be sick. He glanced at his watch, said something about how late it was, he hadn't meant to stay so long. Leaving his beer unfinished, he plucked up the baggie and said his goodbyes — abrupt, even rude, no doubt, despite his best efforts. But he could not stay. He had to go, and now.

Outside, it was cooler.

15

HE THREW UP ANYWAY — just stumbled to the weedy verge of the gravel lot and sank to his knees, expelling the night's beer in two quick heaves. He stayed there a few minutes longer, waiting to see if he was done. Then he stumbled to his feet, wiped the back of his hand across his mouth, and blotted his forehead with the tail of his shirt. He lurched to his car and fumbled open the door. By the illumination of the dome light, he examined the page in its baggie. It appeared unharmed. He deposited it on the passenger seat, closed the door, and stood, unsteady on his feet, his back against the cool metal.

"Your daughter's dead, isn't she?"

He looked up. Trevor Mould stood there, at the edge of the lot. "I'm sorry?"

"I said she's dead, isn't she? Your daughter?"

Charles swallowed. His mouth tasted of bile. "Did Colbeck—"

"Dr. Colbeck has been entirely silent on the matter, I assure you. There in the pub, when that poor lost child came up — it was written on your face, Mr. Hayden." He hesitated. "It's not my place. I wouldn't presume to know what it must be like for you. But if you'll humor an old man, my father used to say that you must focus on doing the next thing in troubled times. Just do the next thing, Mr. Hayden. It's all you can do anyway. If you need to talk, you know where to find me." He started to turn away, then reconsidered. "What happened?"

Charles closed his eyes. Opened them. "An accident. A terrible accident."

"They're all terrible, aren't they?"

"I guess they are."

"It doesn't help to lie, not if you're going to find a place in Yarrow."

"I know."

"Tell the truth. People are kind here. They'll not press you for the details."

"You don't miss very much, do you, Mr. Mould?"

"I try not to," Mould said. "Drive carefully, Mr. Hayden." Then, nodding, the old man went inside.

16

DO THE NEXT THING.

The next thing was sleep. Erin had already gone to bed by the time Charles got home. He'd have to wait until morning to share Silva's find. And he was hardly in any shape to do much with it himself; he was tired and achy from vomiting, logy with beer. So he left the yellowing page safe in its baggie on his bureau, brushed his teeth to get the sour taste out of his mouth, and slipped into bed. But sleep eluded him for a long time, and when he caught up with it at last, Charles woke into a night-drowned forest, wood-lost and afraid.

A child —

— *Lissa* —

— was crying in the faraway darkness, luring him ever deeper into the wild. Yet no matter how hard he chased after, the weeping grew more distant, until finally, desperate, he found himself hurtling through the trees. The woods conspired against him. Paths closed before him and thorns entangled him. Branches clawed at his face. He was spent by the time a malign root snaked out to seize his ankle and send him stumbling to his knees at the edge of a tussocked glade where a great oak grew. Thickets of trees loomed round it like a palisade, and a bloated orange moon brooded overhead, flooding the clearing with spectral light. The child's lament dwindled in the still air and then was gone.

Charles turned in his bed, sobbed himself half awake, settled, and slipped into another dream — a dream of Lissa. Hand in hand, they wandered, hopelessly astray in some vast autumnal wood. Fallen leaves crunched underfoot, and in the twilight shadows, wily, foxlike faces peered out at them from knotholes in the vine-shrouded trees, from the hollow mouths of rotting logs, from the emerald-dark crevices in moss-grown granite outcroppings: there and gone again, the faces always on the move. The air teemed with their whispered colloquies, their laughter and derision. Even the trees seemed alive, skeletal and foreboding. Yet there was a way. There was a path. Charles had marked it as he passed, but it was lost now. The birds had eaten up his breadcrumbs and flown themselves away.

And then, in that strange alchemy of dreams, they stood before a gate with a horned face finely wrought. The gate screeched on rusty hinges when he pulled it back.

You come, too, he said.

You go on without me, she replied. *But tell me a story before you go,* and so he sat on a boulder and took her on his knee.

Once upon a time, he said —

And woke to drowsy darkness, and in waking could not recall the story he had told her, or if he'd told her one at all. Maybe he had not. Maybe it had yet to be written. Or maybe there was no story to tell after all. Maybe things just happened, and we only dreamed the stories we told ourselves. A dream inside a story inside a dream, he thought, bestirring himself. And then he yawned and turned his pillow over and slept again, enmazed by walls and wood, with a horned moon shining over.

17

CHARLES WOKE WITH no memory of dreams.

He would not sleep again that night. His legs were restless, eager to be up and walking themselves about. And so as dawn pinked the eastern horizon, he stood at the mouth of a tunnel high above Hollow House. The Eorl Wood towered overhead, an endless sea of trees that seemed as if it might any moment burst through its enormous retaining wall and sweep down into the vale below. The house stood against it in a show of magnificent defiance, but nothing could forever hold that green tide at bay. Walls and grassy moats might last another hundred years — they might last longer still — but in the end, root and branch, stealthy and implacable as time, would breach them. Hollow House would fall into ruin. Hawks would nest in the shattered tower, deer graze its broken rooms.

Not yet, though. There was time.

Thus solaced, Charles turned away and ducked into the curving passageway under the wall. The floor was damp even in this dry week, and the horned gate squealed upon its hinges as he opened it.

On the other side, the enduring trees aspired to seize the sky.

18

"DO YOU EVER see anything in the wood?" Erin asked, broaching the question at last, long pondered and long delayed, driven by desperation,

her growing sense of entrapment in a daily ritual that she could not lib-
erate herself from, driven even — why not admit it? — by fear.

A shadow passed over his face. He'd embraced her fresh from his
morning walk, the leafy green smell of the wood still clinging to his
clothes, and she had borne it. He was bursting with good news that he
had not yet divulged. She could see it in his eyes — see the pleasure he
had in withholding it until after breakfast, coveting its secret for half an
hour longer, like a boy putting off unwrapping the final Christmas present until the last possible moment, spinning out the pleasure of anticipation. And even after everything that had happened, she still would
not deprive him this small thing. So she'd borne it.

Charles looked down at his plate: scrambled eggs and sausage, fried
tomatoes, a ramekin of mushrooms — Mrs. Ramsden's standard English
fare. She'd served it up and called them to the table and evaporated like
the cobbler's elves. So there were these smells, and the smell of coffee
besides, overwhelming that woodsy scent. Yet the shadow on his face
betrayed the lie.

"No," he said. "Squirrels and rabbits. Trees." He looked up. "Why?"

What to say? I saw a child —

— *I saw Lissa* —

— on the day we arrived. Saw her watching us pass from the shoulder of the road.

And in the days since?

Erin had dreamed her. In her dreams they had walked the night
wood together, she and a child who might or might not have been Lissa,
who seemed somehow to be a dozen and more children at once, all of
them in flight from some minatory pursuer. Who woke her in tears and
left her bereft at her midnight window, staring out at the forest behind
its wall, a black mass against the starlit heavens. By day, she paced off an
obsessive circuit, sketchbook to window and beyond the window wall
and beyond that the Eorl Wood, and back to sketchbook to start all over
again. No pill could free her of this compulsion, though God knows
she'd tried them all, every day and in myriad combinations — to no avail,
except that she felt more and more that she was tethered somewhere
above her own body, numb and divorced from her self.

And the drawings.

Erin shuddered to look at them. She wanted to set them aside. She wanted to stop working on them.

But she could not.

Worst of all, she sensed something in the wood staring back. Not the child, either. The wood itself maybe, sentient and malign. She couldn't say how she knew this. But she did know it, and she knew also that it was irrational to know such a thing when such a thing could not be. Yet she knew it all the same.

Why? he wanted to know.

Because I'm going crazy, that's why.

"Just curious," she said aloud, which is how they left it.

"What did she have for you, this woman?" she asked as they finished eating.

"Silva," he said. "I'll show you."

She cleared the table — despite Mrs. Ramsden's prohibition — while he vaulted upstairs to retrieve his talisman: the single page of age-yellowed paper inside a plastic bag. The sketch of the Horned King, the coded writing. Cold dread rolled over in her heart, cetacean in its slow dominion.

"What is it?"

"We don't exactly know," he said.

"You think Caedmon Hollow wrote it?"

"The date is right," he said, putting on his teacher's voice, which never failed to annoy her. "And the sketch is plenty suggestive. The Horned King—"

"I know. I've read the book, Charles." She paused. "What about the writing?"

"Some kind of cipher. That's the challenge, isn't it?" Enthusiasm undimmed.

And she meant to indulge it, his enthusiasm, to respond as he clearly hoped she would, but when she opened her mouth what came out was "And she just gave it to you?"

A moment of hesitation. Another lie, then.

"She loaned it to me," he said. "I'll have to return it — today, in fact. I need to call her. But I'm going to digitize it first."

What she heard was: I need to call her.

Erin forced a smile. "Well, I'm glad you've gotten a break," she said. "If that's what it is. You should probably get busy, shouldn't you?" And then, she couldn't help herself: "No doubt Silva is anxious to hear from you."

But if he noticed the edge in her voice, he didn't let on. He just smiled with that same boyish enthusiasm. "You're right," he said, adding without irony, "You're the best, Erin," and she felt a torrent of guilt and regret flood through her, washing all before it. She started to speak again, to apologize for thoughts he didn't know she had, to find a way to invite him back into her heart, but before any words came — and what was there to say? — he was gone.

She stood by the table, listening to the silence ring her round, more than halfway hoping that Mrs. Ramsden would sense her misery and find her way back from whatever corner of the house she'd retreated to.

But Mrs. Ramsden didn't come. So Erin left the dishes unfinished — how pleased Mrs. Ramsden would be! — and drifted through the lofty rooms, window to window to window, looking for a little girl who wasn't there and feeling the forest's malign intent impress itself upon her, until at last she found herself at the dining room table. With trembling hands, she twisted off a bottle cap, shook out a Valium, and dry-swallowed it, thinking that she would soon have to hide her little pharmacy away in her bedroom. It wouldn't do for Charles to discover just how much she was using. That decided, she opened her sketchbook to a clean page and bent to the work that had claimed her for its own.

19

IN THE LIBRARY, Charles pulled a chair up to the long table, heavy and dark and polished to a high shine, its legs ornamented with that familiar motif of vines and leaves and impish faces. He slid the page on its cardboard backing out of the baggie and squared it up beside his laptop. He stared at it in wonder. Then he leaned down and drew in its scent, pregnant with history: the touch of Caedmon Hollow's hand (maybe), the scratch of his nib (also maybe) — the enigma of time, in any case, connections forged across eras by simple words upon a page, mysteries waiting to be unfolded.

"Excuse me, sir."

Cillian Harris stood in the doorway, disheveled in his suit, hair awry, eyes bloodshot.

"Good morning, Mr. Harris."

"I'm told you were at the pub last night."

"Yes."

"I wish to apologize, sir. My behavior did not reflect well upon the estate."

"We all slip from time to time. You don't owe me an apology." Trying not to think of his own slips and their awful consequences. "Mr. Harris," he said, "are you okay? Is there anything I can do for you?"

Harris didn't speak. A heartbeat passed, and another. Then, dipping his head: "Thank you for your understanding, Mr. Hayden. I'll leave you to your work."

And then, before Charles could formulate a reply, he was gone, closing the door behind him.

20

"I'M SORRY ABOUT the incident at the pub," Silva North said when Charles returned the enciphered page that afternoon.

They sat at the kitchen table in her modest apartment above the historical society, drinking tea and eating cookies — biscuits, she called them. Flats and lifts, windscreens and crisps. Charles supposed the words would all come naturally in time.

Her apartment — her *flat* — was clean, but not much neater than the would-be museum below: books stuffed haphazardly onto shelves, books in piles on the tables and in heaps on the floor. And toys everywhere: on the rug and the sofa and in baskets, Lorna on her knees at play in the living room, lost in her own private world. Afternoon light hung in the windows, watery and cool, but the kitchen projected the same comfortable warmth that Silva herself did. She might have her prickles—

—*don't patronize me, Charles*—

—but he sensed (or thought he did) an essential kindness in her—in her reaction when Lorna had startled him that first day: the steadying hand upon his back, the invitation to tea. And now an apology when none was necessary.

He said as much.

She smiled. "It wasn't nice to abandon you."

"I don't think you had much choice. No one else was making any headway with him."

"I seem to have the touch. He still carries the torch, I'm afraid."

"For how long now?"

"A long time. Lorna was still in diapers."

He nodded, knowing it was none of his business, helpless to ask. "The drinking?"

"No, not at all, that's a recent development. Very recent. The last few months, actually. It's a mystery to everyone, me most of all. He wouldn't even talk to me when I got him out of the pub last night. Won't have anything to do with Lorna."

"Are they close?"

"Very. And she needs him right now."

"She's very quiet."

"All the children have been quiet since Mary disappeared. They're terrified." Silva frowned. "It's tearing the whole village apart because it must have been one of us that did it, right? It's not like a stranger would have gone unnoticed."

"Maybe no one took her."

"What do you mean?" She stood, collected the empty mugs, and carried them to the sink.

"Maybe she wandered off, got lost in the wood. Mould told me people called it the Elf Wood in Yarrow."

"They do," she said, rinsing the cups. "It's a handy story, the Elf Wood and the Fairy King. Like a lot of children's tales, isn't it? The Big Bad Wolf is never just a wolf. He's a warning about responsibil-

ity. Build wisely—which is itself a metaphor—or something or other
will come along and blow your whole life down. Or Little Red Riding Hood. Don't talk to strangers, much less crawl into bed with them.
Perrault made that clear enough. And that's just scratching the surface.
Once the Freudians get ahold of it . . . Well, I presume you know your
Bettelheim. These are deep waters we're swimming in. Caedmon Hollow, too. Whatever other sources he drew upon, he clearly knew his local folklore."

Silva sat across the table from him, drying her hands on a dishcloth.
She had long, delicate fingers with blunt, practical nails—a pianist's fingers, Charles thought, and he felt once again the warmth of her hand
upon his back. He stole a glance at her. She raised a skeptical eyebrow,
and he felt his cheeks grow hot. He looked down, touched the age-yellowed page in its baggie on the table.

"The Elf Wood is the wrong etymology," he said.

"I don't think people are worrying about etymology when they warn
their kids off the wood."

"Probably not. The name comes from Old English, in any case: *eorl*,
a warrior chieftain. Like Arthur, the real Arthur, not the guy in all the
shiny armor. If there was an Arthur."

"He'll return when we need him most," Silva said. "Like we don't
bloody need him now."

They sat in silence for a moment.

Silva leaned back in her chair to glance into the living room. "You
okay, sweetie?" she called to Lorna.

"Yes, Mum."

"You're very quiet."

"I'm okay. Can I watch *Frozen*?"

"Sure. Let me get it set up for you," she said, adding, to Charles, "If
you'll excuse me."

"Of course."

Charles needed a minute anyway. *Frozen* had been in high rotation
at Casa Hayden. The lyrics to "Let It Go" had been chiseled into his
brain. But he hadn't expected to encounter the movie here, any more
than he'd expected to encounter not one but two little girls who looked
so much like Lissa that they could have passed for twins. Just walking

into Silva's apartment and seeing Lorna there had shaken him all over again.

"Are you all right?" Silva asked from the doorway.

"The movie reminds me of home, that's all."

"Your daughter?"

He looked up. "She played that movie until I thought I'd go mad."

"You miss her."

He blinked back tears. Jesus, was he really going to fall apart like this, in a virtual stranger's home? "I do." And then, recalling Mould's words about lying, he said, "She died. Nearly a year ago now. I'm sorry that I misled you."

"Oh, Charles —"

He held up a hand. "I can't talk about it."

"We don't have to talk about it," she said. She took her place at the table and simply sat with him in silence. There was only the sound of the movie and nothing else. Fucking Disney. Fucking Elsa, imperious and cold, imprisoned by ice. Alone.

Charles asked for the restroom so he could pull himself together. Splashed water on his face. Studied himself in the mirror and didn't like what he saw. Switched off the light and turned away. On his way back to the kitchen, he stopped to watch Lorna watching *Frozen*. She was wedged into a cushion on the sofa, chewing at a nail, mesmerized by story.

She felt his gaze and looked up at him.

"Do you want to watch the movie?" she asked.

"Sure," he said. He sat down beside her, and she curled into the shelter of his arm as if she'd known him for years.

Onscreen, the adventures of Elsa and Anna unfolded. Watching, a man made of ice.

21

THE ONE-YEAR ANNIVERSARY of Lissa's death fell a week later: May 12, what had been, if only briefly, her sixth birthday.

On that morning, before everything had gone so terribly and irrevocably wrong, Charles had woken in a state of pervasive dread — not because he had any foreboding of the looming catastrophe, but because his own life had careened out of control some weeks earlier. What had begun as a chance remark about Christina Rossetti to his colleague Syrah Nagle had by degrees grown into a collaborative essay (never finished) and then into something else altogether, an infidelity of the heart that had culminated in infidelity outright. How long the thing might have continued he could not say, but Syrah had issued her ultimatum (the usual ultimatum) and Charles had made his decision (the usual decision). Lissa's birthday had been one of the driving forces — perhaps *the* driving force — behind that decision. A party had been planned for the following Saturday. A pony had been engaged, an inflatable bouncy house acquired from a local party rental. He was scheduled to pick up the cake (the theme was *Frozen,* what else?) on Saturday morning at ten, with the chaos to commence at two. He found that he'd been looking forward to it almost as much as Lissa was.

Did he really want to write himself out of the story of his daughter's life?

And so he'd planned to break it off with Syrah that day: a private birthday gift to his daughter, an unspoken reaffirmation of the happily-ever-after he'd promised Erin a dozen years before.

Despite all this, he'd managed to maintain a pretense of normality from the time the alarm went off at six thirty. Erin had gotten Lissa up half an hour later, and — enthusiastic birthday wishes aside — the standard morning routine, never especially pleasant, had gotten under way. Lissa had not been engineered to wake up early. She scrubbed at her sleepy eyes with knotted fists. She threatened tantrums (and sometimes followed through). She refused to eat, declined to dress, and had to be coaxed into even a cursory brush of her teeth. By the time they'd cajoled her into Erin's car and Charles himself got away, he was running late for an eight o'clock final exam, too hurried and harried to say much in the way of goodbyes. He forgot to tell Lissa that he loved her, a matter of no great consequence at the time, though he would remember it clearly and with vast dismay twelve hours later, when she was dead.

Such were the memories that stirred him awake in the soul's dead hour, such the memories that drove him out of his sweat-sodden sheets and into the dooryard, to sip of the cool night air. He parked himself on the top step of the portico and looked out at the shadowy throng of the Eorl Wood. At last — it might have been an hour, it might have been longer still — a ruddy dawn blazed up above the trees and cast down its light upon the distant rampart of the mighty wall. A tall figure stood in silhouette upon it, black horns branching and a blood-red disc of sun. Charles's breath caught in his lungs. He felt the beam of the thing's scrutiny, baleful and malign.

The sun hove itself higher and a flight of birds printed itself upon the morning sky.

The breeze quickened.

Charles blinked the thing away. He must have dozed or dreamed it, or drifted into some nightmare fantasy. But a black certainty persisted all the same: the Horned King had stood upon the wall and fixed him with its dire appraisal.

Lissa was dead.

He'd fallen into some vile story from which he could not escape.

22

ERIN WOKE SUDDENLY from a drugged sleep with the red sun at her window.

If she'd stood at the glass and pulled back the curtains, perhaps she too would have seen the thing upon the wall. But who can say for sure? She did not get up. She stayed in bed, pinned to the mattress by the stark fact of the thing: on this, the day that she would have turned seven, Lissa Hayden was dead. Had been dead for an entire year, would be dead for the entire span of the year to come, and for the year after that, and for all the years of Erin's life, and more. This fact rang in Erin's thoughts like some jump-rope chant of Lissa's kindergarten friends, who had been invited to a party that would never come, who somehow, by some chance or fate, still lived. *Lissa is dead,* the chant ran —

> *Lissa is dead.*
> *Lissa is dead.*
> *Lissa is dead.*

Melissa Prudence Hayden (*Prudence?* Charles had asked incredulously) had celebrated her last birthday. She would be six years old forever. And what Erin found herself thinking of most were the eight little buckets of party favors that she'd left on the kitchen counter for more than a month afterward, before Charles had finally (infuriatingly) thrown them away: a pocket-sized *Frozen* notebook and a matching pen, half a dozen *Frozen* erasers, a *Frozen* sticker book, and a plastic snowflake necklace, all of them chosen with lip-biting concentration by her then five-year-old daughter in the *Frozen* section of Party City. Because *Frozen* was so big with the five-year-old set it practically had its own aisle: *Frozen, Frozen, Frozen,* everywhere you looked.

She thought of that and she thought of the placental miracle of the baby, swimming in its amniotic sea, and she thought of the agony of the endless labor to usher it into the world — Lissa insistent on a rump-first debut — until at last the doctor had rolled Erin off to surgery. She still had the scar, a tiny white streak at the base of her belly. You could stroke your finger across it and feel the exit wound Lissa'd left behind, a cicatrix of joy and loss.

> *Lissa is dead.*

Erin could see the grave marker in her head, the awful symmetry of the dates, the stone half a world away from her. She'd asked a friend — Mina, her former legal assistant — to take care of it in her absence, but she knew that even the best such intentions went astray. Mina had her own life, her own two children, her husband, a position with another firm: everything Erin had lost or given up. Erin couldn't help envisioning the grave overgrown, untended, though of course the cemetery was impeccably manicured. But who would leave flowers there, or little *Fro-*

zen trinkets? And who would be there to talk to Lissa, down there in all that cold earth?

Erin looked at the picture propped on her nightstand.

Pushing back the sheets, she sat up and reached for the frame. She held it in her lap, trying to sketch the lines of her daughter's face in her mind, before the other and more terrible images that had seized her imagination crowded them out.

No use. No good.

She could not bear to look at it. She could not bear to face the torment of the day: the awkward meals with Charles, their makeshift conversation, the appalling fact of Lissa's death hanging unspoken between them. There were no words big enough to speak of or contain it, though in the end, she supposed, words were all anyone ever had, and the stories that they fashioned of them. She wondered what story she was writing about herself, or whether she was writing one at all. Perhaps it had all been written for her. Maybe it was all blind chance.

All she knew was that her daughter had passed into darkness, she herself into despair.

And that her marriage had collapsed. The horror had both divided them and drawn them irrevocably together, binding them up in knots of guilt and recrimination and grief that could not yet (and maybe never) be undone. Erin did not know if they could heal the breach between them. She did not know if she even wanted to. But Charles alone had known Lissa as she had known her, and so she could not leave him, and dreaded that he might leave her — this the torment that today of all days she would abjure.

And so she put the picture down, fumbled open the nightstand drawer, and with blind, trembling fingers, shook a handful of pills out of the bottles she'd secreted there, safe from prying eyes. Xanax and Ativan and Klonopin, a bottle of fucking Seroquel, for Christ's sake. Ambien. Trazodone. Effexor for the depression. She did not know what she took. She didn't care. She just wanted to sleep through the day, and so she swallowed them down, two and three at a time, chasing them with the glass of warm water on the bedside table. Only as the darkness closed in upon her did she wonder if she'd ingested some fatal quantity or combination — she'd grasped then, too late, for the receding light. She didn't want to die. She hated herself for wanting to live.

Then darkness, dreamless and all-encompassing.

23

CHARLES SAT ON the portico for a long time after his vision or hallucination of the Horned King passed. But as the sun climbed higher into the morning sky, he forced himself to his feet, made his way down the yard to the stile, and climbed the sloping meadow beyond. The image of the Horned King came back to him as he stood at the mouth of the tunnel under the wall. He even paused in trepidation, and then, as if to prove to himself that the figure upon the rampart had been a mere trick of the morning light, he ducked inside and under. He emerged on the other side into a sea of clear emerald air that tasted of leaf and bough and mossy, ancient trees. And everywhere massive outcroppings of rock, chilly to the touch, and thick, gnarled roots, and, in the distance, penetrating the murmurous canopy high above, a shaft of slanting, golden sunlight, like the fleeting radiance of heaven.

There was no threat here. There could be no threat in this burgeoning green sanctuary.

Something Emerson had written came back to him: *Nature. The transparent eyeball. The currents of the Universal Being circulating through him.*

Charles was not a religious man, but he suddenly understood, for the first time in his life, what Emerson had been trying to get at. The language of transcendence was alone adequate to the Eorl Wood's mystery and beauty. He could not put a name to what he felt, but Lissa's death —his own deep-rooted guilt and sorrow—was for a time subsumed in splendor, and if other, darker tints lay threaded through the light, if some sinister power sought to seduce him by illusion, Charles could neither see nor sense them.

So he walked the outer circuit of the wall in peace, at least for a little while, and when he surfaced on the other side and headed back to Hollow House, some trace of the peace lingered. It accompanied him through the vast empty rooms to the house inside the house. When he didn't find Erin at breakfast, he walked up the stairs to stand at the door of her room, across the hall from his own. He felt the need, on this day of all days, to reach out to her, to drink together from the well of their shared sorrow — to make some reparation where there could be no reparation. But he vacillated before he knocked. And when she did not answer, he dithered longer still. Her bedroom had been closed to him for a year now, so it was with some reluctance that he turned the knob at last, and stepped inside.

"Erin?" A whisper.

The room was shrouded in shadow, the curtained windows dimly aglow. She was little more than a shape in the gloom, the suggestion of a figure curled under her comforter. But he heard her respiration, deep and slow. When he whispered her name again, she did not stir.

Let her sleep, then.

Downstairs, Mrs. Ramsden had set two places for breakfast. "It's just yourself this morning?" she asked as she poured him coffee and settled him at the table.

"Just me."

"I hope Mrs. Hayden isn't unwell."

"I'm sure she'll be fine," he said, though he was sure of nothing of the sort.

24

"Excuse me, mr. hayden," Mrs. Ramsden said.

Charles looked up from his computer. He must have been sitting there for hours. He felt the ache of it in his muscles and in his bones. He'd drifted into reverie, he supposed, pondering the mysterious page that he'd pulled up on the screen — but his thoughts hadn't been on the coded language or the sketch of the Horned King. Whatever his thoughts had been, they were lost to him now. He felt enervated and at a loss, asea in some unmapped region between full wakefulness and sleep. Hic sunt dracones.

Mrs. Ramsden stood swathed in gloom, a dark figure in the doorway of the library, well beyond the bright circle of light over the table. He flashed on that dire silhouette atop the wall. Then he was awake.

"What time is it?"

"It's close on five now," she said, her voice hollow across the long silence of the room. "I'll be going home soon. I'll leave your dinner warming in the oven. But I wanted to say . . ."

"Yes?"

"Well, I don't want to overstep my bounds, sir."

"Please, Mrs. Ramsden."

Mrs. Ramsden hesitated. She cleared her throat. "I'm worried about your wife, sir. I haven't seen her today."

Charles felt a cold shadow sweep the ambit of his heart. "She isn't up?"

"I haven't seen her, sir," Mrs. Ramsden said.

Then, with a brisk cheeriness he didn't feel: "Let's have a look, shall we?"

The cheeriness wasn't enough to carry them through. Mrs. Ramsden watched him across the length of the room and fell in beside him. He could sense the electrical pulse of her anxiety as they navigated the echoing salon and the passages beyond. It crackled in the air around them, like the charged tension before a storm. She flipped switches on and off as they passed, so that it seemed like the light fled before them and the darkness gave chase.

"We usually have tea at ten," Mrs. Ramsden said on the stairs. "I missed her, of course, and then again at lunch, but I thought she might like to be left alone today. She has a very hard time of it, you know. Walks window to window to window. And then all that time drawing. I worry about her — and you as well. I know it can't be easy for you to bear either, Mr. Hayden. You have my sym —"

"Thank you," he said, though he thought he saw a silent reproach in the rigid set of her shoulders.

Then the residence, a second set of stairs. Mrs. Ramsden paused at the base of them. "I'll wait here, Mr. Hayden. If you could just —"

"Of course."

He went on alone, forcing himself not to take the risers two at a time, thinking that surely nothing had happened. She would never do something to herself. And woven through these thoughts a bleak certainty that she *had* done something, that it had been building toward this awful climax for a year now, and that he'd been too tangled up in his own grief to intervene. Something else to add to the docket of his sins.

He stood at the door, knocked, said her name calmly, nothing but the rising inflection at the end, and nothing in return but silence. He spoke again, louder this time, knocked. When there was no response, he tested the door, half expecting it to be locked. The knob turned in his hand. The room was dark. The light had long since passed on to the other side of the house.

"Erin?"

Nothing.

Charles did not want to see what he would see when he crossed the room. It took him a minute to nerve himself to the task. When he did, he felt like a man wading through mud, or setting concrete. She was curled on her side, unmoving even when he called her name again. But she was alive, breathing audibly the slow, heavy breaths of sleep. He reached out to confirm it all the same, touched her shoulder, shook her.

"Erin?"

And now she did stir. She murmured something unintelligible, pushed at the covers, slipped back into sleep.

Charles sat on the bed, letting the panic draw away from him like a retreating tide. After a moment, feeling his own breath steady inside him, he switched on the bedside lamp. A half-empty glass of water. The school photograph. Otherwise nothing. He picked up the photograph and studied it in the circle of light: Lissa, imprisoned behind her wall of glass.

Then he recalled himself.

Mrs. Ramsden was waiting in a panic of her own.

Charles put the picture down and stood. As he fumbled with the lamp switch, his gaze snagged on a tiny blue disc, light against the royal-blue-and-gold weave of the rug. This was the blue room. His own was a rich, heavy crimson, but this one was blue, complete with its luxurious blue appointments shadowing forth in the gloom, and there in the blue room on the golden fringe of the brocaded blue-and-gold hand-knotted rug — which must be worth somewhere north of $25,000, and therefore an asset barely worthy of note in the plus column of the Hollow fortune — lay a single robin's-egg-blue pill. Charles crouched to retrieve it. It was no bigger than a pencil eraser. When he held the pill under the light, he saw that it was scored neatly down the middle. All of which, given the amount of medication Erin was taking, should have been no big deal; people occasionally dropped a pill, after all, except —

Except why had she slept all day? (*Had* she slept all day?) And why hadn't she woken up when he sat on the bed, touched her shoulder, turned on the lamp? She was a light sleeper, after all. She'd been a light sleeper as long as he'd known her. The meds made her drowsy, but —

"Erin." Louder: "Erin."

That tide of anxiety that had only just retreated came rolling back in. Not panic, exactly, but still —

Charles squatted by the nightstand and slid open the drawer. Half a dozen orange plastic vials of pills rolled away inside, capless, surrendering up their treasures.

Just how much had she taken? And what?

He was reaching out to shake her awake, really shake her this time, and ask her exactly that, when —

"Mr. Hayden?" Mrs. Ramsden said from the doorway.

Charles stood abruptly, shoving the drawer closed. His hand enfolded the lone pill, hiding it away.

"Is she —"

"She's fine," Charles said. "She's only sleeping."

25

HE ATE ALONE.

The meal was tasteless — sustenance, little more — though Charles suspected the fault lay in him and not the food.

When he finished, he washed up and climbed the stairs to look in on Erin. Sat once again on her bed. Touched her hand.

She stirred, but did not wake, and he did not try to rouse her.

He thought — not for the first time — of calling Dr. Colbeck. But what could Colbeck tell him that he didn't already know? He turned on the lamp instead, and sorted the pills into their bottles, keeping back the one he had recovered from the carpet. He capped them off one by one and put them back in the nightstand drawer.

Finally, he turned off the lamp. He left the door open behind him and walked down to the library to retrieve his laptop. The sumptuous rooms were silent. The small staff Cillian Harris employed to keep up the disused sections of the house had long since departed. Charles thought he'd met them all by this time, but he'd not yet been able to sort out their names and stations. Anna, Judith, Alex — he'd get it all sooner or later. He ran into them on his occasional fits of exploration, but rarely saw them otherwise. Despite his misgivings about Harris, he felt detached from the daily management of the estate. Erin had unplugged altogether. They might have been ghosts, the two of them, lost souls adrift, echoes in abandoned corridors.

When he returned to the residence, he checked on Erin once again (still sleeping) and settled himself on a sofa in the study, a more modest echo of the huge library downstairs: bookcases stuffed with glossy old leather-bound volumes, dark antique furniture, the same decorative motif of vine and leaf and sly peering faces. A second door opened into a back living room; the more formal one that opened directly off the foyer had been intended for entertaining, Charles supposed, and should properly be called — what? The parlor? The drawing room? He wondered how the Victorians had distinguished among their various sitting rooms, parlors, and drawing rooms. Caedmon Hollow would have known. Charles supposed he, too, would have to know if he ever came to the point of setting pen to paper. An easy mystery to solve, no doubt.

This one, on the other hand —

Opening his laptop, Charles stared at the copy he'd made of the cryptogram. Aside from the ellipses in the middle section and the date at the bottom, he could discern no pattern in the ciphered text. It all looked like a jumble, a random assortment of letters, numbers, and symbols.

He launched the browser and pulled up Wikipedia, but the page on cryptography only made his head spin: asymmetric key algorithms and frequency analysis and Enigma machines. Surely, Hollow — if it had been him at all — would have used something simple ... Charles clicked on the link to Caesar's cipher, which took him to an explanation of the Roman despot's alphabetic substitution code. But the numbers and symbols in Hollow's cipher ruled out simple alphabetic substitution, didn't they?

He paused, thinking. Unless ...

Unless they were red herrings, deliberate noise in the signal-to-noise ratio. He opened another tab and hunted up an alphabetic cipher decoder. Transcribed a line into the text box, omitting everything but the letters. Surely it couldn't be that easy, he thought, pressing the decrypt button and leaning forward to see —

Gibberish.

Charles set the computer aside in frustration. In a story, the cryptogram's meaning would be unfolded to him in time. He had only to await the revelation.

He stood, stretching, and glanced at his watch. It was just after midnight, the year turning to commence anew its long march toward Lissa's next birthday.

It didn't bear thinking about.

Yet it bore down upon him all the same, with an urgency that he could not brook. He paced once the bright circuit of the room and then wandered out through the sprawling chambers of the residence. He paused at the steps, listening, and he hesitated over Erin's sketchbook in the dining room, his finger poised to flip back the cover. But it felt too invasive. And he could not stand to look into Lissa's face. Not now. Not when he felt so desolate and alone.

So he moved on, down the long table and into the kitchen, thinking he might make a cup of tea. He passed through into the breakfast room instead, and stood at the windows with their panoramic view of the grounds.

Outside, night lay heavy over wood and walls. An enormous moon turned its indifferent face upon him. Clouds scudded overhead, chasing shadows across the lawn. The trees swayed like drunken giants. The downstairs windows of Harris's house blazed out into the dark. And then the wind rose higher still and blew the steward's bright windows black, like a miser stingy of the light. Ill at ease, Charles stood a moment longer.

Had he only turned away, he would not have seen what followed. But he stayed, half beguiled, and so it was that he saw Cillian Harris's front door swing open.

A moment later, the man himself stepped out to take the measure of the night. He hesitated at the threshold for a moment, then shut the door behind him and walked out across the lawn. He climbed the sloping pasture beyond, up through the wind-combed grass, until he disappeared beyond the range of Charles's vision. But Charles didn't need to see where Harris was going. He knew: into the wood, moonstruck and spun with shadow. Charles had felt the midnight lure of it himself as he drifted off to sleep, like a whisper at his drowsing ear, summoning him out into the dark, into the wood, where he could walk in the cool air through vast corridors of trees —

"Charles?"

The voice jolted him out of his reverie. He stepped away from the window, turning.

It was Erin, of course. It was only Erin.

26

SHE TURNED ON the light.

Charles stood there blinking owlishly, like a little boy startled awake, his face still filmed with dream. And then he shifted on his feet and lifted his head to look straight at her, still blinking as his eyes adjusted to the bright room. How long had it been since she'd looked into those eyes, weak behind their thick lenses? How long had it been since she'd looked at him at all?

Erin let herself take him in.

He seemed to have aged five years in the past twelve months. She supposed they both had, but the change was shocking all the same. His hair, sprinkled now with gray and in need of cutting, was mussed. He'd been running his hand through it, a habit of both concentration and distraction — his default modes. From the day they'd met, from the moment she'd handed him his glasses as he stood blinking in mild confusion after their collision in the university library, Charles had only ever been halfway in the world. But now he seemed almost entirely disconnected, his face strange, his expression distant.

And how changed he was. He was haggard and thin, his clothes — faded jeans and a pale green oxford, tail out, sleeves rolled back over his forearms — hanging loose upon him. He looked almost emaciated. His daily walks in the Eorl Wood, no doubt, obsessive as her own circuit inside the prison of this house, but there was something else as well: Lissa's death, she supposed, eating him from the inside out. Erin felt a wave of compassion for him. If she hadn't been imprisoned inside her own grief and sorrow — and, yes, anger, with him and with the world that had allowed all this to come to pass — she might have reached out to him.

Instead: "You've been in my room. You left the door open."

"I was worried."

She nodded.

He said nothing, only stood there. After a moment, he dug something out of his pocket and extended it to her on his outstretched palm.

Erin stepped closer. A sleepy lassitude enmeshed her. Could you even call it sleep, that drugged and dreamless coma? It had left her no refreshment, only this aching, bone-deep weariness. She felt disconnected from her own body, a stranger marooned inside the echoing vault of her own skull. Rip Van Winkle must have felt this way after his long slumber, or Sleeping Beauty, awoken with a kiss. She blinked and stepped still closer and looked into his outstretched hand. A Klonopin.

"I found this," he said. "It was on the rug, beside the bed."

"I must have dropped it," she said, but when she reached for it he closed his hand.

"You must have."

They stood in silence.

"It's just a pill, Charles."

"I opened the drawer in your nightstand."

Ah. So that's where this was going. Aloud, she said only, "I don't want you to go through my things."

"I think someone needs to. I cleaned them up, by the way — the pills. What are you thinking, Erin? Do you want to die?"

She remembered that vertiginous sense of falling away into the dark as the drugs took hold, how she'd tried to claw her way back to the light. "No. Do you?"

He didn't answer, not for a long time. Then: "No."

He opened his fist and let the Klonopin drop into her palm.

Erin slipped the pill into the pocket of her pajama bottoms.

"I think you should talk to someone," he said. "Colbeck gave me some names. We could go together if you want."

"Not yet, Charles. I'm not ready."

"When do you think you will be?"

Never, she did not say, though she felt the truth of the statement chime inside her. I will never be ready. I will never be ready, because being ready would mean that I have accepted the awful truth that I will never see my daughter again. Being ready would mean letting go, letting her fade into memory at last, letting her become just a passage in my life rather than my life itself. Being ready would be a betrayal of my love, and I have had enough of betrayal. I have had all I can take of it. But aloud, only this: "I don't know, Charles."

He nodded. "Promise me one thing," he said.

"I don't know what promises I can make."

"Just promise you won't do it again. The pills."

And once again it smote her, the terror she'd felt as that circle of light receded and the pills dragged her endlessly down into a drugged sleep that was more like death than any sleep she had ever known before. "Okay," she said. "I can promise that."

He let his breath out slowly. "Okay, then. We'll wait on the rest of it. We'll wait until you're ready. I can do that." And then: "I couldn't bear to lose you, too, Erin." And the reminder of what they'd already lost was like a punch in the gut.

The word lodged in her head. *Too.* I couldn't bear to lose you, *too.*

"No," she said, "I guess not." But he'd lost her already. He could never get her back, no matter how much she longed to come home to him. She could never give that much of herself again. Never trust. Never risk.

Such was the paradox of love: out of fear of losing it, you willingly relinquished it.

You inflicted upon yourself the wound you dreaded most of all.

"You should get some sleep," she said. "It's late."

"Okay. Yeah. You going to stay up for a while?"

"I thought I would."

"Maybe I'll stay up with you."

"Okay," she said.

"Erin."

"Yes?"

"I miss her."

You don't have the right to miss her, she thought, but she left these words, too, unspoken. So many things unspoken.

So many things she could not say.

27

SHE NEED NOT HAVE said them. Charles had heard them anyway, in the awkward cadences of their conversation, more eloquent in its silences than any words they might have given voice to.

They retreated to the kitchen, where they drank coffee until dawn stole up in the windows, reminding Charles of his vision of the Horned King upon the wall, antlered dark against a crimson sun. *Do you ever see anything in the wood?* Erin had asked not long ago, and there had been a time when he would have told her the truth — that he'd twice seen that horned figure, that he feared he might be going mad. There had been a time when he would have responded with a question of his own:

Why do you ask? he might have said. *Have you?*

But there was too much between them now. Too much history, too much blame and grief, too many inarticulate resentments for such intimacy.

So stillness reigned until Mrs. Ramsden bustled in at seven, relentlessly cheerful, ignoring what she could not have failed to see. "Early morning, then?" she asked as she set about making breakfast.

"Long night," Charles said.

Erin was more direct. "I'm sorry I frightened you, Helen."

Mrs. Ramsden smiled from the stove. "Never mind that. I'm sorry that you were ill."

Ill, Charles thought. It worked as well as any other euphemism. Thus it was papered over.

The smells of breakfast crowded the air — sausage and eggs, a fresh pot of coffee. And Mrs. Ramsden's talk as well. If Erin had succeeded in anything at Hollow House, she had succeeded in breaching Mrs. Ramsden's reserve — or had, at least, given her license to speak when speech would be of service. Helen Ramsden had an unerring sense of the house's fraught emotional weather and how best to respond to it. She made herself invisible when they needed her to be invisible. She made herself present when she could ameliorate their suffering.

So she served up breakfast with a side of benevolent gossip. The Dawsons were renovating their house, the Robinsons celebrating their golden anniversary. And though the Dawsons and the Robinsons were utter strangers to Erin and Charles alike, this happy news gave them at least an illusion of normalcy, a sense that they too were woven into the fabric of a larger community.

But underneath, dark currents coursed. What of Mary Babbing? Charles did not ask. What news of her? And more, what had the Dawsons and the Robinsons done to earn these mundane blessings?

Somewhere Icarus fell to the sea, and the ploughman turned away.

Charles thanked Mrs. Ramsden and pushed himself back from the table, his eyes grainy with exhaustion.

"Going to work, then?" she asked.

He went to lie down instead, set an alarm for noon, pulled shut the heavy curtains in his room. But sleep proved difficult to find. Too much caffeine in his bloodstream, too much on his mind. And when at last he did doze off, his rest was unquiet. Images swirled like fog through his half-unconscious thoughts. Voices clamored. An enveloping wood and a faraway whisper, an insidious command that he could not yet decipher.

You go on without me, Lissa said, and he awoke.

28

CHARLES DROVE TO RIPON to consult Ann Merrow.

She worked out of a Victorian house, impeccably restored. When her assistant ushered him into the inner sanctum — a large, ground-floor room with bright sunlight in the windows — she came around her desk to greet him, shook his hand briskly, seated him in a leather chair by the fireplace. She sat across from him, a legal pad on her knee and a pen at ready. The air smelled of some floral effusion, a scent warmer, perhaps, tucked away in some far corner.

The assistant came in with tea, and Charles and Merrow exchanged pleasantries over the steaming cups. She trusted the Haydens were settling in all right (they were) and that the natives had proved friendly (they had). "You've begun your research, then?" she asked. And when he allowed that he had, she said, "Has it begun to pay dividends?"

Charles laughed and set his tea on the table at his elbow. "It has not," he said. "Or only a little. I found — well, Silva North — do you know her?"

"I do."

"She turned it up, actually. She was kind enough to share it."

"What is it?"

"A document that might or might not have been written by Caedmon Hollow."

"Might or might not have?"

"It's difficult to authenticate. It's a cipher. We haven't figured out how to solve it yet."

"I see. Well, that's odd, isn't it? I suppose there are experts you could consult. You might try the university in York. Though you've already thought of that, I'm sure."

"I have."

"But you've elected not to?"

"It seems . . . premature. I'd like to have a manuscript in hand before I begin to make anything public. I may have no other choice, I guess."

"Of course. Well, you may be sure that I will maintain your confidence." She smiled dryly. "But you haven't come here to talk about secret codes that may or may not have been written by your man Caedmon Hollow, have you? So what is it that I can do for you, Mr. Hayden?"

"I'm curious about Cillian Harris."

"Ah, Mr. Harris. He's quite capable, I assure you. He looks a bit like a ruffian, but he can't help that, can he? He's well educated, he grew up on the estate, and he knows its workings about as well as it's possible to know something like that."

"He said his father preceded him as steward."

"And his grandfather before that. And *his* father as well, for all I know. It may go back further still. I sometimes think he knows the estate's business better than Mr. Hollow's solicitors."

"I thought you were the estate's solicitor."

"Ah." She smiled. "I serve at the pleasure of Mr. Hollow's London firm. To whom Mr. Harris also reports. Though they all report to you — or, more accurately, to Mrs. Hayden — in the end. But I take it you have some other inquiry or you wouldn't have driven all the way into Ripon."

"I do." Charles paused. "I noticed it on the day we arrived, actually. He'd been drinking. I smelled it."

She arched an eyebrow. "Perhaps you smelled his cologne."

"If so, he poured it out of a bottle of scotch." Charles leaned forward. "I was skeptical myself, but he kept turning up with whisky on his breath. And then he showed up at the pub. Very drunk, violently so. He made a scene. He apologized to me the next day, said he'd shamed the estate, but that's not what concerns me. Silva tells me that his drinking has become a problem. I've heard it elsewhere as well. The landlord at the King threatened to ban him. Given that he manages the estate, it seemed wise to . . ." He shrugged and lifted his hands, uncertain how to proceed.

"I see. Perhaps you don't fully understand Mr. Harris's duties. If you're concerned about money, the London firm manages the financial end of things. Mr. Harris's responsibilities are principally local. He takes care of the day-to-day operation of the house and grounds, supervises the staff, oversees maintenance, hires and fires as appropriate."

"Even so."

"Are you thinking of letting him go?"

"I don't know what I'm thinking."

"Well, it's no use thinking about that. You could give him other duties, I imagine, but even then you're on shaky ground. And I don't know how you'd go about replacing him. He's trained for the job his whole life."

"Shaky ground?"

"Yes. You may not remember this — you were pretty boggled with jet lag when we sat down and went through it all — but Mr. Harris comes attached to the estate."

"Attached?"

"Legally, I mean. The position is guaranteed to him in Mr. Hollow's will. The codicil was imposed upon him, as it has been on every generation for some time."

"I don't understand."

"Nor do I. All I know is that as long as the estate is in the hands of the Hollow family — and that includes your wife, Mr. Hayden — the stewardship is guaranteed to the Harrises and their male descendants."

"That's . . . odd."

"It *is* rather unusual," she said. "It is nonetheless the condition imposed upon each successive generation."

"And if the condition is violated?"

"He could bring suit. He would probably win."

"Wow. Do you have any idea why?"

"I don't know the origins of the codicil."

"Can you find out?"

"I'm afraid you're getting into areas where I can be of no service. I fear that I have already overstepped my bounds."

"What do you mean?"

"Your wife inherited the Hollow estate, Mr. Hayden. Simply put, you have no legal standing in the matter."

Charles hesitated. "May I confide something in you?"

"Discretion is my stock in trade."

"The truth is, Erin's in no shape to make such a request. She hasn't recovered from the loss of our daughter. I'm sure this doesn't come as a surprise to you."

"It does not. It took significant research to track you down, after all." She softened. "I'm sorry for your loss, Mr. Hayden. I would have tendered my sympathies before, but condolences from strangers are not always welcome. In any case, I'm sorry to hear that Mrs. Hayden isn't doing well, but without her explicit request, I can't proceed in matters relating to the estate."

They sat in silence for a moment. Charles could sense her turning the matter over in her mind. He sipped his tea, but it had gone cold.

"It is a curious codicil," Merrow said. "I've wondered about it myself." A pause. "You're simply relaying Mrs. Hayden's request, I presume."

"Of course."

Again silence.

"I'm not likely to find anything, you understand," she said. "People aren't obliged to explain the terms of their wills."

"Of course not."

"Most likely I can determine when it was added. The *why* is an entirely different matter. And it's the *why* that you — that is to say, your wife, of course — are interested in, I imagine."

"Of course," Charles said. "Let's just see what you can find out, okay?"

"I'll look into it," Merrow said.

"Thank you."

"I'll be in touch when I know something," she said.

A dismissal. Charles stood. At the door, he turned to face her.

"The money," he said. "The Hollow money. Where did it come from?"

She blinked. "The family has been wealthy for centuries."

"But where did the money come from?"

"I don't know, actually," she said. "I've never really thought about it."

"It's unusual, isn't it — that they've been so wealthy for so long."

"Not in England. Still, their investments have done exceptionally well. Uncommonly so."

"I see."

"Well, then," she said. "When I learn something about the codicil, I'll ring—"

"One more thing, if you don't mind."

"Not at all."

"Do you know anything about the Eorl Wood, Ms. Merrow?"

"Only that it's perhaps the oldest surviving primeval forest in England. And that it, too, has belonged to the Hollows for centuries. And that it now belongs to you, every tree and acorn."

"Nothing else? I've heard . . ."

"Old wives' tales?" she asked.

"Yes."

"I wouldn't let my imagination run away with me, Mr. Hayden."

"Of course not," he said. "I'm interested in tracking down any sources that might have influenced Caedmon Hollow, that's all. Surely he'd have known the local folklore."

"No doubt." Merrow thought for a moment. "If you're really interested in those old tales, there's a man in Yarrow you might talk to: Fergus Gill. He must be ninety years old by now. You'll find him at the pub. He's fond of playing draughts."

"Drinking them, you mean?"

She laughed. "That, too, I suppose. He usually drinks the one while he plays the other, I imagine. Draughts is the game you Americans so quaintly call checkers. In any case, playing or drinking, he should be able to help you with your old wives' tales."

Charles nodded. "I'll talk to him, then."

"Good. Can I do anything else for you today, Mr. Hayden?"

"No, thank you."

And so Charles found himself outside in the bright afternoon sun. He got into his car and put down the window, but he didn't start the engine. He hadn't intended to ask Merrow about the Eorl Wood; he wasn't sure why he'd done so. But there came to him an image of the Horned King upon the wall. There came an image of Cillian Harris, slipping out into the midnight wood — in response perhaps to some malefic bidding.

Nonsense, of course.

Charles wasn't sure why such a thing would occur to him in the first place.

I wouldn't let my imagination run away with me.

Maybe he really was going mad.

Harris hadn't been able to sleep, that's all. He'd been drinking. He'd needed to clear his head. Whatever. But that was the end of it. There was nothing ominous about it, no problem beyond the mundane dilemma of how best to manage his position — if it even needed managing. Maybe it didn't.

He would ask Silva, he decided. She knew Harris better than anyone else. Maybe she would have some suggestions.

That decided, Charles took a deep breath, started the car, and pulled out into the street.

No more crazy thoughts, he vowed. But the crazy thoughts stayed with him all the way back to Yarrow.

29

SILVA HAD MADE no progress with the cipher, either.

She too had tried omitting numbers and symbols and plugging the letters into an online decrypting program — with about as much success as Charles had had himself. "I have some other ideas," she said. "Perhaps if we put our heads together —"

An invitation. It came in the late afternoon, another proposal that he and Erin join her at the pub, this time for dinner, code-breaking to commence after dessert at her flat. "The King's food is indifferent," she said, "but it's the only game in town."

Erin told Charles to go on without her.

"It will do you some good to get out," he protested. "Besides, I think you'll like her."

"I'm sure I would," she said. "But I'm not really in a good place right now."

There were things Charles could have said that he did not say. He might have asked her when she thought she *would* be in a good place, or pointed out that her therapist had told her six months ago that company would help. But it seemed unwise to do so in the shadow of the anniversary a week past. And there was the matter of Lorna. How could he ever prepare Erin to encounter a near doppelgänger of her lost daughter?

"Anyway," Erin added, "I don't think I would be much good at code-breaking."

"I don't seem to be much good at it myself," he said.

"Maybe you'll have better luck tonight."

Perhaps so. Charles wasn't optimistic, though.

He said as much over dinner — a salad for Silva, and for him bangers and mash, which turned out to be sausages and mashed potatoes — not bad, though he could have done without the onion gravy. He consoled himself with a second pint of the Dark Mild.

Silva chuckled. "You'll be too drunk to decrypt anything if you're not careful," she said.

"Maybe being drunk will help. I certainly haven't gotten anywhere while sober."

"Are you making any progress on the research?"

"Also a dry well. I take it you're not having much luck, either."

"Same as ever. Just boxes. I'd let you know if I found anything."

"Likewise."

They were silent a moment. Charles looked around the pub. There was a bigger crowd tonight than on his prior visit, Armitage busy behind the bar. Several old men had gathered to play checkers at the fireplace. He wondered if Fergus Gill was among them. He was just getting ready to ask Silva when —

"I do wish your wife had been able to join us."

"I think the code-breaking did not appeal."

"Well, we could have put the code-breaking off for another time. That cryptogram has been hanging around in a box for the last hundred years. It's not going anywhere. I'm sure she must be lonely out there, rattling around in that great house."

Lonely didn't really do it justice, Charles thought. Isolated might have been closer to the mark. Desolate and forlorn.

"Is she okay, Charles?"

"No," he said, the word rising unbidden to his lips. "No, she's not okay."

Silva held his gaze. "I didn't think so. You're neither one of you okay, are you?"

"We're getting by."

"I can't imagine what it must be like for you. If I lost Lorna . . ."

This was a road Charles did not want to travel down. "Where is Lorna?" he asked.

"My parents took her for the afternoon. Every Wednesday after school. She'll be home soon." Silva looked at her watch. "We should go, actually, get in a few minutes with our cryptogram before she arrives. Drink up, why don't you?"

Charles drank up.

Outside, in the cool, blue dusk, Charles said, "I envy you this weather."

"I don't think anyone has ever said that about Yorkshire weather."

"Back home in North Carolina, it would be miserable already. Humid. Temperatures into the eighties."

"Well, this is your home now, isn't it?"

"Is it?"

"You're gentry."

He laughed. "I fear I'm an interloper."

"Do you miss it? North Carolina, the States?"

He thought about it as they walked. "No," he said finally. "There's nothing there for me anymore."

"What about your wife? Erin?"

Yes, what about her?

"I think she'd like to go back," he said.

But why? To tend Lissa's grave? Was that any kind of life? And what would they do? Erin had given up her practice. He had no job. And even if they no longer had to worry about money—and he supposed they didn't—how could they ever go home to Ransom again? How could they return to the house they'd left behind, where Lissa's presence haunted every room, her voice every breath of air? And how walk those streets, where everyone in town knew the whole sordid story? In Ransom they would be forever mired in the past, defined by the horror of Lissa's death. There could be no future there.

The future was here. Erin would have to come to see that.

He said nothing of this, but perhaps Silva sensed it. A shadow passed across her face. She nodded, and they walked on in silence through the gathering night.

30

"You said you had some other ideas," Charles said.

They sat across from each other at the cluttered kitchen table — laptop, books, a photocopy of the enciphered page between them. The light suspended overhead shed a radiant circle down upon it. The room was otherwise dim: full night behind the shades and a flickering fluorescent bar buzzing quietly over the sink.

"I've been reading up on ciphers," Silva said.

"Me too. Not that it's done me much good."

"Really? You haven't come up with anything?"

"Well, alphabetic substitution was still the state of the art. Not Caesar's simple alphabetic shift, obviously. We've tried that. But something that employs multiple alphabets keyed to a single word, a — what was the guy's name?"

"Vigenère," she said. "A Vigenère cipher. Secure and relatively easy to encode. That's my bet, too."

"Not that it helps. We've got the numbers and symbols to contend with, for one thing. And we don't know the keyword."

"Think positive," Silva said. She propped her elbows on the table and rested her chin on her clasped hands. "Let's assume it really was written by Caedmon Hollow. Why would he be using code in the first place?"

"And who would he be writing to?"

"Precisely. Most ciphers, you're communicating with someone who already possesses the keyword. If that's the case, we're in trouble."

"A specialist could break it," Charles said.

"But you don't want to do that, do you?"

"No. I want the book to be fresh. And an encrypted document — that could be a real hook."

"Especially if it contains something juicy."

"Especially," he said. "Assuming it was Caedmon Hollow, of course. Problem is, we don't have a clue. And if we did, he would be too dead to tell us the key."

"Unless Hollow was writing to *us*," Silva said.

"I don't understand."

"What if there was something he didn't want his contemporaries to know, something he wanted to preserve?"

"It's a long shot."

"I guess," Silva said. "I've been thinking about those numbers, though. If he's writing for posterity — his children, his children's children, whatever — then he'd need a way to pass along the keyword, wouldn't he? I'm thinking that's where the numbers might come in. But I can't figure out how they work."

Charles picked up the yellowing page. "Some kind of alphabetic correspondence?"

"Tried it," she said. "A number of different ways, actually. I couldn't figure out what to do with numbers like 112. Not to mention the symbols."

"They all appear in the second paragraph, in these lines that are bracketed off by ellipses," he said. "I noticed that earlier. That has to be important. Say each pair of ellipses sets off a separate unit of meaning — a phrase — then we'd have to consider the numbers in each phrase independently . . ."

"And the symbols?"

Charles studied the page. "You have a notebook handy?"

"Sure," she said. But as she stood to retrieve it, someone knocked on the door.

"Hello!" A woman's voice.

"Lorna's home," Silva said. "Come on, you can meet my mum."

Charles put the page back on the table and got to his feet. He followed her into the living room. When he saw Lorna, he felt once again that sense of dislocation, the earth unsteady beneath his feet, as if time had slipped its sprocket, dropping him into a past that he'd believed irretrievably lost. What had Faulkner said? *The past isn't dead. It isn't even past.* Here, then, was a glimpse into Erin's inner life, marooned beyond the reach of human rescue in a past that was forever present. What if she had joined them tonight? he wondered. He hadn't mentioned Lorna to her, much less her uncanny resemblance to their lost daughter — had not been able to bring himself to do so. He recognized in this his own duplicity: come, join us, he'd encouraged her, relying on her emotional paralysis to bar her from actually doing so. Why? Out of some misbegotten idea of protecting her? Or because he wanted to preserve Lorna and Silva for himself? He couldn't say. But he thought of Syrah Nagle and was ashamed.

He found his voice. He crouched and said hello to Lorna in the stilted cadence of someone who didn't know how to speak to a child, or had forgotten. Then, smiling, he stood to greet the woman in the doorway. She looked like Silva three decades further on, tall and angular, with the same wide mouth and straight nose, the same hazel eyes. Introductions followed: Isla, she said, her hand cool in his. It was very nice to meet him. Silva spoke highly of him.

"She's very generous, then," Charles said.

"Is she?" Isla seemed to consider him for a moment. "I'd hoped to meet your wife," she said.

"She couldn't make it tonight. She's not feeling well."

"I see. Well, please send her my best wishes for a swift recovery. I trust you're both adjusting to your new home."

"It's a little overwhelming," Charles said. "Everyone has been very kind."

"Wonderful."

"Stay for a drink, Mum," Silva said.

"Another night. I'll leave you to your puzzle. You're making progress, I hope."

"Yet to be determined," Silva said. "We'll see."

"Well. I'll go, then. Very nice meeting you, Mr. Hayden."

"Likewise."

She knelt to say goodbye to Lorna and then, with a final smile for Charles, saw herself out.

"All right, kiddo," Silva said, ruffling Lorna's hair. "It's a bath and bed for you."

"But Mum —"

"No buts." Then, to Charles: "You can be self-sufficient for a few minutes?"

"Sure."

"Notebook on the counter," she said. "Beer in the fridge. Help yourself."

Charles did. The beer was easy to locate—he snagged one called Taddy Porter—but the promised notebook proved somewhat more difficult. He strolled the length of the counter looking for it, pausing to examine a framed school photo of Lorna, so much like Lissa that he felt something twist inside him. And then there it was, a spiral-bound composition book, buried under a stack of tomes on mythology. Campbell, Jung, Eliade—shopworn scholars, their reputations much in decline. Yet their ideas had stuck with him all the same. Though he hadn't read them since college, Charles could still recall some of their touchstone phrases. The monomyth and the collective unconscious. The eternal return. What has been is, what was will be: the marvelous everywhere erupting into the mundane.

Charles picked up a much-worn paperback, lavishly illustrated. Jung's *Man and His Symbols.* Thumbing through it, he happened across an image of a snake biting its own tail: Ouroboros, the Midgard Serpent, time forever renewing itself. Nietzsche had called it eternal recurrence, the cosmic wheel turning in its course. What we have done we will do again, endlessly anew. The iron fist of necessity gripped us every one. Amor fati.

The idea was intolerable.

Charles could not learn to love this fate. He did not want to read the story he'd been written into.

He put the book down. Picked up the notebook. Fished a pencil out of the clutter.

At the table, he opened the composition book to a clean page, took a sip of the porter, and studied the cipher. Silva was right. The key had to be in the numbers.

Not noise, but signal.

The question was, what were they saying? He transcribed three of the enciphered lines from the fragmented phrases of the second block of text, jotting the numbers and symbols from each phrase immediately underneath it —

$$... pw2xa\ la-isl\ zgmvo11gm\ wi<dvq\ l>$$
$$cdzw\ s-x+uu\ bciay\ dqyranyb16minlca\ ...$$
$$2-11<>-+16$$

$$... xz2xbj-pz4waux6a<jr\ wcv>$$
$$zt\ xjlv5xkpgcvf-kp1gcv1f\ kpg2cvf\ ...$$
$$2-46<>5-112$$

$$... gmcl3xjwhi\ tlc-ioiv3wvin2efa\ z\ av<a\ gy\ uzzeelu\ q\ neo\ hk\ a>$$
$$omds\ dqyran-yb\ rmlo2xyqn\ kjl+rb\ meyn'u\ pj8vfz\ ...$$
$$3-32<>-2+8$$

Charles took a swig of beer. He scratched his head. Written out this way, they resembled equa —

"Charles —"

He looked up, startled.

Silva stood in the doorway, one arm draped over her daughter's shoulder. "Lorna has a request."

"What's that?"

"Go ahead, Lorna."

"I want you . . ." She turned away, burying her face against her mother's hip.

"Lorna," Silva said. "You can ask him. He's a very nice man. You're very nice, aren't you, Charles?"

Charles had his doubts on that score. Sometimes he felt that he had nothing *but* doubts on that score. Yet he forced a smile all the same. "Absolutely," he said. "I'm nice."

Lorna stole a glance at him and then hid her face away again. "I want you to read me a story," she whispered.

Something came unlashed within him. He felt weightless, cut adrift a hundred miles above the planet.

He swallowed. "Sure, I'd like that," he said.

"I told you, silly," Silva said. "All right, then. Come on."

Lorna led them to her bedroom, a bower of purple and white. The lights had been draped in swaths of gauzy violet fabric, imparting to the air a cool, lavender glow. A tucking-in ritual involving much giggling and many kisses followed. "One book," Silva said. "Understand?"

"Three."

"Two," Charles said, and that settled it. After a final set of air kisses and still more giggling, Silva left them to their own devices.

Charles perched on the edge of the bed. With much silliness — "Come on, mister," she said — Lorna tugged him all the way aboard.

"Choose your book," he said, and in the interest of delaying the inevitable, she chose, as Lissa would have chosen, the longest of the books fanned out across the comforter. This tactic had once annoyed Charles, who'd usually hastened through story time in order to get back to whatever task had otherwise been occupying his attention for the night. Grading papers or preparing for class. Reading. Whatever. Now he found himself tearing up. He'd let too many of the small moments slip by.

"Are you sad?" Lorna asked.

"A little bit, I guess. But I'm very happy, too," he told her, and he realized that, in this fleeting instant anyway, he really was.

"You're funny."

"Am I?"

"You can't be happy and sad at the same time."

Sure you can, he thought. But aloud, "Okay, I'll be happy, then." As if you could choose. As if joy and sorrow didn't select you at their whim.

Lorna snuggled in under his arm. She smelled of soap and shampoo. She smelled of little girl. She smelled like Lissa. "Read," she said with a wiggle. "Read, read."

Helpless to resist, Charles opened the book. "Once upon a time," he said.

31

HE WAS LOST in a forest. He could hear Lissa (Lorna?) crying in the distance, but when he tried to go to her, her voice drew away, deeper into the wood. And then — there was no transition — he found himself in a moonshot clearing. The Horned King — Cernunnos, he thought — stood in the wind-dappled shadows of the surrounding trees. He was saying something. Charles could hear his thin voice echoing inside his skull, but he couldn't make out the words. Icy dread pierced him.

And then he felt a hand gentle upon his shoulder and he was awake.

He opened his eyes.

Silva held a finger to her lips.

"C'mon," she whispered. He eased off the bed and together they negotiated the minefield of toys that Lorna had planted across the threadbare rug. Silva snapped off the light. He followed her down the hall into the living room.

"What time is it?" he asked, rubbing his eyes.

"Almost ten."

"I need to go. What happened?"

"You fell asleep. Too much beer."

True enough, he supposed. By the time he'd finished reading the second book, Lorna had nodded off. She'd curled into him, breathing deeply, and he'd let his own respiration relax into a matching rhythm, enjoying a moment's respite, as if the present, with all its dolor and regrets, had fallen away and everything was as it had been and might be again, time turning back upon itself, Lorna his own lost daughter. A moment, a moment.

Now he had a dull, beery headache. His mouth tasted sour.

"Can you stay a little while longer?" Silva asked.

"A few minutes, I guess. Why?"

"I'll show you."

"I need a glass of water."

"Okay."

She sat him at the kitchen table, fetched him the water — lukewarm; they had yet to discover the virtues of ice in this benighted country — and pulled her chair around beside him.

"Look," she said, pointing at the notebook.

He looked. She'd jotted down the rest of the phrases that contained numbers and symbols — six of them — and highlighted the numbers in each line. "X marks the spot," she said.

"What do you mean?" he said, and then he saw it for himself. Roughly half of the numbers were followed by an x, and if you counted the last two x's she'd highlighted, both of them bracketed by symbols —

Six phrases. Twelve x's. Which felt a little too symmetrical to be entirely random.

"So there are six phrases in the cipher that include numbers," she said. "If you pull them all out, together with the x's that immediately follow, plus the x's enclosed by symbols, you get" — she turned the page — "these":

$$2x-11<>-x+16$$
$$2x-46<>5x-112$$
$$3x-32<>-2x+8$$
$$-3x+11<>x-9$$
$$-4x+78<>-3x+60$$
$$5x-103<>4x-84$$

"And they look an awful lot like —"

"Equations," he said.

"Right. Replace the little caret thingies with an equals sign, and that's exactly what you have."

"So what did you do?"

She flipped the page. Numbers, each one inscribed in her small, neat hand, filled the next three sheets.

"I solved them," she said.

He looked at the numbers again, impressed. "You *solved* them?"

"Math always came easy to me." She flipped another page. Six numbers — the solutions, he supposed — had been written there:

$$9, 22, 8, 5, 18, 19$$

"Let me guess," he said. "Those numbers correspond to letters in the alphabet."

"That's what I was thinking." She flipped another page:

$$I, V, H, E, R, S$$

She said, "Unscramble it and you get —"

"Shiver," Charles said.

"Right, that's what I thought. So I put the encrypted text into an on-line decrypting tool, plugged the keyword in, and got —"

"More nonsense," he said.

Silva gave him a look and turned the laptop so that he could see it for himself.

"How did you know?" she asked.

32

"IT'S NOT REALLY a Hollow kind of word, is it?" Charles said.

"What do you mean?"

"He was a guy who never used a fifty-cent word when a five-dollar one would do." He studied the letters, moving them around inside his head. Not "shiver," but —

"Do you remember the Badger?" he asked.

"What are you talking about?"

"I'm talking about *In the Night Wood*. The Helpful Badger. One of the creatures Laura meets in the Wood."

"I guess I've forgotten the Badger. But what does that —"

"Just a hunch," Charles said, picking up the pencil, and then, hesitating, he wrote a word beneath the scrambled letters —

SHRIVE

"What's that got to do with badgers?" Silva asked.

"Just try it," Charles said.

"Okay."

She reached for the laptop, deleted SHIVER from the keyword text box, and punched in SHRIVE. She clicked the decrypt icon.

Charles leaned forward — they leaned forward at the same time — and in the instant before the decrypted text came up on the screen, he was suddenly, achingly aware of the proximity of her face to his own: the steady rise and fall of breath in her lungs, the scent of her skin. Too close, he thought, and an image of Syrah Nagle fleeted through his mind.

Then —

"Got it," Silva whispered.

They had. Words — actual, comprehensible words — scrolled up the screen.

Charles hunched closer to read them:

That which I have most feared — which I have dreamed of and so long resisted — has come to pass. My mind is much disordered now. I have so often slaked my thirst upon nepenthe that I can no longer distinguish reality from lunatic phantasmagoria. But this morning I woke to find mud on my boots and the lines below scrawled in my journal. I have here enciphered and preserved them, together with their key, in the hope that some future auditor might adduce in these incoherent echoes evidence for a posthumous absolution that I cannot see myself. I will say no more. The original I have out of cowardice destroyed, but the lines ran thus —

. . . let us not speak of fairy elves and their midnight revels . . . like some belated peasant I saw or dreamed I saw at still midnight with his great ragg'd horns . . . Herne . . . the king has come dost thou not hear the words that he breathes in mine ear . . . when daisies pied, and violets blue and lady-smocks do paint the meadows with delight . . . dost thou not hear them . . . thus he sings on every tree cuckoo . . . sweet cuckoos hatch in sparrow's nest . . . dost thou not . . . midway through the journey of my life I wandered from the straight path . . . most foul most foul . . . my heart rebounds with fear . . . let us not speak of it . . . I woke to find myself in a night wood . . . tiend most foul . . . my pretty cuckoo bird . . . death could scarce be more bitter . . . tiend while overhead the moon sits arbitress, and nearer to the earth wheels her pale course . . .

There was nothing more. Let me only pray that Mr. De Quincey is correct in asserting that this subtle tincture which has so many nights assuaged my restless spirit can also do that which all the perfumes of Araby in concert cannot do: restore to me — for even one night — the hopes of my youth, and my hands washed pure from blood. CH 24 June 1843

"It's him," Charles said.

He laughed in shock and disbelief, in jubilation, and sat back to look at Silva. But he couldn't be still. Adrenaline had flushed away his boozy fatigue. He stood and paced the room, unable to contain his excitement. He had to shake it out of his bones, had to give it voice. This was what he'd been looking for, what he'd barely dared hope he'd find: a genuine hook that would draw in a commercial publisher, not some academic also-ran.

An actual, honest-to-God mystery, a crime and a cryptogram, a shadowy secret history. It was like something out of a story. "It's really him, Silva," he said. "It has to be. Absolutely has to be. The initials, the date, the picture. It all adds up."

"But what does it add up *to?*"

"I don't know, I guess." Then, thinking: "It's some kind of crazy confession. Don't you think? He's talking about absolution and bloody hands. Even the keyword—"

"The Helpful Badger," Silva said, raising her eyebrows.

"Right. The story takes place on the Night of Shrives."

"Remind me."

"To shrive means to make confession. That's what the Helpful Badger tells Laura. Once upon a time, long ago, the small folk betrayed the Lord of the Wood to the tyrant Horned King. On the anniversary of their betrayal they gather throughout the Wood to make ritual confession of their sin." Charles stopped pacing and turned to face her. "Do you realize what this means, Silva? There's real potential here. I mean, this is major, major stuff."

And now she was laughing, too. At him, he supposed, but not unkindly. "Don't get ahead of yourself."

"I'm not. This is really big—big for you, too. Big for the historical society. If this really is a confession—" He broke off. "It is, don't you think? It has to be. What else could it be?"

"Charles—"

"No, I'm serious. What else could it be?"

"Okay, let's say you're right, then. Hypothetically, okay? There's still so much we don't know. Granted, he thinks he's guilty of something, but he doesn't say what."

"Murder," Charles said. "That bit about the perfumes of Araby— see it?"

"What about it?"

"It's an allusion to *Macbeth*. Lady Macbeth says that all the perfumes of Arabia won't wash the stench of Duncan's blood off her hands."

"Okay," Silva said, leaning over the screen to reread the cryptogram. "But he also says he can't tell the difference between fantasy and reality," she said. "If that's the case, then the entire — confession, for lack of a better word — the entire confession could be the product of some delusion. Or even some early impulse toward fiction." She paused. "What's nepenthe?"

"A drug," Charles said. "It's more of a generic literary formulation than a real thing. Did you ever have to memorize 'The Raven'?"

"'The Raven'?"

"Edgar Allan Poe. This awful poem I had to memorize in high school. It's an American thing, I guess. Shall I recite it?"

"Not if it's awful."

"Well, let me at least give you the relevant line," he said. "The speaker of the poem is grieving for his lover, Lenore. And at one point he says, 'Quaff this kind nepenthe and forget this lost Lenore!'"

"Quaff? He actually uses the word 'quaff'?"

"Quaff," Charles said, adding in a sepulchral voice: "'Quoth the Raven "Nevermore."'"

"But obviously Caedmon Hollow was talking about quaffing something real."

"Well, he alludes to De Quincey in the last paragraph. He must be talking about *Confessions of an English Opium-Eater,* right?"

"Laudanum?"

"That's what I'm thinking." He took his seat beside her and scrolled through the cryptogram again. De Quincey, *Macbeth.* The thing was full of allusions. "There's a reference to *The Divine Comedy* in the second paragraph," he said. "The first canto of *Inferno.* 'Midway through the journey of my life I woke to find myself in a dark wood for I had strayed from the straight path.'"

"Only he's translated 'dark wood' as 'night wood.'"

"He has. Could he really have been thinking about the book six years before he wrote it?"

"Maybe so," she said. "Maybe this is the root of it. Eighteen forty-three is a crucial year, isn't it? There's this — confession, or whatever this thing is — in June. And Hollow House burned at the end of August. Plus, he's said to have set the fire himself, right?"

"'My mind is much disordered now,'" Charles said.

"Exactly. And here I'd hoped solving the thing might provide answers."

"Me too. Instead, everything just gets murkier." Charles glanced at his watch. It was nearly midnight. He should have checked in with Erin. He supposed he still could, but she might already be in bed. He didn't want to wake her. Better just to get on the road. "Listen," he said, "I should have been home hours ago. I should go. Can you print me a copy of this?"

"Of course," she said, and as she turned to the computer, Charles resumed pacing. Silva's caution was unwarranted, he thought. The cryptogram was the start of something, or maybe it was the middle, the turning point in a grand story that had languished untold for more than a century: a story that was his to write, a story that he must write himself into.

He'd been trapped for so long. A door had opened, or a window.

33

SILVA WALKED HIM DOWN through the dark museum.

Outside, the air had cooled. The village slept. A breeze moved through the high street to touch his face as he stood on the stoop, and the stars blazed out in the cloudless heavens, like a thousand pinholes punched through the black curtain of the night and behind it something radiant and true.

He had to go. He thought of the white rabbit, pulling his watch from his waistcoat pocket and saying, *Oh dear! Oh dear! I shall be late!* Only he was already late. Yet he stood there a moment longer all the same, and Silva stood opposite, the threshold alone dividing them. And if another fleeting image of Syrah Nagle came to him — if he thought of the taste of her lips upon his own, or the length of her pale body — he did not acknowledge it even to himself. He became brusque and hearty instead. Held up the confession in his hand. Said, "Progress. Thank you, Silva."

"You don't owe me any thanks."

"I do. This was your find. Plus" — he smiled — "you did the math. I'm lousy at math."

"You're welcome, then. I will do the math should any further need arise."

"Deal." And then — Syrah ghosted through his mind once again — he started to say — what? He didn't know, would never know. Silva saved him from some awful temptation; she saved him from himself. "Good night, Charles," she said.

"Yes, well, good night." And he turned away.

He'd reached the gate — his hand was upon the latch — when she said, "Charles." He turned to look back at her. She'd stepped out across the threshold. She'd stepped into the night. "I meant to say earlier, I owe you some thanks as well."

"For what?"

"You were very kind to Lorna tonight."

"I read her a story. Nothing out of the line of duty."

"But it was what she needed, I think — a male voice, a male presence. I guess that sounds odd. But it's been hard on her, this thing with her father, the way he's held himself aloof from her recently. And then Mary's disappearance. Well, she's afraid, isn't she? People are vanishing on her."

"It's hard on you, too, I imagine."

"Anything that's hard on Lorna is hard on me."

I know, he thought. I know, I know. And he felt a yawning abyss open up underneath his feet, Lissa's loss, a lacuna in his soul. How he had hurt for her. A scraped knee, a bad day at school, a bully — he'd felt her small sorrows like mortal wounds, like they had been his own. Hard lessons for them both: the indifference of heaven, the indifference of the sky. Love, hope, joy — the world stole it piecemeal away until there was nothing left to steal. At some level, he must have known this all along, but he had not known it in his blood — he had not owned it — until Lissa died. Your children were supposed to outlive you. But that was just wishful thinking. There were no guarantees, just chance or fate, though maybe it came to the same thing in the end.

You could not know.

All this in an instant, and him saying, "If there's anything I can do —"

"You've done a lot," she said. "I just wanted you to know."

He nodded and opened the gate. On the sidewalk beyond, he turned once again. "Did you know Cillian was attached to the estate?"

"Attached?"

"Attached. As in, his position is guaranteed by the terms of the will."

"Whose will?"

"That's unclear. Apparently the codicil goes back some generations."

"How do you know?"

"I asked Ann Merrow."

"How did you come to ask that? You weren't thinking of firing him, were you?"

"I'm concerned about his drinking."

"We all are, Charles." She came down into the yard. "You mustn't do anything, though. Losing his position at the estate — that would destroy him."

"Well, he's in no danger of losing it, it seems, even if I were so inclined. Which I'm not, entirely. I asked him what I could do to help him, but . . ." Charles shrugged.

"No, he wouldn't like that. He's too proud for that." Silva came to the gate and stood there on the other side, another threshold between them. "Charles," she said, "you must be patient with him. He's going through something. I don't know what it is, but I know that he's a good man. This will pass."

"Do you still care about him?"

The question came out before he could corral it. He did not know where it had come from, but he knew even as he said it that he'd stepped across some invisible line. He could see it in the set of her face in the starlight. It had closed in upon itself, opaque, impenetrable. Watching it happen was like watching a window shade being drawn down.

"He's the father of my child, Charles."

"Right," he said. "That was . . . I'm sorry. It's none of my business." He sighed. "I shouldn't have brought it up. I can't do anything anyway."

"Just don't shut him out. That would be as bad as firing him. He needs something to hold on to right now."

"Of course." Then: "I really do have to go, Silva."

"Good night, Charles."

"Good night." He hesitated a heartbeat longer, feeling that there was something unfinished between them. But what it was he could not say, so he nodded and turned away. Started up the sidewalk to his car, still parked at the far end of the village, in the pub's empty lot. He sensed that she was watching him as he strode up the street; he could feel the itch of her scrutiny between his shoulder blades. But maybe he'd imagined it. When he reached his car and looked back, the high street was desolate. He was alone.

Charles unlocked the car door and slid inside.

He studied the deciphered confession by the dome light — *I can no longer distinguish reality from lunatic phantasmagoria* — and he thought of that horned figure upon the wall. What was happening to him? Could he anymore distinguish between the two himself? Had grief divided him from reason?

Maybe there was something to the Poe poem after all. For hadn't he, Charles, also sought to borrow from his books surcease of sorrow? And hadn't he, too, failed? Perhaps he wasn't that different from Erin in the end, the both of them imprisoned by Lissa's death, alike entrapped by the awful gravity of that black star. When would his soul be lifted from that darkness?

Quoth the Raven "Nevermore."

34

"It's late, Charles."

Her voice surprised him as he closed the door. He put his keys on the table.

"Erin?"

"In the study," she said.

When he stepped into the room, she switched on a lamp. A host of impish faces retreated muttering into the foliage graven onto every wooden surface.

She met his gaze from a chair by the cold fireplace.

She'd been drinking. Charles would have known it even had he not seen the wine glass and the half-empty bottle at her elbow. He'd have heard it in her voice, the just barely perceptible way her tongue glided over her sibilants. He'd have seen it in the glassy sheen of her eyes. Yes. Drinking and more than drinking, he supposed. He wondered what she'd taken, and how much. Wondered if she even knew herself.

"What are you doing sitting here in the dark?" he asked.

"Waiting for you. Come in. Sit down. We should talk."

"We should go to bed. We can talk in the morning." When you're sober, he did not add. When you won't say things neither one of us wants to hear.

"I expected you home earlier."

"I know," he said. "I should have called. It's — time got away from me. We got caught up with the cryptogram."

"Did you solve it, then?"

"Yes."

"You and — what's her name?"

"Silva."

"You and Silva." She nodded. "Are you going to let me see it?"

Charles dug the cipher out of a back pocket and walked it across the room to her. As she read it, he stood at the window, uncertain what he hoped to see. In any case, it wasn't there. The lamp drowned out the night. His own reflection stared back at him, gaunt and hollow-eyed, inscrutable.

"What does it mean?" she asked.

He turned away from the window. "I don't know. I think it's a confession."

"To what?"

"Murder," he said, "if you can believe it."

"Most foul," she said.

"I'm sorry?"

"Most foul. That's what it says." She glanced down at the printout. "Murder most foul. Isn't that the phrase?"

"It is. It's Shakespeare," he said, wondering how he'd missed it. Murder most foul and strange. Murder most unnatural. Something like that.

"It's Hamlet's father," he added. "The ghost upon the rampart of El-sinore."

"What's this other word? Tiend? Is that Shakespeare, too?"

"I don't think so."

"What's it mean?"

"I don't know yet."

"Well." She rattled the page, set it on the table before her. "I guess this is what you've been hoping for."

"More than I'd hoped for. If it pans out."

"We should celebrate."

"It's late," he said. "We can celebrate tomorrow."

"It's never too late to celebrate your successes, Charles. To you and Silva," she said, lifting her glass. "To the scholars triumphant."

And then the light went out.

35

HER TOAST HUNG unanswered between them, brittle in the other-worldly dark.

"Erin," he said.

"I'm here," she said, an unconscious echo of the words he'd used all those years ago as they lay curled together in her narrow twin bed, not much smaller than the student-ghetto apartment that had contained it. It had been dark then, too, and into the dark, for the first time outside a therapist's office (therapy had done no good then, either), she had uttered the story of her parents' death. And if he'd begun by amusing her in those days, bumbling around, his glasses forever sliding down the bridge of his nose, he'd passed from that into consoling her, and from that, unspooling the long skein of their relationship, they'd slipped to-gether into the easy comfort of a good marriage — not one without its doldrums and its discontents, to be sure, but solid earth beneath her feet, the first she'd ever had.

Now, as those words reverberated across the years, it seemed to her that he had plunged them into a still deeper dark, a gelid, clinging blackness of the soul that intensified even as the study's windows unveiled themselves as opalescent blue squares.

She heard him fumbling for a switch. "Well, it's not the bulb," he said. "This one's out, too."

A moment later, the room grew brighter — marginally. His phone.

"I think I saw some candles in the kitchen," she said.

"All right. I'll be back. You'll be okay?"

As though she was afraid of the dark. As though she didn't have other, more pressing things to fear. "I'll be fine, Charles."

A shadow among the shadows, he made his way into the foyer, passing out of earshot, but not imagination. Thus she accompanied him: the broad hallway, the dining room to one side, the breakfast room to the other, and thence into the realm of conjecture, Schrödinger's cat, for he would have to circle around through one side or the other into the renewed certainty of the kitchen, where he would rattle around in the drawers and cabinets for candles that might or might not be there.

He was gone for a long time, or what felt like a long time. It was hard to say. And then a light stabbed out of the darkness. Erin winced, struck momentarily blind. "Success," he said from the doorway. "I even found a flashlight."

"Do you have to shine it in my face?"

"Sorry." The beam swung away like the beacon of some night-borne insect. It alighted on the table, summoning a shadowy facsimile of the room, like a third-generation photocopy, out of the void. Puckish faces peered at her from behind forests of sculpted foliage. She imagined their whispered consultations, a ripple of quiet merriment.

"Here we go," he said, setting out a row of candles. The flare of a lighter imprinted itself on her retinas as he lit them, one, two, three.

"Where's the fuse box?" she asked.

"Christ, I have no idea. A house this size might have three or four of them for all I know. I guess I'll have to rouse Harris."

"It can wait till morning."

"I don't want to wake up to cold water if I can help it. Besides, who knows where he'll be in the morning. I only hope he's sober. Do you want me to take you up to your room before I go?"

"I'll be fine. I'll wait."

"It might be a while. Who knows how long it will take."

"I'll be fine, Charles."

"All right."

He left her at sea among the tiny flames of a dozen tea-light candles, like the Lady of Shalott adrift among the lilies. Erin sat there dazzled, her eyes swimming with floaters, and whether it was the candles or tears she could not say for sure: only that she was in fact afraid — not of the dark and not of the old house creaking around her like a wooden ship under weigh, but of Charles and this woman, Silva. Afraid for her ruined marriage. Afraid of the ghosts of her own heart. She felt dizzy with wine and drugs and loss.

She reached for her glass. Drank.

Her toast — she had regretted it the minute she'd said it — lingered in her mind. Was she jealous? Perhaps. Resentful might be a more accurate term. Resentful that he hadn't considered how his partnership with Silva might remind her of his disastrous collaboration with Syrah Nagle (and it did), or, worse yet, that he had not cared. Yet hadn't he twice, at least twice, invited her to accompany him on his forays into Yarrow? Hadn't he wanted to introduce her to Silva? And didn't that mean something? Erin couldn't decide. She had been friends — or friendly, anyway — with Syrah, but that had prevented nothing. It had only doubled the betrayal. And then Lissa, the third betrayal, and the most horrific. She could still remember Charles's screams. And the water threaded with her daughter's blood.

Enough. Her therapist had told her not to brood.

She resolved that she would not, that she would try to mend things with Charles, that she would try to forgive him, and in so resolving knew that she would fail, that she had already failed. She drained the wine — it was bitter in her throat — and poured another glass. The drinking, which had begun as a simple dinner ritual, had gradually insinuated itself into her every hour. She woke up already looking forward to the day's first glass of wine. She liked the way it amplified the effects of the meds, the way it dulled (but, alas, did not extinguish) the compulsion to put down on paper the awful images that had lately more and more possessed her. And though she usually managed to hold off until after dinner (she didn't like to drink in front of Mrs. Ramsden), the mere anticipation rendered each day marginally more tolerable. Was this what it had been like for her parents, this constant guilty craving? Did she carry their curse in her genes? At this point, she thought it was probably safe to say that she did. She hated this weakness in herself. She committed herself to curbing the habit every morning and failed to do so every evening.

She stood, lightheaded, the world wheeling around her. She touched the end table to steady herself and wound her way by candlelight to the window. Charles was crossing the lawn below. She watched him as he drew closer to Harris's dark cottage, the bright spark of the flashlight beam wavering with each step, not much more than a candle itself beneath the enormous starry vault of the sky. Was this to be it, then? Would she lose everything yet, or was there anything left to lose?

She thought of Lissa cruising down the canned fruit aisle or gazing back at her from the bus stop or standing in the kitchen doorway of the B&B where they'd stayed their first night in this dreadful country. She thought most of all of the child in the wood, staring at her from the verge of that narrow snaky road — gone, all of them gone, these apparitions of her heart. And so she turned her eyes away from Charles — he'd almost reached Harris's cottage — and lifted her gaze past the dooryard and wall, past the encircling moat of pasture, to the vast surrounding fortification.

Lissa was there.

She stood atop the rampart, the white dress they had buried her in hanging still in the windless night. Stifling a cry, Erin brought her hand to her mouth. She bit her knuckle so hard that pain flashed through her in a white sheet.

Yet the child did not disappear.

Erin pressed closer to the window. Her breath fogged the glass. And still Lissa was there. She was there, and it seemed to Erin that a lean, horned shadow loomed over her, a danger more than mortal, and she would have reeled away from the window and stumbled out through the house into the darkness beyond — would have gone to her lost daughter, taken her in her arms, and somehow, she didn't know how, driven that threatening shadow back into the cursed wood that had birthed it or granted it passage from some other, darker realm.

But a wind rose up, lashing the trees of the Eorl Wood. The blast whipped Lissa's dress around her knees and sent her blonde hair streaming. In the next instant, it tore her apart, so many snowy rags whipping away into the sky. For a heartbeat the lean, horned shadow lingered. Then it, too, blew away and was gone.

Outside was only darkness. Outside was only night.

36

CHARLES SAW NOTHING but the yellow beam of the flashlight, illuminating tussocks of grass at his feet. Now that the adrenaline rush of solving the cryptogram had receded, the fatigue had redoubled itself. The first, faint pulse of an oncoming headache had started up behind his forehead. And though he felt the wind's breath upon his neck, he did not look up. He did not see what stood upon the wall, if indeed anything stood there at all.

He brooded on Erin's toast instead. He should have come home earlier, should at least have called, should most of all have foreseen how his collaboration with Silva might trigger — justifiably — Erin's memories of Syrah and the horror that had followed. Should have, should have, should have. Sometimes it seemed that his life was one long sequence of should haves: failures of action and perception, failures of empathy, failures of the heart — a carelessness rooted not in the grandiose illusions of narcissism but in the soil of simple preoccupation.

He was a creature of libraries. He thought about poetry more than he thought about people. Did he love Erin? He did. Did he hope that he could repair things with her? He did. Absolutely. But even in this resolve he sensed the ghost of that selfish inclination. For didn't he also fear losing access to whatever traces remained of Caedmon Hollow, opium addicted and haunted by some yet-undiscovered crime as he dreamed into being his terrible vision? Yes. And deeper still, where our true motivations exist, unexamined and perhaps unknown, there was the matter of

Lissa: her death bound him to Erin in a Gordian tangle of grief, memory, and regret. Charles had come to love his guilt, as men will; he nour-
ished it in the most secret chambers of his heart.

He glanced up at the milky wash of stars. He hadn't really known
darkness before he'd come to Hollow House, so far away from the glow
that prevailed where humans clustered like their ancient forebears, hud-
dled about a fire against the night. Now, he felt the vast maw of the uni-
verse above him and knew that the world was stranger, and more fearful,
than he could imagine.

He knocked on Harris's door.

Waited. Knocked again.

Still no answer.

"Mr. Harris!" This time Charles rapped harder. The door, apparently unlatched, swung open before the force of the blow. Uneasiness
flickered within him, lightning on the far horizon of thoughts. If Harris wasn't home, where was he? And why hadn't he bothered to secure
the door? The answer came unbidden: he was in the wood, of course.
Charles, too, had felt that midnight summons.

Still . . .

"Mr. Harris!"

Charles hesitated, ancient taboos echoing inside his head, and then,
despite these prohibitions — and despite the aura of contained violence
Harris had radiated that night in the pub — he stepped inside.

The odors of whisky and, strangely, glue assailed him as he moved
through the foyer and into the living room beyond. The darting beam
of the flashlight unveiled snatches of dark furniture, that same motif of
leaf and vine and clever watching faces here prevailing.

A half-eaten sandwich moldered on a plate. A bottle of whisky stood
open beside it. And the coffee table —

Charles trained the flashlight on it. The coffee table looked like
ground zero for a kid's art project: an open jar of paste, a drift of magazines, a pair of scissors, blades edged in blue. He took a step deeper into
the room, swept the light in a long arc across the far wall, and drew in a
sharp breath. A tapestry hung there, and though it was threadbare and
faded, the woven motif was all too clear: Cernunnos, the Horned God
or King, mounted on a rearing white stallion, his enormous rack curl-

ing up into the skeletal trees that towered overhead, so that it was impossible to determine where the horns gave off and the branches began. The thing's cruel yellow eyes blazed out from a face of stylized oak leaves, and a long cloak flowed out behind it. In one hand it brandished a sword. With the other —

Light blazed up around Charles.

Startled, he twisted toward the door, shielding his eyes. He stepped backward, his feet tangling, and then he was going down. He threw out a hand to catch himself — the flashlight spun away — and cracked his head against the edge of an end table. For a moment, blackness. And when he opened his eyes, groaning, Cillian Harris stood over him, his face lean and haunted. He looked stunned himself, glassy-eyed and unshaven, like a man entranced or half drowned in a well of sleep. He raised his hands, curling them into fists. Charles had a fleeting thought that the other man might strike him. "Mr. Harris," he said sharply.

Harris's eyes cleared. He shook his head. "What are you doing here, Mr. Hayden?" he said. "You gave me a scare."

Charles sat up, vertiginous, unable to reply. The earth wobbled on its axis; everything seemed slightly out of focus. A wave of nausea rolled through him. If he'd felt the pulse of a nascent headache before, he had the full-blown article now, an angry throb radiating from a point at the back of his skull. He probed the spot gingerly, unleashing another wave of nausea. He was sweating. He swallowed bile. Christ, he was going to be sick.

Charles lurched to his feet.

"Are you all right?" Harris asked.

Without answering — he could not answer — Charles stumbled past the other man, through the foyer and into the night. He went to his knees and dragged in a long breath, thinking maybe he was going to be okay, maybe the tide of nausea had passed. And then it all came up, Dark Mild and Taddy Porter, bangers and mash, once, twice, three times. When he was done — the whole thing seemed to go on for an unreasonably long time — he clambered to his feet, staggered maybe a dozen feet away, and sat down in the cool grass, his head drooping between his upraised knees.

Harris had followed him out. "Are you okay?" he asked.

"I've been better."

Harris laughed mirthlessly. "Aye, Mr. Hayden, so have I. So have I."

Charles snorted. He spat, wiped his mouth with the tail of his shirt, and, wincing, touched the back of his head again. A knot was already rising there.

Harris dropped down beside him. The steward exuded the peaty musk of scotch, and something else, something deeper, and still earthier: black soil and green leaf and cool water running. He smelled of the forest, and looking at him, Charles recalled that night when he'd watched Harris pass through his door into the dark and climb the moonlit moat of pasture, and beyond it wall and wood.

This morning I woke to find mud on my boots. I woke to find myself in a night wood, from the straight path gone astray.

What had the man been doing out there at this hour?

"How is the head, Mr. Hayden?"

"It feels like somebody hit me with a bat."

"It was a nasty spill. I didn't mean to startle you. I didn't realize it was you."

"Why would you? I shouldn't have been there in the first place."

Harris nodded, neither denying nor confirming this point—which was confirmation enough, Charles supposed. "The lights are out in the main house," Charles said. "I thought you might be able to point me toward the fuse box."

"I can do better than that. I can show you." Harris got to his feet. "Let me just get a torch. I'll be back directly."

Harris stepped inside and closed the door, shutting the cottage's mysteries within: the glue, the scissors, that drift of magazines; the tapestry upon the wall. Though Charles had barely glimpsed it before the light had blinded him, he could remember the tapestry with utter clarity: the Horned King astride his rampant white courser, gripping a sword in one hand. The other hand had been knotted in the golden hair of the terrified little girl that he dragged alongside. The image had been highly stylized, without depth or perspective, yet it came alive in Charles's mind. He could see the steam at the horse's nostrils, hear its hooves pounding the earth as its baleful rider hauled the screaming child up before him.

Behold a pale horse: and his name that sat on him was Death, and Hell followed with him.

Charles shuddered, still queasy. He thought of *In the Night Wood*.

When the Horned King had hunted Laura down in the final pages, when the fell creature had seized her up, Caedmon Hollow had dropped the book's closing curtain. Finis. But what had followed for Laura in the chapter he'd left unwritten?

What followed for us all?

You didn't always find the things you'd lost. Sometimes the wood swallowed you whole.

The book is true to life that way, Inspector McGavick had told him, and Charles thought of Mary Babbing and of Lissa and of all lost children, and he shuddered again, and then Harris was saying, "Shall we go, Mr. Hayden?"

Charles looked up, his head aching and everything slightly askew. "When I came down here," he said, "where were you?"

Harris hesitated. "Sometimes I walk in the wood at night," he said at last. "It quiets my mind."

"What's in the wood?" Charles asked.

And though Harris managed a smile, there was nothing happy in it. "Trees, Mr. Hayden," he said. "Just trees."

37

HARRIS HAD RETRIEVED Charles's flashlight as well, and the intersecting beams of the two torches lit their way up the yard to the great house that rose in silhouette before them, black against the sky, like the vast wreckage of some ancient, night-voyaging ship. They walked in silence, though the wind talked betimes among the trees, and they went up the stairs and into the back hall without speaking, and spoke only in spare whispers afterward as Harris led the way into one of the narrow servants' corridors that honeycombed the house, and thence to the basement, down stone risers smoothed by long decades of use.

They emerged into a wide corridor. It had been cool outside; it was cooler still down here, though Charles imagined that it must once have been warm enough, perhaps more than comfortably so, to those who worked in the subterranean kitchen, with cook fires roaring in the hearths. How changed those long-dead servants would have found these abandoned rooms, the once-beating heart of the house, long since fallen still.

Charles had been down here to raid the wine cellar — all too frequently of late — but the basement seemed more ominous in the dark, unfamiliar and possibly dangerous. He played his flashlight beam over the stone walls and arched ceiling, veined with ancient electrical cables. At some point, lights had been installed, affixed overhead in rusty iron cages at fifteen-foot intervals, but the whole network looked primitive, and less than entirely safe. Charles wondered when the wiring had last been updated. The 1940s? Earlier? Impossible to know. Harris said it had been well before his time, at any rate, and the iron bands holding the cables aloft had long since corroded.

Yet they flipped switches all the same as they went. Their way back would at least be well lit.

For now, though, darkness.

On either side of the corridor, arched doorways opened up, more sensed than seen — the kitchen and the neighboring scullery, pantries where empty root and apple bins stood rotting into dust, the servants' dining room, and beyond it a small suite set aside for the cook and her staff. Deeper, then, to the capacious storage space that Mrs. Ramsden had called the archive — a junk room, really, clogged with discarded furniture and boxes stacked in some places four and five high. Banded cables snaked out of each room to join the main trunk overhead.

And finally, farther into the basement than Charles had ever previously explored, an electrical room, little more than a closet: four oversized fuse boxes, a tangle of cables and wires. Harris opened them by turn — once he used the butt of his flashlight to jar loose a stuck door, knocking free a cloud of oxidized dust — and examined the interior of each box. From the corridor, Charles watched over the steward's shoulder: corroding green leads, antiquated breaker switches.

"Ah. Here we are," Harris said.

"What is it?"

"Master switch."

"What happened?"

"Power surge, maybe," the steward said. "Your guess is as good as mine." With one hand, he reached out to take the breaker switch between his fingers.

"Careful," Charles whispered, envisioning a shower of sparks, Harris stiffening as electricity leapt through him and through the old house alike, fire in hibernation roused to hunger, awakened after all these years to gut Hollow House afresh.

"Nothing to fear," Harris said, but he hesitated nonetheless, and then — the breaker hung at the tension point — flipped it home. Overhead, the lights stuttered on, reversing their path through the house as they skipped the length of the passageway, up the dark stairs, and down the servants' corridor.

Charles flinched, the bright flare ratcheting his headache up a notch, and Harris shut the box, and in the residence far above them, Erin turned from the window where she kept her vigil as the lamp flickered to life and drowned out the night.

Lissa was gone. She'd never been there at all.

Erin began one by one to blow out the candles.

38

NEITHER OF THEM slept well that night.

That vision of Lissa haunted Erin — and Charles, too, was haunted, adrift in thin dreams woven from the tapestry on Harris's wall: the Horned King upon his pale horse, the child swept up before him. A gentle rain came somewhere in the small hours, and a wind out of the dark sky, bearing some cryptic summons or command; they stirred in response, wakeful or awake, each thinking of the other, Lissa's death like the blow of an ax, cleaving their lives neatly in two, before and after, then and now, a bifurcation of the heart, perhaps irreparable, solace thus denied.

Morning was no better. Coffee and eggs in the breakfast room, Mrs. Ramsden's cheery gossip, and little conversation to bridge the fissure between them. They didn't speak of the cipher. To speak of it would be to invoke Erin's toast — to you and Silva, to the scholars triumphant — and all the misery that it implied. Already Erin had failed in her resolution. She could not bring herself to start the long process of mending things between them. Not today, and maybe never. Too much anger and resentment. Too much sorrow.

And Charles? He was riven with guilt for a crime he could not forgive himself, and betrayals too numerous to count. Set aside Syrah for a moment. How could he tell Erin about Lorna? Reading her the story, watching her sleep, her small hand curled under her chin, and matching to the rhythm of her respiration the cadence of his own, until at last he, too, dozed off — these things, this fugitive comfort, felt like a violation of everything he and Erin had lost, a betrayal far worse than mere infidelity. He should have told her about the child, so like Lissa, from the start. He could tell himself that he had intended only to save her another measure of pain — and given her fragility, that might have been true — to begin with. But concealed inside his omission, like a worm in the heart of a rose, was a more selfish truth: that for a moment he'd relinquished Lissa's death and every nightmarish moment that had followed, that he'd let himself pretend that Lorna was his own lost daughter, that fugitive comfort was better than none at all. He'd hedged himself in with lies. He had built of them a wall, and he didn't know how to tear it down.

So they went their own ways, each to their separate enterprise, as much curse as consolation.

In the dining room, Erin turned to a fresh sheet in her sketchbook and let her hand find its way, roughing in yet further iterations of the images that had come to possess her, finding in this repetition both some momentary release from obsession and some confirmation of it.

For his part, Charles drifted into the study and picked up the cryptogram where Erin had left it on the table. His head — speaking of bifurcation by an ax — felt as if it had been cloven in two. He could barely focus on reading the thing, much less trying to solve the puzzle — yet another puzzle — that it posed. Shakespeare and De Quincey and Dante. Sparrows and fairy elves and cuckoo birds. If there was a key to unlock the mystery, he could not see it. He put the page down. Stared out the window where the sun had started to burn off the morning fog. The wall. The Eorl Wood, a green mass against the sky.

That summons out of sleep, but half remembered, moved through him. He had dreamed of words in the wind, some awful imperative. More, he could not say. But he wondered if Harris, too, had heard it. What had he been doing in the wood so late? And what had he found there that drew him back?

Charles shook his aching head.

He looked in on Erin: her art supplies on the table, the school photo of Lissa. She closed her pad when he came into the room, as if to hide what she was working on. He thought of asking her about it — why the secrecy? — and in the next breath, thinking better of it, said, "I'm going for a walk."

"Okay."

"Why don't you come with me?"

And she considered it. She really did. She recollected again her vow to try healing the breach between them, to bridge the crevasse, to tear down the wall. "I think I'll stay and work," she said, wondering if sketching amounted to work, or if this, too, had become another escape mechanism. Pills and pencils. Her therapist would be proud.

"Are you sure?"

"I'm sure." She looked up, forced a smile. "You go ahead. Enjoy yourself, but . . ."

"But what?"

Stay out of the wood, she wanted to say. And though she also thought, if only halfway consciously, of the voice in the wind, she dismissed it out of hand. Dreams were dreams, not portents. They were only portents in stories. There was no voice in the wind. "Nothing," she said. "You go on without me." And she knew that phrase. She'd heard it somewhere before —

— she'd heard it in a dream —

— which is maybe why she succumbed and made a small concession to superstition, saying, "But, Charles, be careful."

Charles smiled. "Always," he said, and then he was gone from the doorway and she was alone at the table and he alone in the hall. Alone, too, as he went down through the house and into the dooryard and the meadow beyond the stile, and yet not entirely isolated, for the house —where Mrs. Ramsden busied herself with dusting and Cillian Harris with the household accounts, and where Erin stood at the window, watching him walk away—the house was still in sight if he cared to look back. But he did not care to, or anyway did not do so. Instead he ducked into the tunnel under the great wall and emerged on the other side into the encompassing wood, where the house with its promise of human warmth and companionship was gone and he was hard up against the wilderness, without fellowship had he wanted any and without succor should he need it.

39

CHARLES STOPPED JUST the other side of the gate, at the verge of the wood, the wall at his back. It was full morning by then, and cool underneath the trees. Sunlight here and there glimmered through chinks in the leafy canopy, imparting to the air a crepuscular malachite glow. Everything smelled of rain, damp and fresh and newly awake—the low, ferny undergrowth and the soft earth beneath his feet, the moss-enveloped boulders that jutted from the ground like the broken teeth of buried giants.

Charles exhaled. His burdens sloughed away. He felt born anew— yet ungrieved by the world outside the wood. Even the throb in his head retreated. Putting the sun at his back, he struck off through the forest along a narrow trail, the wall on his right hand, and on his left the enormous trees, rising on a slow grade, through dips and folds in the rocky terrain. Harris was right. The wood quieted the mind. There was no threat here. No summons or command from a dream that was only a dream and not (as Erin, too, had told herself) a portent—this his last conscious thought before the wood gathered him in and there was only stillness in his unstill mind, the pleasant ache in his muscles as he scrambled over the occasional knob of upthrust stone or root, the animal vitality of bone, breath, and sinew, the absolute and eternal present, free of past guilt and future anguish.

And then, something — he wasn't sure what — startled him from reverie: a rustle of leaves or a movement at the corner of his eye. Charles paused to catch his breath and take stock of his surroundings. The path here took him deeper into the wood, skirting a dense coppice of thorny underbrush to climb over a small ridge. This was probably his favorite stretch of the hike, for while glimpses of the wall remained visible through gaps in the trees, it was easy to pretend that he had wandered —

— *astray from the straight path* —

— deep into the virgin forest, entirely apart from the complications that elsewhere beleaguered him.

Something stirred in the leaves farther up the ridge, and this time Charles *did* catch a flash of movement, he was sure of it. He turned his head slowly, searching it out. The trees in their multitudes climbed the heavens, titanic columns in the lingering ground mist. Somewhere, a bird called. And then — he felt his heart seize up — there it was, staring back at him from a tangle of undergrowth a stone's throw up the ridge: a face, or something like a face, and what he was reminded of was his childhood, plucking *In the Night Wood* down from its shelf and thereby changing the course of his life, or setting it in motion, as could only happen in a story. What he was reminded of was opening the book to its elaborate frontispiece, the seemingly random intersection of leaf and bough from which peered a dozen sly faces.

But no. There was no one and nothing. The face — had there been a face? — was gone. He'd imagined it.

He stepped off the path all the same.

He stepped off the path despite the prohibitions of a thousand tales — broken every one, as such prohibitions must be, subject like us all to necessity or fate, the grim logic of the stories everywhere and always unfolding. This door you must not open, this fruit you shall not taste. Do not step off the path. There are wolves.

Charles stepped off the path.

He thought he'd seen . . . Yes, *there,* the face, or one so alike it might have been the same, peering down at him from higher up the ridge, half hidden in the low crotch of a huge oak that had thrown up branching trunks, massive with age and overgrown with fairy ladders. And then, there, a gleam from the dark beneath a granite outcropping, some chance beam of sunlight setting afire a sprinkle of quartz — or maybe it was . . . *eyes.* They blinked and disappeared, only to open up anew still farther up the slope, a knowing glitter, a cunning little face like a cat's and yet unlike it, too, inspecting him from the undergrowth behind a deadfall tree. It was gone again in the same breath, stealthy in the branches. Yes. And there another one, withdrawing. And there. And there. A step, and then another, and yet another still. Climbing.

"Is someone there?"

As if in answer, a breeze swirled through the trees, voices whispering woodland tidings that he could not quite decipher, and quiet laughter, too, mocking and capricious, but not unkind, or not entirely so.

Charles paused, looking back. There lay the path, almost out of sight now, winding down the other side of the ridge to resume its circuit of the wall. And here another way, and a choice between them.

I should steer clear of the wood if I were you, Dr. Colbeck had said. *People get lost.*

Yet those faces drew him on: the imperative of shadow and mystery, the inviting dim under the trees. How could he get lost if he stayed to the spine of the ridge as he ascended? It would be a matter only of following the same spine's descent as he returned.

He would not go far.

There was another ripple of laughter that was not laughter but only wind. And another sly goblin face — another chance intersection of light and shadow — scrutinizing him from the dark interior of a crack that sundered the vast bole of an ancient oak, moss-bearded and stern.

He would not go far.

He climbed the ridge through green, dappled light, lured on by faces that could not be faces and voices in the wind that could not be voices. The sun shifted its angle as it slanted down its rays through the canopy. And then the foliage was just foliage (he had surely imagined them, those shrewd little imps); there was only the wood itself, and that was enough, sufficient to him.

Why had he ever been afraid?

Bracken thrashed as a deer — was it a stag? — leapt away. He watched, bemazed, its white tail flashing in the murk. High on the ridge now, he found a grove of young birch, arrow-straight against the sky. He looked out from a gap among them. The site commanded a view of the folded landscape below. The Eorl Wood stretched as far as he could see. Hollow House was gone, or hidden. The wall, too. There were no walls here, only the primeval forest: trees and rocks and the eternal return of newborn green piercing the damp ferment of the old year's leavings.

Charles sighed. It was time to return, but he was weary with walking, reluctant to face once more the complexities that awaited him outside the wood. Surely, it wouldn't hurt to sit down and rest for a few minutes. Leaving the straight path — he hardly thought about it; he might have been summoned there — Charles slipped down through a ring of ancient yews. Like a child in an enchanted forest from some half-forgotten tale, he emerged into a beautiful glade of green grass where stood a lone oak, regal and old beyond reckoning. That sense of contentment, of being anchored in the eternal present, once again suffused him. He'd sit here, then, he told himself, though he would later wonder whether he'd chosen the spot of his own accord or whether it had been awaiting him all along, his fate or destiny. And so, as necessity would have it, he lowered himself to the earth, embowered in a thickly moss-grown crevice between two gnarled roots. He leaned against the trunk of the oak. He closed his eyes. Birds tested the still air, and the tree cast down upon him a cool blanket of shade. He might have fallen into a daydream or a doze there — he would later wonder about that, too — but then suddenly he was awake.

Charles sat up.

Full sunlight flooded the clearing, but the darkness under the tree had deepened. And it was cold, unseasonably cold. When had it gotten so cold? And where were the birds? Why this silence, so fathomless and deep that he could hear the pulse of his heart?

He swallowed. Dragged in a breath, blew out a cloud of fog.

And then a curtain parted in the air, and he sensed from a world outside this world or from one that interpenetrated it, some remote, numinous sentience, vigilant and green, turn its attention upon him.

A cloaked figure loomed over him, tall and lean. Had it been there all along, or had it gathered substance from the dark, spinning itself into being out of the emerald shadows under the tree?

Charles lifted his gaze — past the battered leather boots planted in the moss-grown soil before him and past a short leather tunic sewn with interleaved steel scales, much rusted, to the thing's face: its skin of autumnal leaves close-woven, its hooked nose and its cheeks like upturned blades, its great rack outspread. A black imperative burned in its merciless yellow eyes, some terrible command. And though it did not speak, its voice was thin and hateful in his head.

Bring her to me.

Charles three times denied it — *No, never, I will not* — unsure of what he was denying.

Metal rang as the creature unsheathed its sword. The blade hung above Charles, silver flashing in the gloom. The thing gripped tighter the hilt, and everything balanced on a heartbeat.

The killing blow descended in a blue arc.

Just as it cleaved his neck — there was no pain yet, only the kiss of cold steel unseaming his flesh — just then a soft breeze flew up from nowhere and Charles opened his eyes or he didn't open them. He woke up or he had never been asleep, and the dark creature under the tree had never been there at all or it had been and the wind had shredded it into rags and blown them all away.

Charles gasped and touched his neck, and the clearing was sunsplashed, and the green shade under the tree was pleasant and cool. Everything was as it had been, only those words —

— *bring her to me* —

— lingering, and then another breath of wind snatched them out of the air and carried them off into the wood as well.

His heart slowed. The blood pounding at his temples faded to silence. A lone bird called, and then another, and then the air filled up with the woodland chorus of insects and birds and the wind in the grass and the trees muttering among themselves.

Charles pushed himself to his feet. He gazed up into the grandfatherly oak where it aspired to the heavens. The sun was visible in flashes through interstices in the leaves. The morning restored itself. That sense of contentment once again enfolded him.

So it might have remained had he not looked down. But it happened that he did.

And saw a boot print in the moss.

40

THE DAY DARKENED.

The sun was as bright, the breeze as gentle. Birds still choired in the morning air. Yet the day darkened.

He had imagined it, of course. Like the vulpine little faces staring out at him from the leaves and the black places in hollow trees and the overgrown deadfalls in the wood. Like the terrible King, the creature, the thing.

Imagination, nothing more.

Yet Charles knelt all the same. Ran one hand across the moss, thinking that it must be the print of his own hiking boot or that it was some chance pattern in the growth or that it was not there at all, that he'd imagined it. And then he felt —

There was something there, something metal like a coin or —

He pushed aside a tussock of grass, picked the thing up, stumbled out from beneath the shadow of the tree to see it in the light. He laughed, without mirth or joy, a single gout of hysteria, really, for what he held was a thin scale of steel about the size of a fifty-cent piece, rusty, but finely worked into the shape of an oak leaf.

The armor. The thing's armor.

He wheeled around, anxious to be free of the wood, trying to discover where he'd entered the clearing. Yews, he thought. He'd come through the yews, but yews soared up on every side.

Charles pocketed the scale. Disquieted, he scanned the yews once again. More than ever he felt like a child in a tale, as though the birds had eaten up the trail of breadcrumbs he'd scattered at his back to find the way home.

He thought of the lean figure of the Horned King towering over him, the kiss of the blade upon his neck. Anxiety throbbed in his chest.

The grandfatherly oak now seemed malign, as if it might at any moment reach down, snatch him up, and shove him into some knothole
mouth, sealing itself up behind him. The once-inviting clearing seemed
suddenly exposed.

People get lost, Mr. Hayden.

A childhood axiom came back to him: when lost, stay where you
are and await rescue. Instead, Charles picked a direction at random and
trudged into the wood. Enormous trees loomed over him, deep-hol-
lowed and knobbed with growths. Roots cracked stone and furrowed
earth. A breeze whispered in the leaves. He thought of those impish
faces, capricious and mocking and half unkind as they lured him deeper
into the wood. He dammed back a rising tide of panic. It was morning
yet. He would find his way.

After a time — five minutes or so, he reckoned — the ground began to
rise ahead of him. Relief surged through him. Surely this was the slope
he'd descended to the clearing, he told himself, though a doubting inner
voice pointed out that he might have taken the wrong angle through the
yews, that he might be climbing toward the crest of an altogether different ridge — or indeed no ridge at all, only a small fold in the land. After
all, the descent to the clearing hadn't taken him nearly this long, had it?
But he kept climbing, and when at last the ground leveled out again, he
found himself once more in a grove of silvery birch.

They seemed to bend aside before him, willowy as young dryads lav-
ing their hair in the wind. He looked out through a gap among the trees.
Below, the Eorl Wood stretched as far as he could see. He'd stood in this
place before. He was sure of it. And the spine of the ridge seemed to de-
scend gradually southward on his right, just as he remembered.

He soon confirmed this observation. This *must* be the way, he
thought with growing confidence, and, yes, fifteen minutes later he
stumbled across the path — or *a* path, anyway, one that looked familiar. He followed it down the ridge and at last the wall appeared among
the trees. Soon after he found a fallen gate, stepped over it into the tunnel beyond, and ducked in and underneath the wall, the passage bound
at either end by an archway of light. He emerged on the other side into
lambent, late-morning air, with the meadow all peaceful before him and
Hollow House below.

41

CHARLES GAVE UP on the library.

Over the next week or so, he turned his attention to the basement, delving through boxes as through the ringed ages of a tree, each layer inward an era more lost to time. The work was slow going. He sorted and cataloged the contents of every box before storing it away anew, and as he inched his way toward that innermost circle of years, he burrowed ever deeper into the history of Hollow House: through the 1960s and '50s, to the world wars and beyond. The library had been the repository of sentimental keepsakes and photographs; the basement was a storehouse for items that could not easily be kept in the upstairs rooms, or no longer had any function there: cast-off furniture, toys ranging from a rusted tricycle to a canvas sack of miniature lead soldiers decked out as nineteenth-century grenadiers, and endless boxes of financial records —bank and tax statements, real-estate disclosures and account books, all carefully preserved, though Charles could not descry any system of organization by which something once stored could be easily recovered.

And sometimes, shoved into one of these boxes, again for no discernible reason, he found something that might distract him for hours on end. He lost an entire day slumped across a tattered sofa, sneezing from the dust as he read a maid's diary from the Second World War, when the house had served as a refuge for children during the Battle of Britain. Another story. Always more stories, each intersecting with a thousand others. What was the world but a story, he wondered —one vast, improbable, impossibly convoluted tale?

Setting aside the diary, Charles stood and brushed off his jeans. He surveyed the storage room, really a series of three vaulted chambers, each set off from the next by a riveted iron rib; he might have been standing in the vast thorax of a whale, Jonah in the belly of the beast.

He reached into his pocket for the rusty steel leaf. His rational mind insisted that the thing might have lain beneath the great oak for ages, but some deeper, more superstitious self told him otherwise. When he'd returned from the Eorl Wood that morning a week ago, he'd fished the thing out of his pocket with reluctance, half expecting (and more than half hoping) that he would find that it had vanished altogether, that the whole episode, start to finish, had been the product of a nightmare or an overheated imagination. But it had been there, and as he'd stood examining it, with the wood at his back and Hollow House before him, Charles had again wondered if he was going mad.

Maybe he was.

Now he placed the leaf atop the battered antique table he'd cleared off as a basement work space, and squared it up beside the deciphered cryptogram. He studied them both, leaf and cipher, twin mysteries. They'd made some minimal progress with the latter, he and Silva, talking by phone to compare notes. Neither of them knew quite what to do with the allusions to Dante, Shakespeare, and De Quincey, but both of them had tracked down the meaning of "tiend," the mysterious word Erin had asked about the night the lights had gone out.

"It's a tithe or tribute," Charles had told Erin over dinner after he and Silva talked.

"So it's Christian?"

"I don't think so. The word turns up in this Scottish ballad, 'Tam Lin.' In fact, it's about the *only* place it turns up."

Erin put her fork down. She didn't seem to have much interest in eating these days. Wine, on the other hand —

He frowned as she took a sip from the half-empty glass beside her plate.

"If it's not Christian," she said, "what is it?"

"Well, 'Tam Lin' is about the Fairy Queen."

"Tinkerbell fairies?"

"The fey. The fairy folk who seduce mortals and steal their babies. Way scarier than Tinkerbell. And in 'Tam Lin' and some other folklore, they must periodically pay a tribute to hell."

"Why?"

"I don't know. For immortality, maybe, or for the gift of magic." He shrugged.

"And how does the line go in the cipher?"

"Tiend most foul," Charles said.

"Which echoes the line from *Hamlet*. 'Murder most foul.'"

"Exactly."

"So you're saying that Caedmon Hollow was paying a tithe to—what? The fey?"

"'Let us not speak of fairy elves and their midnight revels,'" he said.

"Is that from the cipher too?"

Charles nodded.

"And to pay the tithe he has to murder someone," Erin said.

"The tithe is a soul."

Erin took another sip of wine. "Which makes the cipher a work of fiction. Or part of one, anyway."

"So it would seem," Charles had said.

And so it *did* seem, he thought now. Or at least it seemed that way absent his vision of the Horned King, thrice repeated.

Herne, Herne.

Another line from the cipher, and another Shakespeare allusion, this one to *The Merry Wives of Windsor,* to the horned huntsman of Windsor Forest—and maybe, by association, to Cernunnos, the Wild Hunt, even, perhaps, the Erl-king, the Elf King, the Horned Lord of the Elf Wood, and its avatar. If you started to delve into this stuff, you pretty quickly began to uncover an entire subterranean network of pagan myth, legend, and folklore—this the source, or its localized expression, that Caedmon Hollow must have drawn upon for his own story of the Night Wood and its fairy denizens.

Which was all fine. But what had he, Charles, seen, or dreamed he'd seen, a green thought in a green shade, standing over him in the umbra of that green and embowering oak? For surely it had been but a thought or dream; surely he was not crazy. Charles brushed the rusty steel leaf with the tip of his index finger. It must have been there for long, long years, immemorially long, rusting in the rain and the leaf-mottled shadow of sun and tree, though how it had come to be there, he could not guess.

And so he had spoken of his experience neither to Silva nor Erin; nor had he shown them the leaf, evidence or not of what he'd seen or hadn't.

These thoughts as he stood staring down at it upon the table.

Nor was he alone in holding secrets.

Upstairs, Erin turned to a fresh page in her sketchbook, took up a pencil, and bent to her obsession.

42

CHARLES CALLED ANN MERROW from the old rotary phone in the kitchen.

"I'm sorry, Professor Hayden," she said when she came on the line. "I've been meaning to get back to you, but you know how it is. Busy, busy."

"I'm sure you are," Charles said. "Thanks for taking the time to look into this."

"I trust your wife is well."

"She's anxiously awaiting your report."

"No doubt," Merrow said dryly. She hesitated. A gentle note came into her voice: "Truly, Professor Hayden, how is she?"

Charles grimaced. He wound his finger into the coiled line. Unwound it and wound it up again. Said, "She's doing as well as can be expected," leaving unspoken Erin's slow disintegration, the pills, the wine, the secretive cast her art had taken. And the photograph, of course. The photograph in which he'd tried to prison Lissa, and Erin perpetually to set her free.

Merrow had said something he'd missed. "I'm sorry?"

"Is she seeing anyone? Someone she can talk with."

"No. She saw someone at—" Home, he was going say. But instead: "She saw someone in the States. She said it didn't help."

Merrow paused, as if she might have more to say on the matter. She sighed. "Well," she said, "if there's anything I can do—"

"There's not," he said, and then, realizing he'd been abrupt: "I appreciate the offer. I really do. If something occurs to me, I'll call you. I promise."

Merrow was silent for a minute.

"To business, then," she said. "I think you're going to like this. The codicil you inquired about traces back to your man Caedmon Hollow. He revised the will only months before he committed suicide."

Charles uncoiled his finger from the telephone line. He exhaled. So here was another mystery. Caedmon Hollow's cipher, solved and yet unsolved, the rusting silver leaf, and the horned figure in the wood and on the wall. "So Harris's family has been in service to the Hollows for that long?"

"It's a little more complicated than that."

"How so?"

"The original documents name a man called Tom Sperrow."

"Like the bird?"

"Sperrow with an e."

A breeze passed through the open windows. Outside, the wood gathered beyond the wall, green and flourishing with late-spring verdancy. His mouth was dry. Charles took a glass down from the cabinet and ran it half full of water from the tap. He sipped it, held it cool in his mouth, and swallowed. He put down the glass.

"Professor Hayden?"

"Right here. Please, go on."

"Well," Merrow said, "the codicil guarantees the stewardship of the estate to the eldest son of each succeeding Sperrow generation. It passes to the eldest son of a daughter in the event that there are no sons in the direct line of male descent. Thus Sperrow became Harris."

"When did that happen?"

"During the First World War. It seems the last of the Sperrow boys did not return home from the front. The position then passed to his nephew, and thus it has continued."

"I see. And you don't know why this codicil exists?"

"As I told you the last time we spoke, no one is obligated to explain the terms of their will."

"What if the terms are violated?"

"The estate passes to the nearest relative out of the direct line of descent, on the condition that he, or she, continues to employ the eldest Harris son. If the Hollow line has become entirely extinct — and your wife is the last — Mr. Harris is retained and the estate passes into a trust, to be managed by the London firm I represent."

"For whom?"

"Children's charities. Specific designations to be determined by the firm."

Charles reached into his pocket for the leaf, worrying it between his thumb and forefinger as he might have worried a stone in a moment of distress.

"I think everyone would be best served if you could make your peace with Mr. Harris," Merrow said.

"We're not at war," Charles replied, but he couldn't help recalling that moment when he'd opened his eyes in Harris's cottage to find the other man looming over him, mesmerized, or so it had seemed, his big hands curled into fists. "I'm just concerned."

"Of course. This is not like him."

"How well do you know him?"

"We have occasion to work together. I've found him knowledgeable and well intended and nothing less than professional. I don't know what might be going on, but this is not like him. I think you should give him some time."

"And the estate?"

"Most of his decisions go through me. I've never had reason to doubt them, but I will keep a weather eye. You needn't worry, I assure you."

Charles took in a deep breath. He let it out. "Thank you," he said.

"You're quite welcome," she responded, adding, just as he was getting ready to sign off, "How is your research coming along, Professor Hayden? Have you solved the cipher?"

"We have," he said.

"And did Caedmon Hollow author it?"

"So it would seem."

"Well, that's very good news indeed," she said. "You must be excited. What did you learn?"

"I'm not quite sure," he said. "Everything I learn just raises additional questions."

Merrow laughed. "That's the way of the world, isn't it? Everything is deeper than you think it will be. Everything is bigger on the inside than it is upon the out." And then, without pressing him further, she wished him luck and rang off.

43

"So," SILVA SAID over lunch at the pub, "the Tom Sperrow named in the will is Cillian's direct ancestor, his great-great-whatever-grandfather."

"On paper, anyway," Charles said.

"On paper?"

"I think the reality's a little more complicated." He tapped the cipher on the table between them. "See that phrase?"

Silva read it aloud — "'Sweet cuckoos hatch in sparrow's nest'" — and said, "Sperrow and sparrow, right? What do you call those things, when two words sound the same?"

"A homophone."

"And you think Hollow deliberately used the homophone as an allusion to Tom Sperrow."

"That's my theory."

"Then what do you make of the cuckoos?"

"Adultery," Charles said. "Cuckoos lay their eggs in the nests of other birds. That's where the word 'cuckold' comes from. A cuckold runs the risk of raising another man's child as his own."

"So when Hollow says 'my pretty cuckoo bird' he's talking about his child?"

"His daughter, I would guess," Charles said. "He'd be unlikely to describe his son as pretty."

"So his daughter by this Sperrow's wife? A daughter Sperrow is raising as his own."

"I think so."

"How does that explain the weird codicil in the will?"

"I don't know." Charles pushed his plate aside. "Caedmon Hollow was, what, in his mid-forties in 1843?"

"Thereabouts."

"Okay. Look at this bit: 'midway through the journey of my life I wandered from the straight path.' So midway through his life, he finds himself in the moral thicket of adultery. He has a daughter by another man's wife. And then what?"

Silva pointed at the cipher and read off another phrase. "'Tiend most foul,' I guess. A foul sacrifice," she said. "A tithe or tribute."

"But to whom?"

"Fairies," she said. "Remember 'Tam Lin'?"

"Fairies," Charles said. "Why not? If Arthur Conan Doyle can believe in fairies, I suppose I can at least try." He shook his head. "Who's been sacrificed to the fairies, Silva?"

"Caedmon Hollow's daughter."

Charles laughed. "So what we have is a middle-aged opium addict murdering his illegitimate child as a tribute to the Fairy King. Doesn't seem likely, does it?"

"No, it doesn't," Silva said, "especially since, unlike Conan Doyle, I'm disinclined to believe in fairies. Besides, it's really more complex than that, isn't it?" She ticked off her points on her fingers. "One, we don't know that he actually had an illegitimate child. Two, even *he* doesn't really know whether he murdered anyone, does he? The only real evidence he cites is a pair of muddy boots and a few lines he scrawled down in a blackout. Three, he's anything but a credible witness. As you've already pointed out, the man is an opium addict. How does he say it?" She picked up the cryptogram. "He says his 'mind is much disordered now.' Right? In fact" — she skimmed the cipher — "he admits that he 'can no longer distinguish reality from lunatic phantasmagoria.'" Then, dropping the paper to the table: "Plus, the whole thing could be a fragment of some piece of fiction that has gone missing — if it ever came to fruition in the first place. My point is, if you set aside the Sperrow coincidence, we don't really have any evidence at all. All we have is a bunch of conjecture based on what may or may not be a genuine confession. We need some kind of outside confirmation."

"Surely," said Charles, thinking of Mary Babbing, "there would be some surviving record of a child's murder."

"Where?"

"Parish records? Newspapers? Didn't you say you'd found the cryptogram in a box of newspapers? The *Ripon Gazette*?"

"Not the Ripon paper. It's not that old. It was the *Yorkshire Gazette*."

"The *Yorkshire Gazette*?"

She waved a hand at him impatiently, thinking. "Nineteenth-century paper, long since defunct."

"Are there copies from that era still extant?"

"There are," she said, smiling. She reached out and squeezed his hand where it lay flat on the table. "There are indeed."

44

NOR DID IT TAKE long to locate them.

Charles had imagined laboring over the papers issue by issue, day by day, week by week, threading endless spools of microfilm into antiquated machines in the basement of the Ripon Library. Instead, they walked to Silva's apartment under a growing overcast.

Upstairs, they hunched over her laptop at the cluttered kitchen table. The *Yorkshire Gazette,* along with dozens of other papers, had been digitized, indexed, and posted online as part of a site called the British Newspaper Archive. For thirteen pounds a month, you could search to your heart's content. Charles paid up, all too aware, as he dug a credit card out of his wallet, of Silva's proximity — her long body and the faint floral scent of her shampoo, the heat of her skin when their hands accidentally touched as they both reached for the keyboard. They laughed and he surrendered up the card and she keyed in the numbers.

After that it was easy, a matter of filtering the search by newspaper and relevant years, and plugging Tom Sperrow's name into the search box. Three hits rolled up the screen: digitized images of newspapers yellow with age and utterly unlike their contemporary descendants. No pictures, no banner headlines, no pretense of journalistic objectivity; just column after narrow column of tiny print, with occasional brief headlines, domestic articles of national import giving way to items of local interest, from a report entitled THE CHOLERA (*In consequence of the severity of the visitation of the cholera . . .*) to, more intriguing, one called MARVELOUS ESCAPE FROM DEATH (*On Saturday morning, shortly after eight of clock, John Smith . . .*).

Silva nudged him. She pointed. THE YARROW AGRICULTURAL
FAIR, Charles read, and further down in the seemingly endless block of
text: *the woodworking prize was taken by Tom Sperrow, a hearty young
groom in the service of Mr Caedmon Hollow, of Hollow House, near the
village of Yarrow . . .*

Silva pulled up the next paper: 30 June 1843. Charles scanned this
one with more intent. They found the article at the same time — THE
YARROW MURDER. APPREHENSION OF THE MURDERER, and
below:

> *The inhuman monster responsible for one of the blackest murders
> that ever stained the catalogue of crime is, we are happy to say, appre-
> hended, and is now in safe custody. On the night of Saturday night,
> about 11 o'clock, Tom Sperrow, the father of the pitiful victim, was
> taken into custody at his home on the estate of Hollow House, near
> Yarrow, on the testimony of Mr Caedmon Hollow, who it will be re-
> called had some few days before discovered the dreadful crime dur-
> ing his morning perambulation in the Eorl Wood, which engirdles
> Mr Hollow's hereditary estate. Horrified readers will remember the
> dreadful circumstances of the discovery, which has thrown the neigh-
> bourhood of Yarrow into a state of painful excitement. The lifeless
> body of Sperrow's youngest child Livia, who was five years old at the
> time of her most horrid murder, was discovered in a clearing in the
> Wood; the child's head had been wholly struck from her body with a
> terrible blow and her face was frozen in an expression of helpless ter-
> ror. The intelligence of the horrid deed soon spread throughout the
> peaceful town of Yarrow, the inhabitants clutching their own chil-
> dren to their bosoms as the crime remained unsolved for several days
> afterward. Following the murder's discovery both Sperrow and his
> wife Helen, a housemaid also in the service of Mr Hollow, appeared
> to be in a very desponding state. Sperrow's increasing derangement led
> his wife at last to apply with her surviving child Cedrick for the suc-
> cour and protection of her employer. Mr Hollow sent for the Yarrow
> constable and the arrest was made soon afterward, under the cloak of
> the darkness of night. Murder will out, and this truth was fairly illus-
> trated in the case we are now considering.*

So here it was. Confirmation. Charles had expected to feel jubilant — triumphant, Erin would have said, though he could not share the empty triumph of a child's murder with his bereaved wife. And if it was a triumph, it felt like, well, a hollow one. The pun brought him no pleasure.

He sat back, stunned by the apparent savagery of the crime. "Jesus," he said.

Silva didn't respond. She just pulled up the last newspaper: 2 August 1843. The headline was at the top of the second column: EXECUTION OF THE YARROW MURDERER. Justice had been swift. He scanned the article:

This day at noon the last awful sentence of the law was carried into execution upon Tom Sperrow, who was convicted at the late Yorkshire Assizes of the horrible murder of his young daughter Livia. The trial of the unfortunate man who has thus brought himself to a premature grave by the forfeiture of his life to the injured laws of his country took place . . .

And then, further on, after a recapitulation of the murder and trial:

Sperrow was impenitent to the last, proclaiming his innocence, weeping at the impressive prayers that were offered up on his behalf. He was attended by the Rev. J. Rattenbury, who from the first has shewn great anxiety in regard to the unfortunate man's welfare in another world . . .

The wife and young son of Sperrow visited him on Monday. It may be easily conceived that the interviews were very distressing before they took final farewell of each other, though their powers of Christian forgiveness are a model to us all . . .

. . . when the chaplain engaged in the usual service before the execution Sperrow was loud and earnest in his proclamation of his innocence. He continued to declare his innocence as he walked to the scaffold and afterward, until, after the usual preliminaries, the bolt was drawn and the man was launched into eternity . . .

Enough, Charles thought.

"He cuckolded Tom Sperrow," Silva said in a kind of wonder, taking his hand. "Cuckolded him and murdered his own child and allowed Tom Sperrow to die for it. So he settled the stewardship on Sperrow's heirs out of remorse."

"All this to appease the fairies," Charles said. "I don't believe it."

"I'm not saying I believe it," Silva told him. "I'm saying *he* believed it. He was strung out on opium. He said himself that he could no longer distinguish fantasy from reality."

"No," Charles said, unmoving.

She held his hand in her own. For a long time his denial hung in the air, unanswered.

45

OUTSIDE, UNDER a lowering sky, Charles walked up the high street to his car and thought of Helen Sperrow and Silva North. He thought of Syrah Nagle, and he thought of Lorna and Lissa, and he thought of Erin, too, drifting alone through the rooms of Hollow House. Mostly he thought of the myriad ways the world had of bringing you to ruin.

He had not told Erin that he'd be seeing Silva today, had merely told her he was taking the car into Ripon to see if he could dig up anything in the library there, a lie she'd been too listless to question, whatever she might have suspected. The truth was, he hadn't gone anywhere near Ripon. And if he sensed in this deception the ghost of deceptions past, or the harbinger of deceptions yet to come, he could not admit it even to himself. How could he have done otherwise? Caedmon Hollow would not let him rest. Each new discovery spurred him onward. He stood, or thought he stood, at the threshold of some ultimate revelation.

Charles reached into his pocket for the rusty leaf. He held it in his palm beneath the threatening gray sky: he'd left this, too, undisclosed, a lie by any other name. Another deception.

Bring her to me.

He would not. He would not.

He tucked the thing away and looked up.

His hand still tingled from Silva's touch.

46

THE PICTURE HAD gone missing, the kindergarten portrait that en-trapped Lissa, the laugh upon her lips and in her eyes giving the lie to the demure hands crossed upon the table before her, as if she were con-fined not only behind the glass but within the enforced stillness of her pose and would any instant now burst free, exploding into motion with a joyous shout.

This is what remained to him. Absent Lorna, or Lissa's image to re-mind him, Charles could recall now not so much the precise lineaments of his child's face as a general impression of her, a snatch of smile or the warmth of her small hand in his own, but a sense primarily of motion. Her energy had been boundless, her questions endless and unanswer-able. However much he missed her constant tumult now, it had been ex-hausting at the time. Charles was quiet by nature, clumsy, sedentary, and introverted, essentially blind without his glasses. He preferred books to people (mostly), and libraries to parties (always); if he were to be honest with himself (which was difficult, and exacerbated his guilt), he would admit he had often found his daughter annoying.

And though he missed her every breath and every heartbeat, he still wondered if he missed her *enough* — if there was not more of himself to surrender up to sorrow. In the face of Erin's torrent of grief and re-crimination, his own sense of loss felt inadequate. Erin could not go on. How could *he*? Thus his guilt was redoubled, compounded by the fact that he did not feel more guilt, that he had imprisoned Lissa behind a glass and set the glass aside and did not as often as he felt he should even think of it.

Erin, on the other hand, could not set it aside for so much as a mo-ment. And even though, dulled by drugs and alcohol, she sometimes left the actual photo on the long dining room table, the image itself accompanied her everywhere, even in her sleep. And she slept more often now. She went to bed early, woke late, napped in the middle of the day. In the hours between, she stood at the windows, waiting for that vision of Lissa to return. When it did not, she sought refuge in the photograph.

And then it was gone.

Just gone. Neither propped among the vials upon her bedside table nor among the pencils in the dining room.

"Gone," Charles said. "It can't be gone."

She'd found him in the breakfast room, a cup of coffee in his hand and noon sunlight in the windows. And this, too, was a lie, she thought: that her daughter could be dead and there still be sunlight in the world.

She'd woken thickheaded from a dream of Lissa. They'd stood at the edge of the wood, wall and gate before them, the dark trees behind, and a lean, horned shadow looming. *Come with me,* she'd said, taking the child's hand, and Lissa, responding, *You go on without me.* Then she was awake. Reaching for the photograph to steal a minute's solace, she found it gone.

Nor was it in the dining room when she'd come downstairs.

Now, flatly, "But it is."

She sat across from him.

"How?" Charles said. "You don't even leave the house."

"But it's gone," she said. "You can't argue the matter, Charles. Logic doesn't make it so."

He pushed his coffee away and sighed. "Let's take a look," he said.

They recruited Mrs. Ramsden to the effort and moved through the residence together, taking it slowly, room by room. At every turn Charles expected to see the photograph — in the dining room or the study, or in Erin's bedroom upstairs, which he entered for the first time since Lissa's birthday, throwing aside the curtains and flooding the room with light. A flotilla of plastic orange bottles stood upon her nightstand, and a white nightgown hung upon the post of the yet-unmade bed, but the picture was not there.

And if he felt the frustration of the fruitless search, Erin felt something deeper and still more upsetting, something akin to panic. Though she had long since committed the picture to memory — though she had dozens of other photos, from the chance shots on her phone to the framed prints that Charles, perpetually in flight from the loss that enmired her, had refused to let her put up around the house — though she knew that she was being irrational, that the photo, as Charles insisted, was no doubt just misplaced — despite all this, Erin felt its absence, the sheer physical loss of the thing, like a blow, another dislocation of the soul.

In the week after Lissa's death the sheer number of practical decisions facing them had numbed her horror and despair. An undertaker had to be hired, an obituary written. They had to choose a casket, purchase a burial plot, engage a minister — this, though she and Charles, indifferent to belief, had never attended church (in the months to follow she would often wish for the solace of faith). And last of all, the selection of photos for the slide show the undertaker had proposed — an idea that had never come to fruition.

Erin had only started going through pictures when she realized that the whole thing was intolerable. Was she to choose any photos of Lissa with Charles? Could she in the face of his infidelity perpetuate the lie of a happy family? Instead, she'd settled on a single photo, the first to come to hand. She'd placed it on the small table by the casket, adorned by a single pink rose. After the funeral she'd picked it up, clasped it to her breast during the graveside service, and clutched it close during the fraught drive home, where silence awaited them in forlorn rooms, like the smell of musty coats or the dust that furs the tops of picture frames. So it had become a kind of talisman, a last physical link to everything that she had lost, here in this foreign place, unwidowed but without a husband, mother without a child, bereft of the settled contentment that had often felt like happiness and sometimes had been.

All gone now.

"It will turn up," Charles said. "Look. It will. I promise." He stepped toward her, and for a moment she thought he was going to embrace her. For a moment she almost wanted him to.

But then he turned away.

Alone in the kitchen, Erin shook two Xanaxes into her palm and poured a glass of wine.

It was two o'clock.

Unseen at her back, Mrs. Ramsden hovered in the doorway, fretting.

47

IN THE WEEK that followed, Charles did not return to the wood. Yet the specter of the Horned King haunted him still. He sensed that gaunt shadow leaning over his bed before he slept, and he woke in the silent predawn darkness, bone-weary from unquiet dreams, that phrase—

— *bring her to me* —

— echoing in his thoughts.

Out of bed, then, to pull on a pair of blue jeans and pad in stocking feet downstairs to the breakfast room, where he stood at the windows, drinking coffee and brooding over the wood beyond its walls until Mrs. Ramsden arrived. Each morning she asked him what he'd like for breakfast, inquiring in the next breath if Mrs. Hayden would be joining him today. She would not be, Charles responded, a ritual call-and-response encompassing all that lay unspoken between them, shorthand for Mrs. Ramsden's obvious but unexpressed concern and Charles's mute terror that Erin was on the brink of slipping irretrievably into the abyss.

The loss of the photograph seemed to have precipitated a crisis. She began to drink earlier in the day and more steadily throughout; the pills dulled whatever life remained in her eyes; she ate little, slept often. Yet for still another week, Charles and Mrs. Ramsden didn't speak of it. Then one day the subject at last breached the placid surface of their conversation, like some awful barnacle-encrusted monster from deepest ocean trenches, long hidden, revealing itself at last.

"Will Mrs. Hayden be joining you?" Mrs. Ramsden asked from the kitchen doorway, and Charles, at the windows with his coffee, turned and met her eyes.

"What am I going to do?" he asked.

"I'm not sure what you're asking, Mr. Hayden."

Charles set his cup upon the table.

"Please," he said.

"Well, I think I should see Dr. Colbeck, if I were you. And I would speak to Mrs. Hayden as well."

"Maybe so," he said.

"As you wish, Mr. Hayden." Mrs. Ramsden hesitated. "Sooner rather than later is best, I should think."

No doubt, Charles thought. Yet a kind of paralysis possessed him all the same. He could imagine no intervention that might save her. He felt helpless, impotent as a character in a tale to alter the momentum of the events that had swept him up, Erin and Silva, Lissa, Lorna, that apparition in the woods.

So he neither called Colbeck nor spoke to Erin. He sought comfort in the conviction that she would yet improve; it was only a matter of time. Meanwhile, he retreated to the basement, into his research, if you could call sorting through a century and a half of accumulated rubbish research. Not what he'd bargained for when he went to graduate school, certainly. But then he hadn't bargained on a lot of things.

He made or didn't make progress, which is to say that he had yet to find anything of value to his project down there, and he hadn't run across anything of even general interest since he'd discovered the housemaid's diary. On the other hand, the place looked better, with its battered sofa and table set aside as work space, its neat stacks of boxes (discards and keepers) along either wall, and the alley carved between them, running now almost to the threshold of the third chamber, the deepest of the interconnected storage rooms, the first one to be filled—and therefore, he reasoned, the one most likely to house discoveries relevant to Caedmon Hollow.

Dust and sweat afflicted him. He was filthy, his nose clogged, by the time he went upstairs each day. He often worked late, coming up after eight to shower and change. He nuked the covered plates Mrs. Ramsden left in the refrigerator for him. He ate alone.

It was on one such night that he discovered the pictures.

Mrs. Ramsden had left by the time he returned to the residence. He showered off the grime and took his solitary meal in the kitchen.

Afterward, while Erin bent to her obsession at the dining room table, Charles, susceptible to obsessions of his own, sat in the study, reading and rereading the cipher. He had virtually memorized the thing by this point; surely there was nothing else to find there. Yet he felt that he was missing something all the same.

He scanned it again, sighed, and set it aside.

He stood.

At the built-in bookcase by the fireplace, he let his finger slide across the spines and pulled a book down at random — Sir Thomas Browne's *Urn Burial*. He puzzled briefly over the Roman numerals on the title page, trying to determine how old it was — old anyway. Laid paper, the pages furrowed by time. He thumbed through it and slid it back onto the shelf, thinking of his first real library, with its air of silence and respite from the family Kit had renounced before he was even born, the lacquered aunts and the triumvirate of thuggish cousins. And *In the Night Wood,* of course. What caprice of fate had caused him to stop and pluck it from the shelf as he trailed his finger down the row of books? And why had he stolen it?

What might have been a memory surfaced. A curtain parting in the air, invisible thrones and dominions for a moment revealing themselves. A chorus of whispers in quiet consultation. But in the same breath the memory — if it had been a memory at all — slipped away, leaving him only with a lingering sense that he was but a character in a story — that he had stolen the book because the tale had required it of him. How can you blame Oedipus for his crimes, a student of Charles's had once protested, if he was doomed from the start?

Charles had had no ready response, but the idea of submitting to a larger narrative was not without its comforts. Perhaps his doom, too, had been woven on some loom of destiny he could neither apprehend nor understand; perhaps he was little more than a walking shadow, strutting and fretting his hour upon the stage. *A tale, told by an idiot, signifying nothing.* Why not? Even if it signified nothing in the end, it was still a story of someone else's making: cold comfort, but comfort all the same. Maybe it wasn't his fault. Maybe none of it was his fault. The idea enticed him. Surrender. Surrender.

He drifted along the bookcase, dragging his finger *bump bump bump* along the spines of the books until a tall volume, handsome and thin, summoned him. He withdrew it from the shelf and studied the title, stamped in gold upon a field of soft, lustrous brown. *Sir Gawain and the Green Knight.*

He flipped the book open at random and glanced at a stanza of the medieval verse —

> *For wonder of his hwe men hade,*
> *Set in his semblaunt sene;*
> *He ferde as freke were fade,*
> *And oueral enker-grene.*

Charles had taken only a single Chaucer seminar in grad school, and his mastery of Chaucer's Middle English was more than suspect; the unknown Gawain poet's dialect presented an entirely different magnitude of difficulty. But he could puzzle out the gist of the passage, or deemed he could:

> *Men wondered at his hue,*
> *in his semblance seen;*
> *he acted like an elven knight,*
> *and he was all over green.*

Charles let out a long breath. Here, then, another avatar of the wood, another elf king fleshed foliate, come to bid a knight his fell destiny awaiting. Beneath its superficial gloss of Christianity, he recalled, the poem's plot echoed pagan superstition. Once again he had the sense of stepping into a world infinitely more ancient, and stranger, than his own.

He turned the page.

A sheet of yellowing linen parchment had been slid into the book. Two of them, actually — pictures, executed in confident pen and ink and covered over with pastel strokes of color. One of them depicted a horned man in three-quarter profile: a face of interwoven leaves in their autumnal colors, with piercing eyes and high cheekbones and a cruel hooked nose, like the beak of a raptor. The second was another image of the horned man, this time little more than a distant silhouette, standing atop the great wall and staring down at Hollow House itself. Behind the figure, the massed immensity of the forest; above it, glaring down through thin streamers of cloud, a bloated red sun.

The Horned King.

Charles exhaled slowly, flipped back to the first drawing, and then back again. The same phrase had been scrawled at the bottom of both pages. *I have seen him,* it read, and below that, a set of initials: *CH 1843.* "Jesus," he whispered.

Shaken — Christ, was he going mad? — Charles slotted the volume back into its place upon the shelf. He looked at the rows of books, wondering that he'd discovered the pictures at all. Yet that feeling of inevitability persisted — that feeling that the book, with its elf king and his terrible challenge, had somehow summoned him. It was like something that might happen in a story, and he had once again that sense that he was not truly a free agent, that he was embedded in some larger narrative forever unfolding. And then, still holding the pictures, he walked out through the foyer to the dining room.

"Erin?"

She looked up. Her eyes were distant and unfocused, as if she were coming back to herself from a faraway country, and a strange one. Like Harris, he thought — Harris in the steward's cottage, enchanted or entranced, that same remote cast to the eyes, that sense of slow return.

She closed her sketchbook. Swallowed. "Charles?"

"Look what I found in the study," he said.

He held up the drawings. Pushing aside her half-empty wine glass, he dealt out the pictures like playing cards: the Horned King, in close-up and in silhouette upon the wall.

Erin drew a sharp breath.

"Caedmon Hollow did them," Charles said, tapping the portrait of the Horned King.

Erin studied them. She reached out to touch lightly the initials at the bottom of the second page. When she spoke again, her tone had shifted

its register. It was husky with . . . what? Wonder? Fear? "Charles," she
said. When she looked up at him, her face was white.

"What's wrong?"

She didn't answer him. She opened the sketchbook instead.

Charles felt a moment's cold shock at what he saw there: a sketch
of the Horned King in three-quarter profile. Setting aside the lack of
color—Erin was working in pencil—the picture was in every respect
identical to Caedmon Hollow's pastel: the same piercing eyes, the same
hooked nose, the flesh of woven leaves.

Erin's fingers trembled as she turned the page.

The Horned King in silhouette upon the wall, the swollen morning
sun at his back.

She turned the page: here the Horned King in profile. And here
again, upon the next, the King upon the wall. Page after page the sequence repeated itself, the lines so sharp and precise that the pictures
might have been photocopies, until at last Erin reached the picture she'd
been working on when Charles had come into the room: yet another
portrait of the Horned King, this one half finished, the eyes and the arc
of the nose just roughed in, but otherwise in every line identical to its
predecessors, as if she were not so much drawing the monstrous creature
as transcribing the obsessive dictate of some demonic muse. Or, worse
yet, as if the thing were clawing its way out through the page, each penciled line a rent in the fabric of reality itself, so thin was the membrane
between the everyday world of traffic jams and teacups and the appalling place on the other side, the outer dark, where there was weeping and
gnashing of teeth, and the Horned King held sway.

"I can't stop," Erin said. "I can't stop drawing them. All I have to do
is pick up a pencil and—" She shook her head. "I start out, I tell myself
I'm going to do something else entirely, and then it's like I lose track of
myself, and when I come back I find that I've done"—she waved a hand
at the unfinished page—"this."

"Automatic writing," Charles said.

"What?"

"It sounds like automatic writing. When a medium goes into a trance
and takes down a spirit's dictation."

"God," she said. "What an awful idea."

He sat down beside her, the corner of the table between them, but when he started to speak, she broke in. "I tell myself I'll stay away," she said. "I tell myself I'm done with it, and then I find myself sitting here all over again. The pills, the wine — I thought maybe they'd kill the compulsion. But nothing helps."

"We need to call Colbeck."

"Colbeck? You think a doctor can help, Charles?" She laughed bitterly. "We need a fucking exorcist."

"Erin —"

"This can't be rationalized. This can't be explained away."

"Listen, you're just upset," he said. But he was upset, too, wasn't he? He'd been explaining things away for weeks: the rusty steel leaf he carried in his pocket like a talisman, the Horned King in the wood and on the wall.

Yes.

And the capricious faces in the trees, and the dreams, and that cold voice in his head. And now this.

But it could not be. Such things could not be.

"Maybe the drugs are causing it, Erin. Maybe if you could just get —"

Clean, he was going to say, but she interrupted him again. "I've seen him."

"What?"

"I've seen him."

"Who?"

She nodded at the portrait of the Horned King. "Him."

"Where? You've shut yourself up for weeks inside this —"

"On the wall," she said. "The night the power went out. I saw a child on the wall. I thought it was Lissa and maybe it was. I don't know who she was. But I saw her on the wall, and that thing was there — a thin, dark shadow, like fate or doom. And then the wind rose and they both came apart like rags and blew away."

And what Charles thought of then was the thing standing over him in the woods and him thrice denying it. What he thought of was the blade coming down in retribution — and how even as the edge kissed his flesh, the wind had risen up to tear the thing to pieces and carry the tatters off into the warm morning air.

Erin, who had always been able to read him with almost preternatural accuracy, said, "You've seen him too, haven't you?" She reached out and took his hands where they lay upon the table. "Charles, please. Please be honest with me."

Yes, I have seen him, Charles almost said. It had been so long since she had touched him; her hands were warm upon his own. I too have seen him, he thought. I have seen him on the wall. I have seen him in the wood.

But then — he was not Caedmon Hollow, he would not be mad — Charles shunted the admission away, denied it even to himself. He pulled back from her. He stood. His hands folded themselves into fists and unfolded themselves again. He would not be mad. He would not be afraid.

"I've seen nothing," he told her.

Erin was crying.

"I want to go home," she said.

48

Was he afraid?

Was there reason to be?

After all, he could dismiss the apparition of the Horned King. (He must have dozed beneath that towering oak.) He could rationalize those clever faces in the wood (an overheated imagination, a trick of the light) and shrug off that thin voice in his head (the lingering whisper of a dream). He could even account for the rusty steel leaf he'd found in the wood. Who knows how long it might have lain there in its bed of moss? Years, maybe. Centuries.

Fine.

But how could he explain Erin's reproduction of Caedmon Hollow's pastels? Maybe she'd run across the originals in a drugged-out stupor (though she had no memory, however faint, of doing so). Maybe she'd fixed them in her mind, become at some unconscious level obsessed with them, whatever — but line-by-line duplication? Occam's razor finally cut credulity from underneath your feet.

He could not help recalling his Sherlock Holmes: when you've eliminated the impossible, whatever remains, however improbable, must be the truth.

But what if what remained was *itself* impossible?

Charles sighed.

On the table in the basement, he laid out the pieces of the mystery like a clock at its cardinal hours: Caedmon Hollow's pastels at midnight and Erin's duplicates at six, the rusty steel leaf at three, the cryptogram at nine. He placed the printouts of the three newspaper articles square in the middle. He stared down at this arrangement for a long time, but he could not unravel the mystery encoded there, could not discern the minute or the hour.

He studied the pictures yet again. Brushed the talisman with the tip of his index finger. Read and reread the cryptogram.

The third time through, his eye snagged in the opening paragraph —

> *But this morning I woke to find mud on my boots and the lines below scrawled in my journal. I have here enciphered and preserved them, together with their key, in the hope that some future auditor might adduce in these incoherent echoes evidence for a posthumous absolution that I cannot see myself.*

Echoes, he thought. Incoherent echoes. He'd supposed Hollow was referring to the pattern of allusion in the ciphered text, and surely that was part of it. But what if . . .

Charles pulled out a chair and sat down.

Weren't Erin's penciled duplicates of Caedmon Hollow's pastels echoes in their way?

I have seen him, the caption read. And so had he and Erin, too, so many nightmarish visions calling down the years.

Ouroboros, he thought. Time was a snake that bit its own tail.

The cosmic wheel turned, and Charles Hayden was afraid.

49

"ONCE UPON A TIME," Fergus Gill began, putting one of his pieces into play. Draughts, Ann Merrow had called the game, though Charles knew it better as checkers. He and the old man sat with the board between them at a table close to the pub's hearth.

Behind the bar, Armitage — who'd drawn Charles a beer and pointed him in the right direction — polished glasses. It was three o'clock, the Horned King mostly empty in the dead hour between lunch and dinner: a few dedicated drinkers at the bar; a youngish man with a paperback, reading over his pint in one of the booths along the far wall; a handful of old-timers hunched over their checkerboards at the fire. When Charles had walked over to introduce himself, Fergus Gill, tall and robust, with a shock of iron-gray hair, had been watching a hotly contested game, his own kit tucked under one arm and a pint on the table at his elbow. The old man's face was equine, fleshy and scored with age. His hand, when they shook, was knotted with arthritis; his voice, when he spoke, Yorkshire thick.

"Wondered when you'd come around," he'd said, settling himself across from Charles. He unlatched his board and began setting out the pieces. They were to play, apparently.

"Why is that?" Charles asked.

Gill ignored the question. "Black or white?"

"White, I guess."

"Black moves first."

"Okay."

"You know the rules?"

"More or less."

"That'll have to do." Gill looked up from the board. "You want to know about the wood, I suppose."

"Ann Merrow pointed me in your direction."

"I remember when Ann was a girl. Seems like I remember when *everyone* hereabouts was a child." And then his invocation of the ancient formula: "Once upon a time, of course, I was a child myself. You weren't even a glimmer in your mother's eye then, and she probably wasn't much more than a glimmer in *her* mother's. If even that. This was the decade before the war — the second one, I mean, the bastard Huns and their bombs over London. Seems impossible that all those years have passed. You plan to move?"

Charles looked at the board. He moved a checker.

Fergus Gill shook his head as if Charles had made a fatal mistake. Probably he had.

"Merrow said you knew more about the wood than anyone in Yarrow."

"Old wives' tales," Gill said. "Had them of my great-grandmother, who was older in the 1930s than I am now. We Gills come of long-lived stock, Mr. Hayden. I'm ninety-one. I feel it in my bones. But what's your interest in those old stories?"

Charles took refuge in a lie that was not a lie. "I'm writing — I'm planning to write — a biography of Caedmon Hollow. *In the Night Wood.*"

"So I've heard." Gill pondered his move, then slid a checker forward.

"Have you read it?"

"A long time ago."

"I'm interested in the intersection between local folklore and the book itself. Take the pub's name, the Horned King, for instance. Or the wall around the estate, for that matter. There's a horned man motif in the ironwork of the gates."

"I should be careful of the wood if I were you. People get lost."

"Or kidnapped by fairies," Charles said.

"Folk tell their children that to keep them from going astray."

"Like Mary Babbing?"

"Mary was a sweet child. But I shouldn't think it was a fairy that took her, was it?"

"No," Charles said.

"Your move."

Charles pushed another piece into the fray.

Gill jumped it, and jumped another. He stacked his vanquished opponents to the side. First blood. "So you want to know about the Horned King and his fairy subjects."

"Especially what the Horned King wants with children."

"Ah. Well. He's made a deal with the devil, hasn't he? The story of the wood is a story of two unholy bargains, my gran used to say. The Horned King made a pact with the old fiend to renew his youth, whenever the well of years ran dry. And he'd pay his part of each transaction in coin of the devil's currency."

"With his soul?"

"The fey have no souls to bargain with, my gran always told me, and the devil plays a deeper game. The old Hun set conditions to vex the Horned King." Gill lifted his pint. "Your move."

Charles glanced at the board, considered his options, slid another piece forward. "What conditions?"

"The devil required the soul of a child in exchange for his services, and he deemed a stolen child unacceptable. To fulfill the bargain, the Horned King had to bring him a child that had been surrendered up as tribute in its turn. Thus the old Hun got two souls for the price of one — the child and the child's father that had relinquished her. A wily old bastard, the Hun."

Gill finished his beer. Charles went to the bar for another round. When he returned, the old man jumped another of his checkers and removed it from the board. But this time he'd left an opening for Charles, who returned the favor — realizing too late that Gill, a wily old bastard himself, had set him a trap. Two more checkers down, Charles pushed another piece into play. "You said there were two bargains."

"Ah. That's where the Hollows come in. According to my gran, some Hollow, a thousand years gone and more, traded his daughter for a bounty of fairy gold, the bargain binding upon his sons and their sons after them, to be renewed whenever the Horned King once again grew old."

"Why not a son?"

"Daughters were dispensable. Sons were heirs."

Charles leaned back. Here then was another story. Stories inside stories inside stories, like circles in a pool where a stone has been cast, each expanding ring a correlate of the ring that had preceded it, each act an echo and recapitulation, a renewal of some previous act: time a snake that bit its own tail. Or its *tale,* he thought, his mind seizing upon the homophone, another echo. Had Caedmon Hollow, drunk on laudanum and fear, written himself into this nightmare fantasy? Had he taken his cuckold daughter into the wood and struck her head from her body? Had he allowed another man to hang for the crime? *I have seen him,* he had written, and Charles thought, I, too, have seen him, and Erin also, and he heard that thin imperative —

— *bring her to me* —

— echoing inside his mind.

"Do you believe that story, Mr. Gill?"

"Belief is a funny thing, Mr. Hayden," Gill said. "Sitting here in the pub of a sunny afternoon, with a pint in my hand and a game of draughts before me — well, it's hard to countenance such things, isn't it?"

"But in other circumstances?"

"In other circumstances . . ." Gill shrugged. "What is that you have in your hand, Mr. Hayden?"

Looking down, Charles found that he'd fished from his pocket the leaf of rust-pocked steel, that he was worrying it between his thumb and forefinger. He hesitated, and then, reluctant, though he could not say why, he leaned across the checkerboard to drop it into the old man's palm. But Gill did not extend a hand to receive it. He merely sat there, his gaze fixed on Charles. Charles placed the leaf on the table beside the old man's stack of checkers.

Gill said nothing. His silence magnified the talk of the old men at their games. After a time — a very long time, it seemed to Charles — Gill sighed.

Reaching into his pocket, he produced a matching leaf — silvery and pristine, but otherwise identical.

He placed it upon the table. Unsullied by corrosion, the fine workmanship of the piece was more evident. The delicate fretwork of veins seemed almost to pulse with life, the scalloped edge of every blade to unfold itself to the ministrations of the air.

"He, too, has grown old, then," Fergus Gill said.

"What do you mean?" Charles asked.

Gill didn't answer. His eyes were far away. He had forgotten the checkers game, or had given it up. "My gran used to tell me that there was a forest inside the forest," he said, "or one that lay close beside it — in a place that was not this place but separated from it, as it were, by a curtain in the air. It was nothing you could see or touch, that curtain, but it kept the Eorl Wood apart from the other wood, the wood inside the wood, or alongside of it."

"The Night Wood," Charles said.

"Aye. And she told me once — I would have been fifteen or so, when it looked like England might fall to the bloody Huns — she told me then that I must be careful in the wood, for the curtain between the two forests was thin in some places. In such a place, it might part unseen in the air before you. You could lift your foot in the Eorl Wood and set it down in the Night Wood, and then" — he spread his hands — "then the curtain might fall closed behind you and you would find yourself, in a manner of speaking, lost. 'Be careful, Fergus,' she used to say, 'the wood is deeper than you think it will be. The wood is bigger on the inside than it is upon the out.' And do you know what I did when she told me that, Mr. Hayden?" He did not wait for Charles to reply. "I laughed," he said. "I was fifteen, and I knew the wood like I know the back of my hand, and I laughed at her."

"You knew the wood?"

"So I thought," the old man said. "You Yanks were dithering and wringing your hands, and the Huns were on the offensive. Those were lean times. And young Fergus Gill had fallen to supplementing the family larder."

"You were poaching?"

"Rabbits mostly. A deer once, but it proved more trouble than it was worth. I knew nothing of field-dressing a deer. And it's not easy for a fifteen-year-old boy to haul such a creature out of the woods, especially if he has a care not to be seen doing it."

Fergus Gill took a long, meditative pull on his beer.

"Did you get lost in the Night Wood, Mr. Gill?" Charles asked quietly.

The old man nodded. "I did," he said. "I surely did. Sometimes I wonder if I ever really found my way out."

"What happened?"

"I cannot say. All I know is that I was in the wood, and the wood was as it always had been, and then it was no longer. I began to see faces in the trees, Mr. Hayden. I told myself I was imagining them. But they were there — sly, foxy faces, always at the corner of my eye. When I tried to look at them straight on, they disappeared, only to show up again, deeper in the trees. And whispering, always whispering among themselves."

"You saw the Horned King in the wood, didn't you?"

"Perhaps I only dreamed him."

"Yet you have the scale from his armor."

"Aye, Mr. Hayden. I was lost, led astray. I do not know how long I wandered, trying to find my way back. But I had grown tired when at last I came to a clearing among the yews where an ancient oak grew. Five hundred years old or more that tree must have been. I thought that perhaps if I rested there awhile the day might seem less strange. I was weary, and the shade under the tree beguiled me. So I found a likely spot in a mossy bed between two great roots, and I laid my gun aside. Maybe I dozed, and maybe I did not. But when I came to myself again, the bright June afternoon had grown cold, a piercing, unnatural cold, like none I had ever felt before. And it was quiet, too. There were no birds, and there was no breath of wind. I started to my feet, reaching for my gun, and then I fell back into the arms of the ancient oak, for a figure had spun itself up from the shadows — a tall man, or a thing like a man, cloaked in green and clad in a leather jerkin —"

"Sewn with steel scales like those on the table," Charles said.

The old man nodded. "And then came a wind and unraveled him like smoke."

"I've also been there," Charles said. "In that clearing, I mean. And I've also seen him. I thought I'd gone mad."

"Aye, and maybe you have. Perhaps we both have."

Gill finished his pint. This time Charles did not move to refresh it.

"Tell me," the old man said. "What did he look like, Mr. Hayden?"

"Cruel," Charles said. "He looked cruel. He had the horns of a stag and a hooked nose and high cheekbones, sharp as knives. He had cold yellow eyes."

"And his skin?"

"His skin was made of leaves," Charles said. "Red and gold leaves, woven together like patchwork."

Fergus Gill sighed. "It is as I feared," he said. "He was yet green when I saw him, his face unblemished with fall color, his fairy mail unrusted. And now the winter of his age is upon him."

Charles leaned back, thinking of the pictures he'd taken from between the pages of *Sir Gawain and the Green Knight,* his sense that the book, with its own woodland avatar, had summoned him to pluck it from the shelf. Gill's words echoed in his mind: *And now the winter of his age is upon him.*

"So it's time to renew his compact with the devil," Charles said. He laughed, a brief plosive grunt of disbelief. "Where are all the dead Hollow daughters, then?" he asked, thinking of Livia, decapitated in the wood. If what Gill was saying had any truth to it—

"There would be dozens of them," Charles said.

"Perhaps there are not so many. My gran used to say that the Horned King does not age as men age. Time does not run in the other wood as time runs in ours. There's no saying when the Horned King might return. But the debt must be paid when the debt falls due." Gill drew a long breath and seemed to come back from that far place. "Children's stories, aye?" he said. "Mere once upon a times. Nonetheless, Mr. Hayden, I think I should go home if I were you."

50

YET WHAT HOME were they to go to?

Their home had been in Ransom. They had created it together, a new story, bereft of history and written into being out of sheer determination to provide for their child the life they had never had themselves. They had established inviolable rules and traditions (they ate dinner every evening as a family and watched Bugs Bunny and Sponge-Bob the same way on Saturday mornings, and they opened one present each on Christmas Eve). They had made strong friendships in lieu of family (though these had not survived the upheaval of Charles's adultery and the horror that had followed). They had sought, most of all, to ground Lissa in a place where she could drink deeply of the earth—familiar streets that would always await her foot, no matter how far she roamed, and a room that she could forever call her own. They learned too late that they'd constructed their palace out of straw. Death and betrayal were wolves. With a breath they could blow it all away. As long as Lissa had been alive, Ransom had been their home. After her death, it was just the place where she was buried.

I think I should go home if I were you, Gill had said, and Charles, in reply,

I have no home to go to.

And then:

If such a monster existed, and it does not, I have no daughter to give it. And if I did have one —

If he did, what then? And so it all swept over him, the horror and the grief — for Lissa, and for Erin, too, and for everything that he had lost or given away, and what he'd gained instead, this cursed, pinched existence, chasing down the mystery of another child's death in the company of a woman he'd fallen half in love with, and a child who might have been his own.

If I did have one, he said, I should not pay. The existence of a debt does not determine the fact of its satisfaction.

No, it does not, Fergus Gill said. *Nor does unwillingness to pay deter a debt's collection.*

He'd held Charles's gaze a moment and then returned his attention to the game. He lifted another checker — another ancient story unfolding, governed by rules laid down long centuries before — took two pieces, and placed his checker gently down in Charles's back row. The king's row.

Crown me, he'd said. When Charles stood instead, the old man slid the two leaves across the table. *These are yours,* he said, and, nodding, Charles had pocketed them.

Thank you for your time, Mr. Gill, he said.

You're welcome, the old man said, and then, hesitating, *I am sorry for your loss, Mr. Hayden.*

Nodding once again, Charles had turned away. At the bar, he sent another pint to Gill and made his goodbyes to Armitage, and then he was outside in the bright afternoon light, where he paused to look down the high street, past Petal Pushers and the newsstand and Mould's hardware, at the great stone building that housed the Yarrow Historical Society. Silva would be inside, laboring over her boxes. Why not walk down there, he asked himself, and lay it all out before her: Erin's pictures and the steel leaves and the figure in the wood, that thin voice in his head and its awful command. Share and share alike, she'd said, in this, their common enterprise.

But then Caedmon Hollow's words came back to him—

—*I can no longer distinguish reality from lunatic phantasmagoria*—

—and he turned away.

He was not mad. He would not be.

The same denial echoed in his head now as he stood buried deep in the guts of Hollow House and laid the two metal leaves, one shining and one blooming with rust, at their cardinal point in the clock upon the table.

Not mad, not mad, not mad.

He looked up at the junk stacked in the third chamber of the storeroom. And then he got to work. He labored there the rest of the day and deep into the evening, returning near ten to the silent residence above him, to shower off the grime and microwave the plate Mrs. Ramsden had left in the refrigerator.

He ate alone.

Upstairs in her bed, Erin kicked at her sheets and dreamed unquiet dreams.

51

IN THE MORNINGS that followed, Charles forwent his breakfast ritual with Mrs. Ramsden, opting instead for coffee and toast in the predawn darkness. By the time she arrived, he had already descended into the vast basement. Erin slept late and drank wine in the afternoon. She floated through the residence like a wraith, ethereal and pale, and did not any longer brood over her sketchbooks, or even open them. She took her evening meal alone (she barely ate), and when Mrs. Ramsden spoke to her, full of false cheer, as if by simple bravado alone she could restore things to some semblance of normality, Erin responded in a listless monotone.

Mrs. Ramsden fretted, and not about Erin alone.

One of the housemaids had quit the previous week — she wouldn't tell Mrs. Ramsden why — and during this cursed lull two more resigned. One, like her predecessor, refused to divulge her reasons. The other was more forthcoming. *I don't sleep well,* she confided. *I have strange dreams.* Mrs. Ramsden inquired no further. She didn't need to. Her own dreams had grown queer of late. She slept enmazed in corridors of trees, and woke unsettled. She did not like the look of the Eorl Wood brooding beyond the windows of Hollow House. If it hadn't been for Erin, whom she had come to cherish as she would have cherished her own daughter, she might have quit herself.

In short, a shadow seemed to have fallen over the entire estate, a malady of the spirit or the soul deeper even than the anguish that had afflicted the Haydens when they'd first come to Hollow House. The tension held for a week, ripening.

And then, as the sun set on a long, hot afternoon, the air grew still, gravid with impending storm. It was after midnight when the first peal of thunder rolled out over the trees. Charles stirred and slept again, and then something brushed his cheek, rousing him from a dream of Lissa, in a pathless wood astray, and a horned shadow and a thin voice importuning. *Bring her to me,* it commanded him, but Charles three times denied it, and then he was bleary-eyed and awake and the storm had spent itself and there was only the night and a soft rain drumming outside his open window and a white moth darning the shadows overhead.

Charles held up his hand. The moth alighted on his outstretched finger, fairy-powdered wings poised to renew its flight, tufted antennae testing the rain-gentled air. Reaching up, Charles closed his other hand around it. It batted about inside his fist as he got out of bed, crossed to the window, and released it into the night. He stood there for a moment afterward, but there was nothing to see, only the rain and the cloud-veiled moon, so he turned away and slipped back into bed. When he closed his eyes he found Lissa awaiting him in the darkness on the other side. They stood together before a corroding horned gate, the woods at their back. Charles reached out to open it.

You come, too, he said.

You go on without me, the child said.

The next day, Charles found the box.

52

ONLY "BOX" WASN'T quite the right word. It was a chest, really, maybe a foot deep and half again as long, more like a miniature casket than any kind of box.

Charles's work in the basement had become increasingly onerous as dusty cardboard boxes gave way to plain wooden crates, which he more often than not needed a crowbar or a hammer to pry open. By then he'd acquired a small arsenal of tools from Trevor Mould: an electric drill, an array of screwdrivers, a handful of wrenches. He felt like a safecracker, a particularly luckless one, since the crates never seemed to yield up anything of immediate interest: leather-bound account books with much-faded columns of spidery figures, maybe, or a rat's nest of loose papers, and once, memorably, a real rat — or what was left of one anyway, a desiccated scrap of fur, a stir of yellow bones and teeth.

So Charles had no real expectations when he pulled aside a tattered woolen blanket that had been draped over a stack of boxes in some long-ago year. Nor did he realize that he *had* stumbled across something interesting until he reached out to move the chest — and found that underneath a thick coat of dust the wooden surface was whorled with a complex network of curving grooves.

He swiped his hand across the lid. When he saw what was emerging — the curve of two intersecting leaves carved in low bas-relief, and a sly, elfin face gazing out from the space between — Charles took in a long breath and let it out between pursed lips.

His heart picked up a beat.

He ran one finger around the scalloped edge of another leaf and looked at the clean streak he'd made in the dust. Then he picked up the box and lugged it to the worktable at the other end of the long room.

He set it down and reached for a rag. He took his time wiping the chest clean, working the cloth into each tiny groove and studying the picture that inch by meticulous inch materialized: not precisely the woodcut that served as the frontispiece of *In the Night Wood,* but a first cousin at the very least, and perhaps the inspiration: a maze of interweaving foliage out of which peered the demonic little faces of creatures that were neither human nor animal, but partook somehow, indefinably, of both, foxy and fey.

And something else, half hidden by a wreath of branches in the lower right-hand corner: a tiny songbird.

Charles glanced over at his clock of mysteries — the cryptogram and the steel leaves and Caedmon Hollow's original pastels, once reproduced by a hand a century and a half removed. And in the center, at the heart of it all, the death of a child.

Tiend. Tiend most foul, while overhead the moon sat arbitress.

Death could scarce be more bitter, he thought.

His hand trembled slightly as he reached for the trio of newspaper articles from the *Yorkshire Gazette.* He pushed aside the accounts of the arrest and the execution that had followed, and skimmed the headline of the third piece: THE YARROW AGRICULTURAL FAIR. He'd highlighted the germane sentence, more than halfway through the three long paragraphs underneath: *The woodworking prize was taken by Tom Sperrow, a hearty young groom in the service of Mr Caedmon Hollow, of Hollow House, near the village of Yarrow.*

He set it down and looked back at the intricately carven chest: the tangled foliage and the cunning faces and, hidden away in the corner, like a signature, the songbird.

A cuckoo or a sparrow, Charles thought.

Or both.

53

TIME HAD SLIPPED away from him. The residence was quiet, the hour north of five. Mrs. Ramsden (secretly relieved) had gone for the day, and Erin —

Where was Erin?

Charles climbed the stairs and knocked on her door. When he got no response, he eased it open and stepped into the crepuscular room: a narrow line of evening light between the curtains, the hiss of wind in the trees outside the open window.

"Erin?"

She lay still, eyes closed, breathing deeply. An empty wine glass stood on the nightstand, beside an open plastic vial of — what? He picked it up, turning the bottle so that he could read the label. Klonopin. And almost empty. What would she do when she ran through the last of the stuff?

Charles capped the bottle and put it down.

Once upon a time, he would have woken her to share the news of his find, but now —

He brushed back a strand of hair that had fallen across her cheek and tucked it behind her ear.

Let her sleep.

Downstairs in the kitchen, he picked up the heavy phone with its coiled line and dialed Silva's number. When she answered on the fifth ring — he was just getting ready to hang up — she sounded slightly winded. In the background, Elsa was belting out the chorus of "Let It Go."

"What are you doing?"

Silva laughed. "*Frozen* dance party," she said, nearly shouting, and Charles, who'd more than once danced himself breathless at an impromptu *Frozen* dance party of his own, closed his eyes, thinking of Lissa.

"Hang on a minute," Silva said, and an instant later the volume dropped precipitously.

"Mum!"

"Be still, Lorna, I'm on the phone."

The volume went back up —

"Lorna!"

— and a compromise was negotiated, Elsa launching once again into her signature tune.

"All right?" Silva said, coming back on the line.

"Sure," he said. "It sounds like you're having a good time."

"Put it on repeat and dance your happy feet," she said. "What is it, Charles?"

"Can you come out to Hollow House?"

"Now?"

"Yes."

"Have you found something?"

"I'm not sure," he said, though every cell within him thrummed with certainty. "I'd rather show you."

She was silent, mulling it over. "What time is it, anyway?"

"Just six."

"Why not?" she said and rang off, leaving Charles alone in the kitchen with the declining summer light in the windows and the ancient phone like a club in his hand and Lissa in his heart afresh. Put it on repeat and dance your happy feet, she said.

Charles hung up the phone and went downstairs to wait.

54

"What's inside?" silva asked.

"I didn't open it."

"What do you mean you didn't open it?"

"I didn't open it."

"Why not?"

Yes, why not? he wondered. And what came to him was the touch of her hand upon his own and the rhythm of their breath in synchrony as they leaned over her laptop to study Caedmon Hollow's decrypted confession. Looking at her now — her close-shorn cap of hair, her eyes, the scatter of freckles across her nose — Charles felt a giddy rill of pleasure spill through him. He supposed that, all unconscious, he'd meant it as a gift to her, like hand-cultivated roses or sweet water from some hidden woodland spring, some treat reserved wholly for her pleasure.

This was a revelation to him.

Everything is deeper than you think it will be. Everything is bigger on the inside than it is on the out.

Why not? she'd asked.

"Because," he said.

"Just because?"

"Share and share alike," he said, and he saw her eyes flick over the clock he'd made upon the table, the evidence posted at each cardinal point: the steel tabs shaped like oaken leaves and Caedmon Hollow's pastels and Erin's line-for-line reproductions.

"I rather think you've been holding back on me," Silva said. She ran a finger over the top of the chest, tracing the groove between two leaves and touching lightly the songbird signature, a cuckoo or a sparrow or both: the handiwork of Tom Sperrow (he thought), another mute, inglorious Milton, his sign chiseled out in one corner: the chest a gift from groom to master, perhaps, proffered in good faith, little knowing that his master had betrayed him and would betray him yet again, to plunge from the gallows, neck broken for a crime he had not committed.

Silva picked up the silvery scale, unrusted.

"What's going on, Charles?" she asked, and he did not know what he was going to say in response until he said it.

What he said was, "What if it's true?"

"What if *what's* true?"

"All of it," he said.

55

WHAT IF TIME was a snake that bit its own tail, he said, or a wheel grinding inexorably around the axis of fate? What if what was had been and will be yet again? What if you lived inside a story and the story had already been written?

What if the Horned King was real?

"Real?" Silva said.

"I've seen him," Charles said.

Silva turned the steel leaf in her long fingers. She set it down in exchange for its rusted mate. She said, "You've seen the Horned King?"

Three times, he said. Call the thing Cernunnos, Herne, the Horned God or King, avatar alike of the Eorl Wood and its nightside other aspect — call the thing what you will, he had three times seen it, in the forest and upon the wall and beneath the great oak in the clearing, before the wind had risen and shredded it to rags and blown them all away. Yes, and heard it, too, in his mind and in his dreams, a thin, fell voice as hateful as a blade adjuring. *Bring her to me,* it said, and Silva —

"Bring who?"

— and he, responding, "Lissa."

Lissa, last heir to a curse ancient beyond reckoning, summoned across an ocean to play her role in the Horned King's fatal ritual. But the summons had come too late, Charles told her. "Lissa was already dead."

Silva's face softened, her expression shifting along fault lines of pity and sorrow. He suddenly saw himself as she must see him: a father maddened by grief, no longer able to distinguish reality from the lunatic visions of a man more than a century and a half dead. And maybe she was right. Maybe he was a fool, blind, in a dark wood gone astray. He'd been chasing ghosts while his wife, breath by breath, descended into a morass of drink, drugs, despair.

Silva took his hand. She led him to the rumpsprung sofa he'd dragged out of the rubbish when he'd first started in on the basement. She sat him down, and in the cool silence, with Erin in her bedroom far above them, drugged into an uneasy sleep, Silva said, "What happened to Lissa, Charles?"

I let her die, he told her.

Tell me, she said.

56

BUT WHERE TO START?

Where had it begun, Lissa's tragedy? When he'd crashed headlong into Erin in the university library? Or earlier still, when he'd plucked *In the Night Wood* down from his grandfather's shelf? And why stop there? Why not go further back, to the day when the doomed man who'd written the infernal book sat down and with a stroke of his pen began it? Or further still, deep into the past, when some ancient Hollow forebear met in parley a fey emissary from the wood inside the wood? Stories intersecting stories, endless narratives unfolding. From the butterfly's wing the typhoon that follows, from the acorn the oak.

But no.

Causa proxima non remota spectatur.

A chance remark in the English Department office, that's all: Syrah Nagle at the copier and him waiting his turn behind her, watching the machine spit out stapled duplicates of "Goblin Market" and saying,

> *"Backwards up the mossy glen,*
> *Turn'd and troop'd the goblin men"*

—a half-remembered fragment of the poem from a grad school seminar in the Pre-Raphaelites, the remark entirely innocent (or so he would later tell himself), yet Syrah Nagle laughed in delight. She was new to the department, an assistant professor in her second semester at Ransom, and though he'd been on the committee that had hired her, Charles had seen her then as if for the first time: a long drink of water, Kit would have called her, a tall, blonde contrast to Erin, who was spare and compact, dark.

"It's a wonderful poem," she'd said. "All that barely repressed eroticism. My students never get it until I point it out." She laughed and snatched up a copy still warm from the guts of the machine, flipped it open, and read a couplet aloud:

> *"She suck'd and suck'd and suck'd the more*
> *Fruits which that unknown orchard bore."*

Charles laughed, blushing—he could feel the heat in his face—and she laughed with him. "I know, right?" she said. "All that sucking—'she suck'd until her lips were sore.' You read it aloud and, like, lightbulb moment."

Lightbulb moment indeed. He couldn't help thinking of Erin, who was squeamish when it came to sucking. Syrah Nagle, it turned out, was not. But he wouldn't find that out until a month or so later, after a carefully orchestrated academic flirtation. Before the day was out, he'd contrived a reason to poke his head into her office. Did she happen to have a copy of *Biographia Literaria,* he wanted to know. He was looking for that passage on the "willing suspension of disbelief" —

"Which constitutes poetic faith," she'd said without looking up from her laptop. And then, laughing, she *did* look up. She thought that bit was excerpted in the *Norton,* she said, which is how they wound up in front of her bookshelf, thumbing through *The Norton Anthology of English Literature* and standing closer together than was strictly necessary.

And what Charles remembered of that moment (and he felt a jolt of guilty libidinal energy recalling it) was the clean Ivory soap smell of her skin and the whisper of breath in her lungs. Soon enough — sooner than he really wanted, actually — she'd dispatched him back to his office, book in hand. But she'd leaned in at his door to say goodbye on her way out that afternoon, and she'd stopped by again the next morning, this time bearing coffee. They'd fucked up her order (her words) at Starbucks on the way into the office, so she'd had to go back by the drive-thru window. Why shouldn't he be the benefactor of her misfortune, she asked, dropping into the hideous green wing chair reserved for student supplicants and crossing her long, long legs before her. Which event somehow turned into a daily coffee date, which led to the expedience of inventing a (largely spurious) collaborative project so they could spend more time together, which climaxed, more or less literally, when she pushed closed the door one morning and knelt to take him into her mouth.

Charles had had more than a little trouble concentrating in his English comp course later that morning. In fact, he didn't have much luck concentrating on anything but Syrah for the two months that followed. Before Erin, he'd never had much luck with women — had, in fact, rarely worked up the nerve even to *test* his luck. Bookish and shy and altogether too certain of rejection, he'd slept with only two women in his entire life, and the first one, with whom he'd had a fumbling high school encounter in the back seat of a battered Ford Taurus, hardly counted, it had ended in a disaster so premature.

So the sheer novelty of the thing was alone overwhelming. The considerable range of Syrah's carnal imagination (she was, as far as he could tell, totally without inhibition) and the seemingly boundless scope of her energy clinched the matter. He was doomed, had been from the moment she'd turned laughing from the copier. But as the semester drew to a close, a new tension entered the relationship—a tension greater than that occasioned by their clandestine intimacies on the loathsome wing chair. The summer break loomed. What then?

Maybe it was time to make the break, Syrah said.

The break? he'd asked.

With Erin, she said, as though they'd been planning such a break from the first, fait accompli, and the depth of the trouble he'd gotten himself into broke over Charles with the force of revelation. He hadn't realized a break was necessary, and if a small part of him—the sexual novice who thrilled at the adventure he'd stumbled into—quickened at the idea, his greater self recoiled. He had virtually no desire to leave Erin, to sacrifice their easy harmony upon the altar of his libido, nor did he wish to surrender up the material comforts of his life for some crummy garden apartment in one of the cheap complexes on the edge of town. And then there was Lissa. The mere idea of leaving Lissa triggered a roller-coaster plunge in his gut.

He pled for time.

But time brought him no clarity. He did not know how to do the thing he had to do. He feared the consequences. Never mind the professional fallout—the strained departmental meetings, the awkward encounters in the hall. What would happen at home? Would Erin discover his infidelity? Would she leave him, taking Lissa with her? He thought she would, on both counts. He would be left with nothing.

Syrah pressed.

On the eve of Lissa's birthday, he resolved to end the affair—a secret gift to his daughter, a rededication to his marriage.

Twenty-four hours later, Lissa was dead.

My fault, he told Silva. It was my fault.

And high in the labyrinth of the house above them, a gusty wind belled out the curtains of Erin's bedroom and lay cool fingers upon her cheek, stirring her from a dream of Lissa and a lean horned shadow and an endless sea of trees.

57

OKAY, THEN, Syrah had said when he finally worked up the courage to tell her.

Cool acquiescence, nothing more—this over coffee in the dining hall, thronged at the noon break between finals. He'd invited her to meet him there, hoping by this stratagem to avoid a scene.

"I hope we can be friends," he said.

"Of course," she said.

She stood, extending a hand. Charles took it, struck by the absurdity of this gesture, a handshake in closure to such prolonged physical intimacy, and then she was striding on her long legs across the crowded cafeteria to push her way out into the bright spring afternoon, leaving him to finish his coffee alone.

Was that to be it, then? he wondered. Okay—and nothing more?

The question stayed with him through another endless final exam, where he graded papers at the front of the room as his students labored at their desks to delineate the finer points of High Modernism. It stayed with him through a distracted birthday dinner (stuffed peppers, Lissa's favorite) and accompanied him upstairs, while Erin cleaned up the dishes down below: bath time for the birthday girl, the "big tub," the whirlpool in the master bathroom, a special birthday treat, the question still lingering as he adjusted the water and helped her get undressed.

Then the phone buzzing in his pocket, Syrah's name on the screen. His guts twisted.

"Daddy!" Lissa cried, jealous of his attention.

Charles sent the call to voicemail and put the phone away. He'd just heaved the birthday girl squealing into the tub when the landline went off like a klaxon. Charles lunged out into the bedroom to snatch the phone from its cradle on the nightstand. He thumbed it to life in the middle of the third deafening ring, praying that he'd beaten Erin to the line, that she wasn't on the downstairs extension listening to the tirade that followed: Syrah — not okay after all. Syrah in fury, Syrah in tears, threatening and cajoling by turns, riven by contradiction. She wanted to see him (she could not bear to), she wanted to talk (what was there to say?), she wanted to die (she wanted him to die). Charles remembered every turn of the conversation, every sordid cliché. He remembered the panic reverberating through him like a plucked chord. He remembered swinging closed the bathroom door, vexed by the tumult on the other side — the water still cascading from the spigot, Lissa splashing, her high, sweet voice lifted in song, *let it go, let it go.*

What he did not remember — what he could not remember because he was not present to witness it — was the other doom already hurtling down upon them all. It was that doom that forever fixed his mind. It was that doom that unreeled before him in the nightmare theater of his imagination.

And it was that doom that he voiced to Silva North.

Even now, he could only imagine it (he could not stop imagining it): the play of emotion on Lissa's face when he did not answer to her song — disappointment and resentment at first, followed by grudging acceptance, and then distraction. At last, distraction. He imagined how it might have gone: first the loofah, dipping and squeezing, water over the side of the tub to splash on the tile below, bombs away; and then the soap, up on her feet to send it plunging back into the water, and a submarining dive to retrieve it, singing the whole time. He remembered hearing her voice in counterpoint to Syrah's anxiety —

— *let it go, let it go* —

— and dear God, how was it that he had not noticed when the singing stopped?

Six years old. The birthday girl.

Jesus.

She must have slipped, that's all anybody knew for sure. But he could see how it must have been: her clear blue eyes widening as her feet went out from under her, her arms flailing, and then — fatal chance — the back of her head catching the tiled apron of the tub. There must have been a sharp instant of pain — the edge had opened a deep cut — then nothing at all, just a plunge into absolute and final darkness. She had drowned, that's all, drowned in a fucking bathtub.

And he hadn't even noticed when she stopped singing.

It was the sound of the water thundering from the spigot — she was going to flood the place — that drew him back into the bathroom, still cradling the phone against his ear.

And it was here that imagination and memory reunited, for Charles *did* witness the rest of it. He saw with his own eyes the water-slick tiles, the mirror, and the walls, lashed as with a thousand drops of rain. With his own eyes he stared down through soap-clouded water to see his daughter staring back at him through winding Medusa coils of her own red-black blood, her blue oxygen-deprived face frozen in horror, her eyes empty and dead.

He must have dropped the phone, must have screamed. He had no recollection of that, no recollection of Erin crashing into the bathroom. He knew only that she was there, she had materialized from the humid air. Of the frenzied instants that followed, Charles had only a disco-ball kaleidoscope of memories: the boneless slump of Lissa's body as he dragged her streaming from the water and a flash of Erin's futile attempt to revive her and the phone slick in his hand when he snatched it up. He cut off Syrah and punched out 911, thick-fingered in the pitiless blare of the dial tone — misdialed, and punched it out again, a man in a void, spinning. The dispatcher's preternaturally calm voice —

— *what's your emergency* —

— sent him slamming back into the gravity well of his own body.

Too late.

Lissa was dead.

Dead when he stepped into the bathroom.

Dead when he fished her out of the tub.

Dead when the paramedics arrived, bustling and officious.

Too late.

She was gone, he said, and Silva made some wordless noise of comfort and wrapped her arms around him. He slumped into her embrace, and for a time there was nothing but silence, the forest steadying itself around them, and Erin upstairs, unquiet in her sleep.

58

A LACUNA, THEN. Hiatus of the soul.

59

AFTER A TIME, Silva kissed him gently on the crown of his head, as she might have kissed a child, as she might have kissed Lorna. Charles looked up and she dipped her face to meet him. His lips brushed hers. They trembled on the edge of a precipice.

And then he thought of Syrah Nagle and pulled away.

Silva stood. "I'm sorry," she said. "I shouldn't have —"

Charles laughed, in bitterness or sorrow. Sometimes you do the right thing. Sometimes you do it too late.

He sat on the sofa, watching as she paced. She paused by the table, fingering the steel leaves from armor forged in that night-plunged sister wood.

"You don't have to believe me," he said.

"I don't know what to believe."

She picked up one of Erin's drawings, studied it in silence, put it back on the table.

"What now?" he asked.

"I suppose we open that box."

60

EASIER SAID than done.

The latch had rusted over. The hinges had corroded. When neither responded to gentler persuasion, Charles reached for the hammer.

"Brute," Silva said, holding up a hand. "Stop!" She took the hammer and laid it aside. "How about a screwdriver, a flathead if you have it. I hate to break the lock, but at least we can do it with minimum damage."

Which she did, angling the tip of the screwdriver like a wedge under the lock and tapping it gently with the hammer — no brute, she — until finally —

"Got you," she said.

— the lock popped loose with a shower of red dust, leaving the wood underneath it undamaged.

"Nicely done," Charles said.

"An ill-spent youth," she said. "Shall we?"

"I'll let you do the honors."

She nodded and took a breath, ran her hands over the edges of the box, and then, with the reverence of a monk unsealing a reliquary, she started to lift the lid. The rusty hinges protested, and Charles thought they were going to have to force the thing open after all. But no, with a final groan, the hinges began to turn and Silva pushed the lid upright.

A doll lay inside the chest, her yellowing porcelain head webbed with hairline fractures, her fine hair as dry as straw. Her elaborate Victorian dress was a dry grayish husk, but her pursed rosebud mouth, when Silva wiped the dust away, was still pink, and her eyes still blue. They gazed up at Charles with blank disregard, and he shuddered, thinking once again of Lissa's blind stare through those swirls of slowly dissipating blood. He should never have spoken of it. Lissa had escaped her prison in the telling.

Charles sighed. He looked around the great room: twice-ribbed leviathan and its capacious three-chamber swallow, bellyful with the wreckage of a hundred years and more, half unpacked and sorted along either wall. All this for a doll in a doll's casket, cast-off toys of a rich man's daughter. All this for the ghost of crimes both personal and remote, ghosts he could not lay to rest.

"So that's it," he said. "A doll. Sorry I wasted your time."

Silva lifted the thing out of the box and placed it gingerly on the table. "Not so fast," she said. "There's something inside it. I can feel it."

Charles watched with renewed interest as she flipped the doll over and unbuttoned the dress. The body underneath was made of parched, flaking leather, stuffed and laced up the back like a stitched wound, secured at the neck. Silva untrussed the doll, moving with a sure, delicate grace, and set the lacing aside. She pulled the incision apart, dug with long fingers through the stuffing, and —

"Here we go."

— worked up out of the slit a sheaf of papers, thrice folded to make a thick packet and tied off with twine.

Charles watched at her shoulder as Silva undid the knot.

When she did, a steel leaf, much rusted —

— *he too has grown old* —

— fell ringing to the table.

Charles was reaching for it in disbelief when Silva said, "Look at this." She laid down the innermost page, ivory with age and delicate at the folds. A poem had been inscribed upon it in Caedmon Hollow's pinched hand:

> *When daisies pied, and violets blue,*
> *And lady-smocks all silver-white,*
> *And cuckoo-buds of yellow hue*
> *Do paint the meadows with delight,*
> *The cuckoo then on every tree*
> *Mocks married men; for thus sings he, "Cuckoo;*
> *Cuckoo, cuckoo"— O word of fear,*
> *Unpleasing to a married ear!*

Charles reached for the cryptogram. "This passage," he said. "He alludes to it in —"

"Charles —"

"What —"

And then he saw.

"Lissa," he said.

And she, "Lorna."

It might have been either one of them, this child sketched in strong, sure lines upon the next page she had laid upon the table: the soft curve of her jaw in three-quarter profile, the seashell delicacy of that ear. Charles was struck anew by the uncanny resemblance between his lost daughter and Silva's living one, and now this third, time-lost, gazing out at him from the past, her name inscribed below her likeness in that familiar crabbed handwriting: *Livia, my sweet, my darling, my cuckoo bird.*

Lissa.

Lorna.

Livia.

And Laura, too, he supposed, the night-doomed heroine of Caedmon Hollow's strange fantasy, snatched up and carried away forever into some pathless other wood.

Charles picked up the metal leaf that had fallen from the little packet. He squared it up beside its companion pieces, identical, at this, their cardinal hour.

What if it were true?

It could not be true.

And then he looked at the final sheet Silva had laid out upon the table: another portrait, a boy with a thatch of unruly hair who shared, indefinably, the other child's —

— *Livia's* —

— mien, though he had none of her delicacy of feature. A younger sibling surely, a surmise seemingly confirmed by the lines inscribed at the bottom of the page:

Cedrick —
    Why should the worm intrude the maiden bud?
    Or sweet cuckoo hatch in sparrows' nests?

"Her brother?" Silva said.

"The article about the execution —"

"It mentioned a son."

"Another cuckoo in Tom Sperrow's nest," Charles said. "Another line of descent."

"Cillian?" she said.

And Charles thought, What if it were true?

It could not be true.

But what if it were?

"Where's Lorna?" he asked.

"With her father."

"With *Cillian*? Why?"

But his mind was moving too fast to listen to her answer. Why? *Because,* he thought. Because, because, because. Because the story *required it.* Because time was a snake that bit its own tail. Because what was had been and would be yet again. Because the wheel of fate turned upon the axis of a secret history, eternally returning, and the Horned King's hour had come round at last.

Once upon a time, he thought.

Upstairs, Erin opened her eyes.

61

THE WOOD HAD invaded the dooryard. A curtain had parted in the air or had been torn asunder. An age had turned, a year, a season. A full moon shed down its glow upon the autumnal trees, and the gusty branches chattered among themselves like old men rattling their bones, and Erin, high at a crumbling casement in the ruins of Hollow House, was afraid.

It was a dream, her mind insisted. A strange, otherworldly nightmare.

Outside her window not this baleful wood but the sculpted grounds she had these months grown accustomed to. Outside her window not this bloated monstrosity of a moon but the old familiar moon, swinging in the new moon's cradle. Outside her window —

Erin leaned forward, her breath smoky in the chill.

Outside her window, a child fled through the skeletal trees.

Lissa, she thought with a sharp intake of breath.

Lissa, and a lean, horned shadow pursuing.

62

SILVA SAID, "Mum and Dad were out, so I brought her along."

She said, "We ran into Cillian in the dooryard. Lorna was so excited to see him."

She said, "What harm could it do?" and the words hung in the still air unanswered. She laughed nervously. "It's getting late. I'd best go round and collect her."

"I'll walk with you," Charles said.

They didn't speak as they went up through the basement and into the house. Outside, full dusk had set in, a thin moon riding up behind a ceiling of low clouds. Harris's cottage was dark down the length of the lawn. Snakes coiled in Charles's guts, and when Silva reached for his hand, he let his fingers fold around hers. They walked faster, neither of them speaking, the charade of normalcy forgotten.

"Cillian!" Silva called when they reached the cottage. "Lorna!"

When Charles lifted a hand to knock, the door swung open beneath his fist, and he was stricken by a sense of déjà vu so powerful that he might have stepped through a doorway in time.

Silva's voice caught in her throat, the echoes dying away inside the house. They stood gathering their courage, like children at a threshold in a tale. They could smell the dumpster reek of the interior before they stepped inside. It increased by an order of magnitude in the foyer — a rich organic fetor of whisky and spoiled food — and by the time they reached the living room, it was nearly overwhelming. Charles snapped on the light, sending some black and loathsome insect scuttling into concealment amid the jumble of open paste jars, food-encrusted dishes, and empty liquor bottles on the coffee table. Scraps of newsprint and glossy magazines scissored to confetti littered the floor.

"Dear God," Silva whispered. And then, "Look at this, Charles."

She'd paused before the tapestry. It was worse than Charles remembered: the strange mutant trees of the Night Wood, the terrified child, the Horned King upon his pale horse rampant, his countenance awful to behold. The thing's eyes were yellow slashes, its fingers knotted talons, twice again too long, its mail shirt sewn with overlapping silver leaves.

And then, moved by impulse, by some instinct born of those scissored scraps of paper on the floor, Charles reached up and yanked the tapestry to the floor. A newsprint collage lay underneath, sprawling, huge: five hundred faces, five hundred smiling mouths, a thousand eyes of china blue, all of them pasted to the plaster in a bewildering array of haphazard overlapping angles. Here a single eye peering out from between the jagged intersection of two girlish jaws. There a nose and half an inch of pale flawless cheek.

And in the middle, framed by the crazy replication of scissored features, three perfect faces, whole and unblemished but for the slashes of black marker that obscured their eyes: a school portrait of Lorna — Charles had seen the same picture on Silva's kitchen counter — and the missing photograph of Lissa and (as Charles was lifting a hand, as if to touch his daughter's face) —

"Mary," Silva whispered.

Mary Babbing. The very same newspaper photo Charles had picked up his first full day in Yarrow. And what Charles thought of was Inspector McGavick. *You think she's dead,* Charles had said, and McGavick, *I wouldn't like to say one way or the other* — not that he needed to say it, not that they hadn't both already known.

Sometimes you didn't walk out of the wood, that's all. Sometimes the wood swallowed you whole.

The book is true to life that way, McGavick had said.

And he remembered something else: when the two detectives had walked down to the cottage to talk to Cillian Harris, Harris's door had been closed to them. The three men had conducted their business in the rain.

"What if it's true?" Charles said, and this time Silva didn't ask what he was talking about. "What if it was Cillian that took her?" he said. "What if the . . . what if that thing had demanded he bring it a child. Don't you understand? He couldn't stand that voice in his head all the time. I heard it myself. Erin, too. The pressure of its need. But for him it must have been so much more powerful."

Charles paused, wondering how it must have been with Harris, hearing the summons of the Horned King ever singing in his dreams, his mind boiling with the terrible knowledge of what it was he was being asked to do, until it spilled out through his fingers and splashed itself over the walls of the cottage.

"Why?" Silva said.

"Because he's in the direct line of descent."

Now Silva had caught the drift of his thoughts. "So he tried to drown it out by drinking," she said.

"And maybe that was enough for a while. And when it wasn't —"

"He took Mary," Silva said.

"But that wasn't enough either. The Horned King's bargain required a child in the direct line of descent."

Silence, then — a heartbeat, nothing more, Silva so cold and pale.

"He's taken her into the wood," she said. "We have to call someone. We have to call the police."

"Too late," Charles said, possessed of a sudden grim foreboding.

"What do you mean?"

So Charles once again took her cold hand in his own. He led her outside, through the stench and squalor, past the unseeing eyes of the bizarre collage, and into the dark foyer where the door still stood ajar upon the night — outside, outside where the telephone lines had gone silent and the airways mute, where a swollen orange moon, wreathed in storm, let down its rays. Harris's snug cottage, when they turned to look at it, was an ogre's lair, moss-grown, slit-eyed, dank. The ramparts had fallen, the curtain had been rent. Trees occupied the dooryard.

They were in the Night Wood now.

IN THE NIGHT WOOD

A T LAST LAURA EMERGED FROM THE baleful Wood into a misty avenue of evergreens. She sniffled and wiped her nose. She had been very afraid and she had been very brave and now she was very tired indeed. Her feet were shod in blood from stones and thorns, her lacy white nightgown hung in muddy rags (how angry her mother would be!), and her shoulders ached from the branches the monstrous trees had hurled down upon them. But perhaps all would yet be well. Here was a straight path for little girls to walk upon.

But even a straight path has many turnings.

And so the Story betrayed her, as Stories will, and brought Laura to the End she had most dreaded. The mist curled and parted, and in the cold Moonlight unveiled the Fate she had seen in the Mere of Souls: the Horned King upon his pale steed riding. He wheeled the horse around to face her, his cloak billowing, and brandished his great sword.

Laura stared at Him, frozen in horror.

What would she do now? she asked herself as the fell King spurred his horse into a gallop and hurtled down the corridor of trees. She recalled too late the words the Knight of Ice had imparted to her at the end of his Tale: *When you come to the end of your own Story,* he had said, *you must remember the thing that you have forgotten*. But how could you remember the thing you had forgotten when you had forgotten to remember it? she wondered.

And then the Horned King was upon her.

— CAEDMON HOLLOW, *IN THE NIGHT WOOD*

1

ERIN STUMBLED OVER a tussock of wiry grass as she wound her way up and down a track too narrow to call a path (or even a track). Ancient, leaf-barren trees crowded the way. Her breath clouded the air before her. Goosebumps pebbled her flesh.

Once again, she thought that she had stumbled into a dream — a nightmare kindled by wine and pills. Or perhaps, better still, what if it had *all* been a dream, the whole long year and more? Perhaps her faithless husband had been true. Perhaps she would wake up at home in Ransom to find Lissa snuggled under her comforter, her birthday still before her.

So wake up! Erin told herself, pinching the skin of her forearm and twisting and twisting once again. Wake up, wake up, wake up!

She did not wake up.

She plunged on instead, night-blind, lost.

When Erin had seen the child —

— *Lissa it was Lissa* —

— she had thrown on the clothes she'd left draped over the bedpost — an old Ransom College sweatshirt, a pair of ragged jeans. Then she'd flown down the crumbling stair to the grand salon, weedy and broken, with the great cloud-veiled moon peering down through the shattered roof. Outside, beyond the ruined entrance hall, she'd lunged recklessly into the trees. She didn't know how long she'd thrashed her way through the wood — five minutes? more? — but when she'd finally stopped, breathless with panic, she found herself lost in the omnipresent trees.

Where was she to go now? Whither Lissa and her dread pursuer?

Precious seconds slipped away. How long before the Horned King on his pale horse overtook the fleeing child? How long could Lissa hide? How far could she run? How swiftly? Erin swiped her forearm across her nose and realized that she was sobbing. (How long had she been sobbing?) A clock had started ticking in her head, shaving down the hour.

She searched, fruitlessly, for some sign of her daughter's passage. She bellowed Lissa's name. The night called it back to her in mocking rejoinder.

Then:

Was that a child's cry, lifted in terror or despair?

No. Yes. She did not know.

But it was something, anyway. So she moved off in the direction of the cry, if it *was* a cry, and after a time, that clock still ticking ticking ticking inside her head, her feet found the narrow path that was hardly a path at all.

The trees closed behind her.

She was gone.

2

LETTING GO OF SILVA'S hand, Charles wheeled away from Cillian Harris's witchy lair. Trees and more trees and still more trees, an interposing labyrinth of trees through which he glimpsed in the streaming, storm-torn moonlight the derelict pile that had been Hollow House, an age ago or more in another, sister wood, intersecting this one, or interpenetrating it.

Erin, he thought, stumbling away—

"Charles."

He turned, taking in Silva at a glance. Her face was haggard, pale. She held a muddy gray fleece, a Disney princess imprinted on the breast.

"It's Lorna's," she said. "The zipper's torn."

"I don't—"

"Maybe she got away from him. Maybe she's —"

Lost, he thought, thinking of Lorna wrenching free, leaving her jacket in the grasping hands of her murderous father. Another luckless child, astray in the pathless wood. Another Laura, in flight before her terrible pursuer.

Another Lissa, doomed, drowned, dead.

Not Lorna, too, he thought. Not another child in this long procession of horrors. He would have to save her. He would have to try. And so he turned away from the shell of Hollow House; he turned his face to the Night Wood, and together he and Silva climbed the forested slope that had been a moat of grass once, in some other, better place, where the world had not yet begun to unwind into winter, as had this sister wood, this fey realm afflicted with the mortal woes of its fairy king, and alike awaiting some terrible redemption.

The great wall at the top of the slope had fallen into decay, root-split and eroded, time and the elements running everything down to ruin: such were his grim thoughts as they scrambled over the tumbled, moss-blackened stones and stole deeper into the nightmare trees, vast and misshapen and veiled with shrouds of some withered epiphyte, like black crepe. Shafts of moonlight lanced through the barren branches overhead, illuminating the woodland floor with pale, ghostly radiance. Beside him, as they pushed deeper into the wilderness, Silva clutched the torn fleece and wept.

"We'll find her," he said.

"How?"

Charles didn't answer, didn't know what to say, simply stumbled on, deeper into the wood. Fallen trees checked their progress. Stones jutted from the earth. Wind whipped the night into a froth of moonlit dark. Footing was treacherous, each step a chance — and finally chance undid them.

A few intermittent gusts of rain had begun to billow down through the trees by then. They were scrambling over a shelf of stone, Charles in the lead. He had reached back to pull Silva up when her foot slipped. She was going down before he knew it, dragging him after her. He lost his grip on her rain-slick hand and lurched backward, scrabbling for balance. His breath bloomed in a chill fog before him. His heart slammed against his ribs.

Another sheet of rain blew down, spotting his glasses. The moon hove into view.

He slid down the hummock of rock to kneel beside her, stricken with déjà vu: Silva and Erin, each clutching at an injured ankle, the two moments superimposed one upon the other, and him saying now, as he had said then —

"Are you all right?"

— already knowing the answer.

"I don't know."

"Let me see."

"Help me up."

"Let me have a look at it first."

"We don't have time for that, Charles."

So he hauled her to her feet instead.

Silva took a step, grimacing, and sagged back to the ground. It was all Charles could do to keep her from falling outright. She laughed bitterly. "I can't put any weight on it."

"Maybe if I help you," he said. "If you lean on me, we can —"

"What? Climb the bloody rock?" She shook her head. "There's no time."

Silence then, the night wheeling about them.

"You have to go on without me."

"Silva, I can't just leave you here."

Her voice was fierce when she replied, "Lorna is out there somewhere, Charles! If she's to have any chance, you have to."

"But —"

"*Please*," she said.

Charles sighed. "Okay," he said, and then, just as he was turning away, she reached out to him, took his hand. She clutched it for a moment, squeezing, and then released it. "Don't let her down, Charles," she said. "*Save her.*"

"I will," he said. Another promise, and another promise he was sure to break.

For how could he ever hope to keep it?

3

THIS WAS THE question Charles pondered as he stole on through the forest.

Lorna had left no sign to mark her passage — or none that he could read. Charles did not know how to find her, much less save her. The wood was vast and deep, running on perhaps to the ends of the earth, and when he paused to call for her —

"Lorna! Lorna!"

— the name boomed back at him through the trees, mocking and empty.

Nothing, and again, nothing.

Just the sound of an inquiring owl.

Just the sound of the trees, enmired in earth, whispering tidings of his passage. They flung down their branches in every gust of wind. They shot out roots to entangle him. And when the storm-racked moon hid its face away (as it did now), they went walking in the dark. Charles listened to their ancient bones creak, and when the light returned, the path had almost imperceptibly changed direction. He was sure of it. He wondered, not for the first time, if the wood was steering him away from Lorna.

Perhaps the trees were in league with their fell king. Perhaps he would be wise to turn his feet from the way that seemed to open up before him. But whenever he did so, the wood soon became impassible, thicketed and rocky, steep.

Lost, blind, Charles moved on, avoiding the easy path, fighting his way through snarls of bramble and thorn. There was nothing else to do — no quarter to be had, no solace, and when he called out Lorna's name again, no answers in the wind. Those brief squalls of rain came with increasing frequency now; the streaming clouds more often obscured the moon. And in the weird otherworldly light, the wood became perilous and strange — a whispering wood, a dream wood, a nightmare wood where reality bled out and outer darkness flooded in.

The air grew colder. The trees loomed over him, sentient, malign, and the forest rustled, alive with laughter and uncanny mutterings.

Grim, autumn-blooming blossoms, fleshy and pale, turned their faces to look upon him as he passed. And once — Charles's heart seized in his breast — something terrible, something huge, launched itself into flight from some nesting place high above him. The thunder of wings announced it, beating down a reek of damp earth and decay. Looking up, he glimpsed it in a moonlit patch between the trees: corpse-white against the night sky, a great bird with the face of a woman, lovely and awful to behold. It cried out, and its voice, too, was like a woman's — a wrenching, banshee lament.

Charles fled, fighting through the wood until at last it spilled him sliding into a deep gully choked with brush and deadfall trees. He fought to gain the far slope, but the undergrowth defeated him. He moved down the channel instead, a hundred yards or more, looking for a cranny in the scrub where he could slip through and pick his way up to the other side.

Pausing to catch his breath, Charles lifted his hands to cup his mouth once again, and —

Stopped, breath frozen in his lungs.

The night had fallen utterly silent. The inquiring owl no longer wondered who. Even the wind had died.

He swallowed Lorna's name like a stone.

A great stag stood atop the embankment opposite — ten, maybe fifteen yards away. So close that he could smell the thing, a rank, wild musk, and see the suppurating wound in its side where a hunter's spear must have gone in. So close that he could see, or thought he could see, the expression in its eyes, mournful and proud.

It stood utterly still, its enormous rack outspread against the sky, and stared down into the gully where Charles waited, hidden in shadow and in briar. He felt the weight of the creature's grave scrutiny, and a dire certainty seized him: that there was still another wood inside the wood, or maybe the same wood defiled, a daylit wood held too long in thrall to the night, a wood that might yet be restored if its wounded king could be healed. He held his breath, stunned by the thing's beauty.

And then a cloud crossed the moon, dropping down a curtain of darkness. When the sky cleared a moment later, the stag was gone. Just gone. It might have dissolved into the gloaming.

Some small creature rustled in the brambles. The owl once again commenced its interrogation. But Charles felt clearer and more brave. He would go on. He would find a way. Though the thicket, impassible, encircled him, and the trees themselves conspired to thwart his every step, he would find a way.

And then, in the moonlight, he glimpsed a small face staring out at him from the depths of the tangled undergrowth, a little demon face like a cat's, capricious but not cruel. It was gone in the next heartbeat, but it had opened before him or shown him by its presence a crevice in the brake. Charles slid through it, and there was another face waiting, foxy and sly, to guide him deeper into the undergrowth, and through it, and still another as he clambered at last up the far side of the gully. He heard, or thought he heard, a whispered confabulation and faint laughter in the air, and then there was another face, there and gone again, and farther on, another and another, and thus the wood's secret denizens led him on, or lured him.

He did not stop again to call Lorna's name.

He followed.

4

CHARLES COULDN'T SAY how long he'd been walking—scrambling over rocky outcroppings, slipping through narrow places in the thicket —when he saw the last of the cunning little faces. Time had grown elastic, untethered from any earthly hour. All he could say for certain was that he was soaked—gusts of rain still slashed the air—and weary, bone-weary. His feet ached. His legs ached. His eyes were gritty with exhaustion.

The wood was open here, the trees widely spaced in the moonlight. The ground, slick with the rotting leaf-fall of centuries, sloped gently away before him into a darker wall of yews, ancient and closely grown, their evergreen branches interwoven.

He had been here before. And though he did not wish to be here now, though his every instinct told him to go no farther, to flee this

place, his intuition told him otherwise. Those shrewd woodland creatures, mercurial and shy, had brought him here for a reason. And what
other hope did he have? So he moved on downslope, and as he drew
near the wall of trees, he heard the low, forlorn cry of a child — weeping, hopeless, lost.

Lorna. It was Lorna — and he almost said the name aloud, almost
called her name down through the trees. But an image of Cillian Harris
seized and silenced him, and worse, an image of the Horned King, lean
and cruel. Anxiety snaked through his guts, and he was afraid.

Yet he pressed on.

Branches lashed at him as he pushed through the belt of sentinel
trees. The wind had picked up by then, chasing thin streamers of cloud,
moonlight, and shadow in quick succession, disclosing strobelike flashes
of his surroundings: a clearing with long grass bending in submission to
the tempest and the palisade of vast encircling yews, their ancient limbs
outstretched. The great oak where he had drowsed himself into a living
nightmare printed itself against the sky.

And still the sound of Lorna sobbing, heart-rending, desperate, the
loneliest sound he'd ever heard.

Where was she?

Voicing her name at last —

"Lorna!"

— Charles plunged into the clearing. The world tilted around him,
lurching as something — some grasping root, maybe — tumbled him
earthward. He struck his head on a stone hidden in the grass. Pain flared
at his temple, a stroke of lightning coruscant behind his eyes. He lay
there a moment, stunned and groggy.

When he pushed himself up at last, the ground pitched beneath
his feet. He touched his face; his fingertips came away dark and wet.
And then the sky opened. Rain slammed down, washing blood into his
mouth, coppery and warm. He coughed and spat, reeled back a step,
and saw through a shimmering veil of blood and rain the thing that had
tripped him: not a root, wayward and malign, but the body of a child.

Lissa, he thought, all unconscious, but what he said aloud was
"Lorna."

The child — a girl, a blonde girl no more than five or six years old —

did not respond. She lay curled away from him, the knobby arc of her spine visible through the rain-sheer fabric of her dress.

Dread washed over him.

Still woozy, Charles went to his knees, his thoughts muddled and unclear. He reached out a hand to touch her shoulder.

"Lorna," he said, shaking the child. When she did not respond, he rolled her boneless over on her back. Her head lolled to one side. Her skin was pale and ravaged with rot, her mouth open, her blank eyes upturned toward the sky. A centipede, glistening and black in the rain, slipped across her cheek and wormed its way into her nostril.

Charles jerked away.

Fathomless horror welled up within him.

"Lorna," he gasped, realizing in the next breath that it was not Lorna, could not be, though the two girls might have been sisters. It was the other child, the lost one, Mary, her picture pasted upon Cillian Harris's wall. Charles's conversation with McGavick came back to him unbidden. *You think she's dead,* he'd said, and McGavick, sighing, *I wouldn't like to say one way or the other* — knowing the truth all the time, the hard fact of his profession: the wood — the world — could at any moment open up and swallow you whole.

But a child? Charles thought, recoiling from that bitter truth, Lissa's truth, and Mary Babbing's, too. The truth of the wood and world: dead children, and more of them every day.

And still that sobbing everywhere around him.

Then the clouds once again snuffed out the moon, and the autumn air turned as cold and winter-blue as a crescent of ice skimmed from the top of a deep-February cistern — a cold animate and cruel, charged with malevolent intent.

A thin, inhuman cry rose triumphant in the air behind him.

By instinct more than anything else, Charles threw himself to the left, rolling in the high grass. He sensed something passing close at hand, the whicker of disrupted air.

A black figure stood over him — lean, inhuman, crowned with a rack of enormous horns. That hateful cold emanated from the thing. Charles met its eyes — its awful yellow eyes — and scuttled away in terror.

The Horned King strode after him, unhurried, sure. The thing's blade hissed as it descended through all that swimming dark. Charles hurled himself to the right. The blow that might have decapitated him fell wide, the blade flaying his shoulder, another welter of blood washed clean by the shimmering veils of rain. Clutching the wound, Charles scrambled erect, lost his footing, went down again. Panic tore through him. He clawed his way through the muck and slammed his back into the trunk of that solitary oak —

— and felt the chill prick of the blade beneath his chin.

5

CHARLES SQUEEZED SHUT his eyes, steeling himself for the fatal stroke.

But the sobbing turned to screams: *"No! Don't! No!"* — and the blow did not come.

Silence, then.

And still it did not come.

Charles heard nothing but the rain, felt nothing but the pulse of his own heart and the icy pressure of the sword point at his throat.

"No," Lorna said, sobbing. "Please."

Charles opened his eyes. The moon broke free of the clouds. He could see everything. He could see the long length of the sword and the textured flesh of the Horned King: dead leaves and dying ones, a panoply of late-autumn color, close-woven. He could see Lorna most of all — Lorna on the far side of the clearing, in the shadow of the wood. *Run!* he wanted to scream. *Run!* But she could not run. The trees, dear God, the trees —

The trees themselves — the wood, the whispering wood, the Night Wood — had seized her. Thick, ropy vines snaked down out of the canopy of one of the centuries-old yews that enclosed the clearing. They writhed around her, clutching and caressing, binding her tight to the tree's lichen-bearded trunk. And all around her, the forest bent to the wind, murmuring in sinister consultation.

"No," he whispered, and the Horned King stirred with interest or intent.

The rain slashed the air like silver daggers, hurled down by a bruised and sullen sky.

Charles took a breath. He let his gaze climb the length of his assailant, from the battered leather boots to the tunic sewn with rusty metal leaves, and higher still to the thing's face — and all at once everything went cold and silent inside his head.

It wore his face.

Beneath the spreading rack of horns, the Horned King wore his face.

The old familiar montage possessed him: water gushing into the tub and the shrill summons of the telephone and Syrah Nagle's fury in his ear. And most of all, unforgettable, as if it had been scored into the grooves of his brain, the black Medusa coils of his daughter's blood.

Tiend. Tiend most foul.

What sacrifice had he made? What his return?

A month or two of stolen pleasure on the hideous green wing chair in his office. A moment's spasm, nothing more.

And the price?

Everything. Job, wife, child. Everything.

Even hope.

And then Lissa's voice inside his head: *Not hope.*

It was hope that had brought him to Hollow House, hope that he might salvage his career, his marriage, his life. It was hope that had brought him to this clearing in the wood, hope that he might save the child who could have been his own, they looked so much alike, Lissa and Lorna — Livia, too — that uncanny resemblance echoing across a hundred years and who could say how many long ages before that. Ouroboros. Time was a snake that bit its own tail, the old story grinding round upon the wheel of fate.

Yet he'd never surrendered hope. Not really. He'd only forgotten to remember it, and in remembering that he'd forgotten it, he reclaimed it for his own. You had to forgive. You had to turn your face from the past. You had to soldier on. Maybe what had been didn't have to be. Maybe you could break the circle, renounce fate, write your own story.

All you had to do was begin.

Once upon a time — an incantation against the night.

No more. It had to end.

Charles wrenched himself to the side, the tip of the blade opening a bead of blood across his throat. "No," he screamed as he came to his feet. "No more!" He leapt at the thing, seized it, carried it down to the earth. For a moment he thought he could overcome it. But it was too strong. With a single blow of its hand it dislodged him. And then they were on their feet again. The thing drove him back toward the edge of the clearing, its sword carving blue arcs in the air. The rain hammered down, and still it drove him back, until his feet at last slipped beneath him and he stumbled, turning over in the muck a rain-washed stone the size of a skull. Then the trees had him, vines hissing down to seize him and drag him back against the trunk of one of those ancient yews, to hold him helpless as the Horned King rose before him. The cold, that terrible cold, enfolded him. Charles wrenched his head around to meet the monstrous creature's gaze. With one hand, it drew back its sword for the fatal blow —

Rain gusted in Charles's face, blinding him. And then the wind shifted. The moon bathed the clearing in bright, clear light. Erin rose up behind the Horned King. She was clutching with both hands the stone that Charles had tripped over, and, as Charles looked on in awe, she brought it crashing down upon the Horned King's head. The thing staggered, started to turn, and went down upon its knees. Erin screamed —

"No more! No more!"

— as she drew back the stone for another blow, and then another and another. The dark creature pitched forward, convulsing, and she hurled herself upon it. The stone rose and fell, rose and fell, rose and fell, and the whole time she was screaming out her rage and sorrow.

No more. No more. No more.

And then the thing was still.

The vines holding Charles tightened, lacerating him. The wind shrieked, bearing a final syllable of denial, a word, or what might have been a word —

NO!

—and then it was over.

The wind was just wind. The trees were just trees.

The vines released Charles, if ever they had held him in the first place. He fell to his knees, resting his head against the earth, and the sound of Erin's weeping filled the air. Somehow he summoned the strength to go to her, pushing his way on hands and knees through the mud and the weeds and the rain falling like a blessing down upon him.

They stood together, unsteady on their feet.

He ran his fingers through her hair, lifted her chin, kissed her. He held her until the sobs stopped, and longer still, until she looked up to meet his gaze, her eyes clear now. Undimmed.

"I'm sorry," he said, though he couldn't say for sure what he was apologizing for. Everything, he supposed. "I'm so, so —"

"Hush," she said, laying a finger across his lips, and together they looked down into the face of the Horned King himself. But it was no king after all, it was only a man. It was only Cillian Harris, his face broken and pale and empty of everything but sorrow.

In one outflung hand he clutched a rusted steel tab. Charles bent down to retrieve it.

"What is it?" Erin asked.

It might have been a leaf once, in some other age or wood. Now?

"It's nothing," Charles said, folding his hand around it. "It's nothing."

And then Lorna was there. She was weeping, too, and they drew her wordless into their embrace. They all rocked there together for a time, and it was as if Lissa had returned to them. But no, it wasn't Lissa. Lissa was gone, fallen through a hole in the world, wood-lost and alone.

This was Lorna. He said her name aloud. He said, "Hey, Lorna."

"Lorna, huh," Erin said, and then, pulling the child closer, "It's okay, Lorna, it's over now"—the necessary lie. Because it wasn't over, Charles knew. It would never be over. It would never be okay. There were wounds beyond healing, breakages beyond repair. But he knew something else, too: that in time, with love, it might be a little better, and then, after a while, a little better still. Even wounded, even broken, you found a way to be whole. You went on. That's all. You went on.

They pushed their way through the yews and into the wood beyond, where a great stag stood sentinel. It held Charles's gaze for a moment and then it startled into flight.

Maybe, Charles thought, maybe stories held a germ of truth. Maybe if there weren't really any *happily ever after*s to our *once upon a time*s, there could at least be a hard-won accommodation to the vicious world, a compromise at tale's end with bitterness and suffering.

Maybe.

It was hard to know. He was hurting, and the pain fuzzed out his thoughts. Nothing seemed clear or certain but the terrible ache in his shoulder and Erin's warmth beside him. And then Lorna tore free of them, and he saw her running and Silva limping up to meet them and somewhere out there beyond her, in the gloaming at the woodland's edge, the first gray light of dawn rising up beyond the trees.

Author's Note

In his cryptogram and elsewhere, Caedmon Hollow often alludes to the work of those who came before him. He borrows extensively from William Shakespeare, and, to a lesser degree, from John Milton, Dante, Thomas De Quincey, Goethe, and the Scottish ballad "Tam Lin." Charles Hayden's mind is allusive as well, and in the course of the novel, he quotes, borrows phrases, or alludes to Samuel Taylor Coleridge, Ralph Waldo Emerson, William Faulkner, Thomas Gray, William Blake, Christina Rossetti, Arthur Conan Doyle, Lewis Carroll, W. H. Auden, and Alfred, Lord Tennyson. Most of these passages are attributed to their sources in the text, but some are not, so I want to acknowledge them here. If I have missed others, it is through oversight, not intent, and I beg the reader's forgiveness.

Acknowledgments

Writing this book, as those who were close at hand will attest, was a lot like wandering in the Night Wood. I was lost for a long time, and only through the assistance of many, many people was I able to find my way back to the straight path. Friends and readers who helped blaze the trail include Jack Slay, Nathan Ballingrud, and Durant Haire. Without their careful attention to the manuscript and their generosity of heart, these pages would never have been completed. My agent Matt Bialer and my friend Barry Malzberg also read early drafts and provided cogent and helpful advice; Matt is, additionally, to be commended for his seemingly endless patience. I am grateful for my editor, John Joseph Adams, whose diligence and fine eye for detail immeasurably improved the novel in ways both large and small. I am also indebted to Larry Cooper, who copyedited the manuscript, often saving me from myself; Robert Canipe for helping me sort out some plot issues early on; and Lenoir-Rhyne University for granting me the sabbatical I needed to finish the manuscript. Steve Sanderson talked me through some of the problems posed by grief and addiction. Tim Goldberg did the math. It goes without saying that I am responsible for any errors or infelicities that here remain. Finally, I would be remiss if I didn't thank my family most of all. My father set me on this path many, many years ago; my mother encouraged me along the way. I wish they could have seen this project come to fruition. I am glad that my sisters, Pam and Sally, did. Most of all, my deepest love and gratitude go to my wife, the lovely and talented Jean Singley-Bailey, and my daughter, Carson, for their unstinting love and support even in the darkest hours.